THE GHOST KEEPER

The
Ghost
Keeper

A NOVEL

Natalie Morrill

PATRICK CREAN EDITIONS
An imprint of HarperCollins*PublishersLtd*

Published by Patrick Crean Editions,
an imprint of HarperCollins Publishers Ltd

First edition

HarperCollins Publishers Ltd
Bay Adelaide Centre, East Tower
22 Adelaide Street West, 41st Floor
Toronto, Ontario, Canada
M5H 4E3

www.harpercollins.ca

Library and Archives Canada Cataloguing in Publication
information is available upon request.

ISBN 978-1-44345-045-4

Printed and bound in the United States

LSC/H 9 8 7 6 5 4 3 2 1

For my family

THE GHOST KEEPER

UNDER THE PINES IN THE WÄHRING CEMETERY, A FOX carries the rib of a man in his teeth. He has a burrow under the east wall and he gives me no end of trouble, this fox. I've seen him in the sun, trotting princely atop the brick wall, and his black toes are never cut on the glass and his red coat is never caught on the barbed wire. I have seen him in the rain too, under the trees and along the inner wall, with a vole or mouse or brown collarbone in his mouth and his red coat dripping. And I have seen him in the snow, when he is a streak of light and a bolt of God: then I can't chase him off; he is a miracle. But on this day he's a bone-thief, and I can yell, "Shoo!" and run at him with my arms flapping and hope that he drops the rib as he scampers so I can bury it again.

No one comes here anymore—only the fox and the birds, and only me. The ground is like a beast breathing slowly, with the tree roots writhing and stirring the earth and the headstones tumbled all in a heap, here and there. The wall and the broken glass and the barbed wire keep the vandals out—all but a few, ready to be scratched raw to spray something hateful on a toppled marker; and most of that from some years ago, I think, years ago now.

But nothing can stop this fox, I've learned. He will come here into the quiet to hunt voles and mice and avoid the people and cars, and except for his bone-stealing habit I can't blame him. Here are two green acres where no one ever goes, and certainly he could scamp up the street in the night, through yards and past houses, and make it to the Türkenschanzpark if he tried, but why try, I grant him, why try? No reason to leave except, on occasion, one middle-aged man and his flapping coat, and he—I—have to go home soon enough. But I will make his bad habit a nuisance for him while I can.

"Shoo!"

He doesn't drop the bone this time. Scoots under the wall—*Aha!*—and the last swish of his red-brush bottom is a grin and a laugh at me, old fellow, who can't squish like that under the stone. I stand panting by the wall.

On this day it's spring, April. Green and grey-brown. The air is bright and keen like running water. And I get the feeling, then, the feeling I get too often in the cemetery, that there is a little red coal underneath my ribs, here.

I don't know why, but in my heart all the dead become children. They are very small, and quiet, and they don't know why no one comes to them anymore, and I can't explain it so that they understand. But the heaps of headstones like the rubble of a shelled-out warehouse are themselves heaps of bones to me now, heaps of bodies, dry bones. The earth alive.

Is this what it's meant to be? Some kind of narrative, one would expect, something with a beginning, and yet I can't find the beginning. All I can see is April light and the red-brush tail, and they hold me, but reason would shout, "Give me the beginning, Josef, the true beginning." And what would I write? Daniel begat Mendel who begat Josef who begat Daniel who begat Josef Tobak, and that's me, and I begat Tobias Tobak, and maybe this ought rather to be his story, but I hear, "Set it down, Tobak," so I write. And maybe I should start back there somewhere, as in, *I was born in Vienna, in the Leopoldstadt, in May of 1909*, and my mother and father had wanted me to be born in a hospital but no, I was born in my mother's mother's house, in a bedroom on the third floor. That building is long gone, though, shot to rubble, something new and concrete-faced standing there now.

Or I could start with the *Anschluss*, because everyone knows about that, or I could start with Anna's eyes on a New Year's Eve, the first time I saw them, like cool fire and like a home half-forgot. Or I could start with Friedrich Zimmel that awful night. Is that the beginning? There, that ended in the Währing cemetery too. But maybe it was before that, back in New York with the Schwartzes, or maybe Lena or her mother was the beginning.

It's only that it's complex, you see. I may have to come at it from the side.

PART I

1

'VE WALKED AWAY FROM THIS FOR A WHILE, AND I'VE
thought about it, and I find the whole thing hinges on a moment:
this final conversation with Friedrich Zimmel, years after the
war, years after I came back to Vienna. It begins in the night, with
Friedrich under the yellow light in his kitchen. He's called me here
very late, after many nights of wanting to call me but sitting alone
with his drink instead. And now his face is purpled, and his eyes
are yellowed, and his fingers wrapped round his drink are shaking
and he says to me:

"You're going to hate me."

Because I love him, and because by then I've made a kind of
peace with his betrayal that followed the *Anschluss*, I say to him,
"Never. Please."

And he, looking dark beyond dark, says, "You know about my
Lena."

BUT HERE I'VE stopped again. I see I'll have to tell you about
Lena, and for that I have to write about Friedrich, and to tell you
things about Friedrich, I must tell you first about my family. And

I don't write this to condemn him—Friedrich, that is—so surely it's not right to begin there, in that kitchen on that night, when it remains that he did so much for us before then. And if it's a thing that must be set down, then let me set it down in such a way that I won't grow ashamed of how I've treated his memory, nor that of any person. There are none so powerless as the dead, and I believe one must in some way show mercy to memories as much as to bones.

HERE IS ANOTHER way to begin.

I am a little boy in Vienna. Papa is an accountant for the company Geisman–Zimmel, and we (my sister, Zilla, my parents, my mother's parents and I) live together in an apartment in the second district. My papa is still a young man, and Geisman–Zimmel is a sprawling, self-confident kind of manufacturer, owned jointly by Hans Zimmel, a Catholic, and Otto Geisman, a Jew. Perhaps this is unusual, even then. But take note: when Papa comes home, he speaks of his department boss, Nussbaum, as a shiftless lecher, but when he talks about Mr. Zimmel or Mr. Geisman, they are heroes—men who, like my city's statues, I only ever see as if from below and backlit by the sun. Perhaps it's because these men are liberal in the sense that only dogmatic capitalists can be liberal: any man who can turn a profit under duress has their respect. Papa loves them for that. Hans Zimmel is Friedrich Zimmel's father.

Daily Papa travels from the second district to the company offices (across the Danube canal, catch the tram, hop off on Rechte Bahngasse and then up to the great broad doors on Strohgasse), and then back to our apartment at the end of the day. Ours isn't a small apartment, by neighbourhood standards: we have two floors to ourselves, the second (which is really the third, above the mezzanine) and the one above that. Oma and Opa were fairly well off to begin with, besides which, Papa's job pays well, and he works furiously—all his pride is in it.

As a boy in the Leopoldstadt, I can run down to the canal, past the bakeries and grocers and coffee houses on Taborstrasse, and right up to the water, which is green or grey or brown, depending on the season and the sky. I can lean over and see the shadow my head makes on the surface of the water, shuddering. It's a shadow that carries down through the green beyond the surface, like a tunnel I could fall through, fitting perfectly.

Sometimes, at the canal, there are processions from the Orthodox synagogue, and these fascinate me. By the rail on the bridge I crouch and watch them. The reflection of the bodies in the canal is black on green, like my shadow, but it seems sometimes like it is the water reaffirming this crowd, doubling them and praying along.

(We are not religious, my family, and this is thanks mainly to Papa, though Mutti supports him in it. She lights candles on Fridays, yes; but that's for my grandparents' sake. Papa's lips are always tight as she does it. Some weeks he sits and reads the whole way through the prayer. Even then, though, the veins snake out over his temples and he flips the pages of his book or newspaper forward and back as if at random.)

Run south along the canal and you come eventually to the fairgrounds at the Prater, with its shouting and garbage and light, and the immense Riesenrad Ferris wheel with red boxcar pods arcing snail-slow across the sky. Until I'm about five years old I can hardly stand to look at it. This monster, I imagine then, is bigger than God, and it seems always just about to topple over onto me.

Of course I don't tell my friends that it scares me. There are a lot of things I don't tell my friends, many things beautiful or frightening—these I carry inside, like coins in my pocket that only my own fingertips know.

IN MY CHILDHOOD home, Papa does not let any of us speak Yiddish, and because of that I never learn it well. We speak German, like "proper Austrians." Mutti says "vulgar" when she talks about the way our neighbours speak, and the one time my sister, Zilla, curses Papa, at the dinner table, in Yiddish (in a moment of rebellion more than hatred, when she is twelve and I am seven), her punishment confirms this: Mutti shouts and sends her straight to her bedroom, and though she tells my father that Zilla is too old to be spanked, after dinner Papa goes up to Zilla's room with his belt folded in two. And I know he would not be half so furious if she had cursed in German.

There, see: Zilla is another person to whom I owe justice here. Begin with Zilla, then.

When I am a boy, my sister, five years my senior, is tall, striking, fearless and alien. Papa and Mutti want her to mix with the right people—that is, high-society Viennese, not our Leopoldstadt rabble. Our father makes introductions through his work, but he never, in the end, thinks quite the way she does. Zilla's particular rebellion is to take our father's direction and press it to extremes he doesn't dare consider. At fifteen she spends her evenings in coffee houses, tucked up against men three times her age. She laughs with and at women who wouldn't have a word to say to our mother. And she is intelligent, too—too smart to have much patience for her average admirer.

"He's just boring." This is the worst she can say about anyone. She thrives on scandal; she keeps pace with the most controversial ideologies; she courts playwrights and psychologists and musicians and diplomats, Communists and Catholics—but to be boring is unforgivable. For most of our lives together I live with the terrible suspicion that I too am "boring." It keeps my mouth clapped shut most of the time, my believing that.

Oh, but remember—she is also tender. And has such love for the good that her heart is set for breaking. How many people see that? I wonder. Even I could forget it, sometimes.

FRIEDRICH ZIMMEL IS one of the men in love with Zilla. The first time I go with her to a party at Friedrich's downtown flat (when I am an awkward sixteen, and she is twenty-one and very much in her element), he comes straight up to me and tumbles into what must be, I assume, a stylish psychoanalytic dispute.

"Here, Josef, listen to this one and ask Zilla what she thinks." He keeps glancing in her direction as he talks, but Zilla is laughing with a neurotic-looking Spaniard who wipes his mouth on the back of his hand between grins, and she doesn't once look at us. "I was reading the *Zeitschrift für Psychologie* yesterday, and there was another letter on Adler's birth-order theories, and despite all the anecdotal evidence I can't help but take issue with the assumption that—"

I nod and nod, but there is no hope. Friedrich is an amateur psychologist, if such a thing exists. He studied philosophy at university and would have liked, he tells me, to become a medical doctor, but the fact that his father is grooming him to take over his business leaves him stuck. He reads everything, though, and whenever he can he meets with the gentlemen in Doctors Freud and Adler's circles; but Friedrich is a manufacturer and a manufacturer's son, and no matter how wealthy he might be, he is not especially fascinating to the people who fascinate him most.

IN THESE CONVERSATIONS, though, I will argue that there was something gained. Certainly Friedrich began inviting Zilla to parties soon after he met her, when they were both very young, and certainly his inviting me had (at first) more to do with his feelings for her than for me. But see this: he could speak to me in her place, when he was nervous, or she cold. And though I suspect that at first and for a long time he saw me as a surrogate for her and a path towards her, as I became an adult there were times—and as time went on, it became common—that he'd come to me asking or telling things that I knew weren't meant for my sister's ears.

We would sit in his father's library, and he'd talk, one of those psychiatric treatises spread over his knees, but he'd hardly glance at it. He let me borrow his books of poetry. He let me read the poems aloud to myself. They seemed sometimes to sharpen him for a moment, as if some light in a far window had caught his eye.

It's strange, I would think; because I wasn't the kind of person he ought to have made time for, and yet he seemed, more and more, to depend on me, and not simply for access to Zilla. Me—why? I never asked him. As if the question might jerk us both into wakefulness, into a world of sense, where a person had no time for such friendships and where we'd recognize each other as strangers, and myself as useless to him. Isn't it so? I would ask the night, walking home from his place; yes, it must be so.

2

WAIT—I'VE GONE ASTRAY ALREADY. YES, SET THESE lives down; they're part of it—but if this culminates with the cemeteries, Tobak, find the place they enter in.

SO BACK, FOR a moment, to an earlier time, when I'm still a child. This would be 1915, during the Great War, when Geisman–Zimmel has switched from metal fixtures for sinks and bathtubs to arms manufacturing. Before deprivations hit us hard, I suppose—though to children these differences need to be parsed in retrospect. The world is full of strangeness, then, but to me the biggest change is that my father's mother has moved from the countryside out in the east, the region that's Czechoslovakia now, to the city. When her Viennese husband died, she'd moved back to be with her sister, but now that sister too has died, and so back she comes to be near her son. At the train station, when we go to meet her, I stare and stare for a lady who looks like Papa, but am embraced instead by a tiny old woman with a face like a turnip. Papa never smiles at her, though he carries her bag to the tram.

Papa tells his mother that there is no room in our apartment for another person, and perhaps it's true. He helps her get a room in a boarding house two streets away from us, farther from the canal, and she settles in well.

And she isn't like Oma and Opa, my mother's parents, who are just about the type of Austrian citizens Papa would like us all to be. She tells me to call her Babka, which is also the name for a kind of cake, and I always think of her as cake-coloured after that, or of cake as grandmother-coloured. Her tiny apartment is sectioned in two—into a kind of sitting room and a bedroom—and though she isn't supposed to cook in her rooms, she has a Primus alcohol stove that sits in the corner and she almost always has a coffee pot heating on it when I visit.

HERE I AM, a child sitting in an armchair across from my grandmother. Outside there is grey rain and feet and wheels and horses making noise on the roads. My shoes are by the door and my feet, in blue wool socks, are wet from the ankles down. The room smells of pickles and also, today, of rum, because Babka is heating some milk with rum for me, to take off the chill. Her cat, Liba, another thing not really allowed in the boarding house, is curled next to me on the armchair, her long grey leg stretched out straight to just barely touch the blanket over my legs. She will uncurl if I move, I know, and so I am sitting very still.

Babka is talking to me in Yiddish as she watches the little stove. She is explaining something about when she was a girl, but I don't really follow. I know what Papa would think, and it makes me nervous—so much so that I don't let myself understand half of what she's saying, though I suspect I could, if I tried. I think instead about Liba, watch the way her coat shifts in the soft light like smoke in the cold autumn air. I am not allowed to have a pet.

Out on the street, a man shouts, "Almost too late!" And now Babka is telling me the story about the fish.

It's hard for me not to listen to the story about the fish. I can understand almost all of it. In the story, which she will tell me at least a dozen times as I grow up, a man named Simeon goes fishing. He lives in Vienna, in the second district, like us, but the story takes place many, many years before.

As he does every day, Simeon wakes up very early in the morning, while his wife is still sleeping and the children are still in their beds. He does not light a lamp, but dresses in the dark, slips into his boots, picks up his fishing rod and tackle by the door and pads out into the still-dark morning.

Simeon walks northward up the river towards a spot he knows, where there's a little sloping beach and the cover of trees. He baits the hook with an earthworm plucked from the grass. He casts his line. The morning is quiet. Simeon, Babka explains, says something or thinks something about God, something I don't understand and probably would not understand in German either.

The man is just finishing this thought, or this sentence, when there is a fierce tug on the line, and the pole nearly shoots out from his hands. He plants his feet, grips the rod and begins to reel in the fish. Such a big fish! Fat and silvery and as long as Simeon's arm. It takes him five minutes to land it, and when he does, it seems that both man and fish are panting with exhaustion.

Our hero is thrilled. He plops the great fish in his net, and he struts with the net over his shoulder, struts straight back home where there's a great, keen cleaving knife in his kitchen and a hard wooden cutting board. He slaps the fish down on the countertop. His children are awake now, and they gather round his legs, rubbing their eyes, to see the fish as big as a papa's arm.

Then, as a fisherman must do (although it makes me squeamish as a boy to think about it), Simeon takes the great, keen cleaving knife and raises it above the fish's head.

And then the most amazing thing happens. Just as Simeon is swinging his knife down to behead the fish, the fish screams out with a man's voice, *"Shema Ysrael!"*

"WHAT?"

I ask because Babka speaks the words in her most dramatic, agonized voice, so that it seems the story is worthless without them.

"Oh!" For a moment she looks scandalized, and I wonder if I have said something wrong. But then she clucks, leans forward and touches my cheek with her right hand. Her hand smells like hard yellow soap. She leans back in her chair and swirls a hand in the air, looking for the German words that seem, by her expression as she speaks them, to be always inadequate.

"Like, *'Hear, Israel!'* Except about God, and the people, and you say it also at the end, at death," she explains, "but in Hebrew," and I say, "Oh." The milk and rum is bubbling, and she pulls it off the heat to pour me a cup, pan tilted over a chipped mug, and the rain still hissing against the window.

I raise the mug to my mouth but don't drink it, just rest my lip against the rim and let the steam rise up over my face. I am sure I must have heard someone say those words before, but I never knew them as words; I never guessed they had meaning until my grandmother placed them in the mouth of a dying fish. The fact that this fish speaks Hebrew seems to place it within the realm of the biblical, and that, as far as I understand, means history.

=

AND, DO YOU know, I'm not sure why I had such respect for sacred texts at that point in my life. Papa, of course, did not send me to Hebrew school. But in the second district, surrounded by voices and bodies and smells and tastes that were something more than simply Austrian, no matter how much Papa wished it otherwise, you could not *not* know things.

But the story—back to that. It's very important that I set down the story about the fish.

SO THE RAIN taps like idle fingertips against the glass, and I let the rum warm me up a little as Babka folds her skirts under her legs and presses on.

Though the fish screams in Hebrew, Babka says, our hero does not have time to avert his cleaving knife and so it falls—*whack!*—against the cutting board, and the fish's voice is cut off mid-scream, and its head bounces off the wood, mouth agape, one dead eye staring sightless up to heaven.

The little children yelp. The father gasps. The family leaps back from the counter as if they themselves were pricked by the knife. The father wrings his hands and prays aloud for protection, for forgiveness, for help. He runs to get his wife, who is nursing the baby upstairs. Throughout the first few moments of his explanation she is sure her husband has lost his mind, but then the older children huddle in, some wailing, some simply wide-eyed, but all relating the same strange story about the fish.

The parents confer over the nursing baby, with the children huddled in a semicircle around them. What is to be done? Has Simeon murdered a holy being? Was the fish a monster? At length the wife points out that they are talking in circles, the husband is still wringing his hands and the fish isn't getting any fresher. He needs to go ask the rabbi.

So Simeon wraps the fish's body and head together in a cloth and carries it against his chest out into the street, where the neighbourhood is coming alive with fishermen and bakers, grocers and carpenters, wives and children running errands before the sun gets hot. His children trail behind him in a broken line. The man with the dead fish pressed against his heart feels that this bundle in the cloth, this thing in his arms, is somehow his most secret shame, and that the cloth only barely hides it and that the fish's blood seeping through it is a testament against him. His neighbours are staring, he knows. He keeps his eyes down and does not speak to anyone.

At the rabbi's house, he walks in on the family having breakfast. He babbles a brief apology and a briefer explanation, which of course he is forced to repeat fifteen times before anyone quite understands what has happened. His children have diffused in among the rabbi's many children, but each when prompted repeats the same story the father has told many times already, to the point where even the rabbi's children, in chorus with their young guests, begin repeating the story as if they too were witnesses.

The wife pushes the breakfast dishes to the side of the table. The fisherman places the fish on the table and unwraps the cloth. Fallen scales frame the fractured body like leaves scattered round a tree in autumn. A child is sent to fetch a string against which they can measure the fish. The rabbi picks up the head and looks in the fish's eyes, in its mouth, straight down through the back of its throat, open now to the air. They touch the fins and the spine, pluck scales and hold them up to the light. The room is full of watchers, children and women and a pair of cats just beginning to catch the scent, mewling and weaving among the many legs.

At last the rabbi sits in his chair at the table and gestures for his guest to do the same. They lean in close to each other. The room is silent.

("But the cats . . . ?")

(The wife has swept the cats out of the room and the mewling comes muffled through the front door.)

And the rabbi tells Simeon:

"It was a dybbuk."

I am a small boy and I have only the barest excuse for a religious formation: I could barely tell Moses from the mayor, and I hardly know what a dybbuk is meant to be. But it is certainly something frightening, because Babka leans in when she says it, whispers the word and then puts a hand to her mouth. The skin at the back of my neck seems to twist. I take a long drink of milk without blinking.

The rabbi tells the fisherman that the fish has to be buried, like a man, and not eaten. The whole family nods, and there is a collective sigh in the room at the justness of this verdict. The fisherman bows his head, and the rabbi lays a hand on his shoulder. There is a plot of land, he says, in the graveyard in the city, where they can put the fish to rest.

And that is just what they do.

"AND HE WILL not bother anyone after that," says Babka, and slaps her thigh. I jump a little in place, and Liba pulls back her paw, yawns and uncurls beside me.

"That's the end?" I still have half a cup of milk left, I realize, and take a deep gulp of it.

Babka clucks at me and waves a hand. "Yes, that's the end. They bury the fish in the graveyard. They give it a proper funeral." She rubs her chin and peers out the window at the rain. "The grave is still there today."

Here again is that twist at the back of my neck, the hairs coming awake against my skin. She speaks in Yiddish, but I reply in German. "There's a grave?"

"Yes, yes. In the ninth district, in the Seegasse cemetery. In a courtyard behind a hospital, I think. It's marked with a stone fish."

"Can I see it?"

"Why not? Get Papa to take you." She picks her tooth with a fingernail. She doesn't have many teeth left, my Babka, but she has most of the front ones so her smile is half-full, half-yellow, like a cob of dried corn.

I don't finish my cup of milk. I stare out the window, through the film of water beyond the glass, and I pull the blanket closer around me. Babka meanwhile takes the cup from my hands and gulps down the last of my drink, quite calmly, as if nothing at all has changed.

3

THE SEEGASSE CEMETERY IS NOT SO VERY FAR FROM
where we lived, as I see it now, but when I am a child it is
impossibly far and I despair of ever seeing the fish's grave. I
start to think about all the other graves I would like to see there, the
graves that, I feel, *must* be there: the fisherman's, and the rabbi's,
and the children's graves, and those of the cats as well. I feel when
I wake every morning, and when I go to bed at night, that there is
someone expecting to meet me in the graveyard across the canal.
With every moment I keep them waiting, it seems, the apologies I
owe grow heavier and heavier.

Zilla is the one who crosses our parents; I am so shy it seems
my family can sometimes forget I'm there. But I need to ask about
this; I'll burst if I don't. I tell Papa at the dinner table that I want to
go to Seegasse to look at the cemetery. He doesn't turn to me, but
raises an eyebrow as he cuts into his chicken.

"Why would you want to go there, Josef." It's not a question,
the way he says it. I feel the heat bubbling up into my cheeks, but
I can't go back to eating.

"There's a fish," I tell my father. Zilla looks at me, but I will not
let my eyes meet hers. I feel I'll burn up like a sheet of paper, *poof,*

nothing. And oh, I wish I were someone else just now, someone who could speak.

"There's a fish pond?" Mutti doesn't smile at me, but there is something in her tone that suggests yielding, or at the very least, real interest.

"No. It's not alive. It's buried."

Zilla laughs at this, and Papa rubs his forehead. From down the table, Oma blinks at me, chewing slowly.

Mutti says, "People don't bury fish, Josef. They eat them."

"Not this one." My heart is beating fast again, and I feel I can see with an inward eye a whole host of people, standing, waiting for me across the canal, people who have no notion of why I haven't come to them yet. "This one talked."

Mutti frowns at me now. "Josef, I think the boys at school have been telling you stories."

"I didn't hear it at school," I say. But then my face goes red as if my cheeks have been boiled, and I hope with all my heart I won't have to tell them that Babka is the one who told me about the fish.

"I wonder where you did hear it, then." Papa still hasn't really looked at me.

Then Oma says, "Perhaps he heard it in the market, Daniel."

Now Papa does look up. We all look up at Oma when she says that, even Opa, who is mostly deaf.

My father blinks at his mother-in-law. "Why would he have heard it in the market?"

"It's an old legend," says Oma, and though her voice isn't strong, her every word makes my heart thrum harder, stronger. "I remember Helena's aunt telling it to me once, when I was a little girl."

Now Papa's forehead turns hard and rutted. "I won't have my son traipsing about after fairy-tale creatures."

Oma picks up her fork. I hate the sound of eating when I'm not hungry, when no one is shouting or shushing and it feels as if the food is just there to fill people's mouths and bury the things waiting to be said.

"What was the story, Oma?" Zilla is leaning forward now.

"We're eating, Zilla. You may save the nursery-room talk for the nursery," Papa says.

Zilla has hazel eyes that are long and slanted and bright, and when she narrows them at my father it seems that the reason he keeps his eyes on his food is so he won't have to meet her gaze.

"Josef will tell us if Oma won't," Zilla says.

Papa says, "Josef will finish his supper in silence, as children should."

"Josef," says my sister, sitting straight in her seat, staring hard at me, "tell us about the fish."

I burn red again. I stare at my plate. I can't eat or speak.

"Zilla, listen to your father," Mutti says.

"I just want to learn something about local history," Zilla says to our mother, but the words, her choice of them, are meant for Papa.

"You may hear all you like about local *history*," my father snaps, "but fairy stories aren't adult conversation."

"I don't even know if it is a fairy tale. I don't know the first thing about it." Zilla is on the cusp of shouting. "Besides, you didn't mind talking about the *Christkind* when Fritz visited."

"The *Christkind*," says my father, "*is* local history, in that it's a notable cultural phenomenon, an interesting element of pseudo-Christian apocrypha, and worth remarking on by men and women who have anything remarkable to say." Papa's voice is rising with every word. "Neither Fritz Reiter, nor your mother, nor I were at all interested in the *Christkind* per se. But we were interested in the way Christians incorporate pagan stories into their own histories and then convert cultural phenomena into market opportunities. If you have anything intelligent to add on that topic, by all means, speak up."

Zilla, across the table from me, is hunched in silence, and though I don't look at her I can feel her tension. Someone's fork taps at a plate.

"Maybe," says Zilla, "I'm curious about this story of the fish as a cultural phenomenon."

I look up as Papa sweeps his napkin up from the table, dabs his moustache as if the little hairs pain him, his face reddening. He then presses his napkin down hard into the tablecloth. He says:

"The damned fish isn't a phenomenon. It's six-hundred-year-old stupidity beloved by second-district idiots who've kept their heads buried since they were children."

Zilla says, "But Josef *is* a child."

And Papa says, "Not that kind of child, he's not."

And I expect Zilla to stand up, or throw something or break something, so fierce is the tightness in her jaw and the heat in her eye—but she doesn't, she sits still, quiet, stares at her plate. Except that now she glances up at me, and I see in the steadiness of her gaze that her fierceness is a slow-burning thing, something that need not be spent tonight.

Papa and Mutti speak about a friend of Papa's who is hosting a party. Oma and Opa take small bites of food, and Zilla and I sit and shift our dinner around in front of us.

I want, just then, to fall into the river and fly away underwater. There it wouldn't matter that I couldn't make anyone understand me.

THAT EVENING I cry, but in my heart I can't muster the courage to face the silent dead who wait across the canal. I don't apologize. I don't say anything. I'm like I was at the supper table, unable to meet anyone's eye, wishing I could be more invisible than a thought.

In the morning I still have trouble eating. I sit and look at my feet in their wool socks, at the blue knit that's ridged and grated, little *V*s all the way down to my toes, *V* for *Vater*, for *Verschuldung*, for *verboten*.

But Zilla walks me to school that morning. She walks me in silence for two blocks, holding my mittened hand in hers, and her fingers are tight and hard around my hand. I know she is angry at our parents, at Papa specifically, but in my mind it becomes me whom she can't stand. And it's another reason to say sorry, her walking there beside me; it's another reason to make myself speak, but I can't. My throat is dry and I choke on the word.

When we reach a cross street on Pappenheimgasse, we wait for the traffic in the road to slow before we cross. A man with a horse and cart has pulled over by the curb. He stands with his face towards the animal's tail and reaches down to the horse's muddied hoof. Before consenting to lift it, the horse makes a noise like a chair creaking under someone heavy, and lowers its lips almost down to the mud. With one hoof against its master's thigh the horse seems to lean on the man; they prop each other up in the street.

And as I am watching them, Zilla says into my ear, "I'll take you to the cemetery." And she tugs my hand to walk across the street.

At first I trot beside and a little behind her, tugged along, chewing on words. She will take me to the cemetery. She will take me there? I splash through slush without thinking of it. Though Papa doesn't want it? I nearly trip over an old woman's boot as she stands in a shop doorway. Now?

"Now?" I say.

"No, not now." Zilla is looking straight ahead, and her face is like a statue, a proud statue, fierce. "On Saturday afternoon, after school. I'll tell Papa we're going to the Prater. He won't mind. He won't care." She rips up the last words in her mouth.

Leaping along beside her, there are a thousand things I want to ask her, but I just say, "He might be mad."

"Let me handle that," Zilla tells me, and finally she does look down at me, hazel eyes on fire, and her gaze is on something beyond or within me, something I've not yet seen. But she smiles. And she says, "Aren't you going to thank me?"

But "thank you" is another of those things my tight, dry throat won't let me say, so I just press my cheek hard against her mitten. All around us is the great noisy world of people, but in my heart there is a stillness and a light, and I am a lamp cupped in my sister's hand, a warm bright hidden light.

ON SATURDAY AFTERNOON, after school and through the rain, my sister takes me down towards the canal, and our feet slapping against wet pavement sound like someone applauding at a concert. The canal today is itself a grey-green pavement of ripples under mist and I drag back a little on Zilla's arm, staring at it, as we cross the bridge. Water pools in the iron grooves tracing the main streets, the slots that guide the trams, but when our own streetcar comes the rain has slowed to a drizzle.

We step off and turn onto Seegasse, towards the cemetery, and then I can't tell you what the world looks like. Zilla leads me by the hand through wide hospital doors. There are people murmuring all around us, and a tile floor against which our shoes tap out clear and sharp. At a desk she asks how to access the graveyard. A male voice rumbles above me then, and next come footfalls, which we follow. Then down a few stairs, and then the far doors. A key turning in a lock. Dark earth and grass underfoot, and the sharp, damp air in my mouth.

I can't look up at first. I can't stand to see it. This little world is a place I don't dare to meet with my eyes, perhaps because it's real, it's here, finally, when it was too deep and too powerful to be real before. There's this trembling in my middle, in the deepest place, where feelings meet my body and become real. In that place I am Simeon with the fish; I am he, with his shame or his fear pressed against his heart, not yet knowing how to lay it down.

But Zilla squeezes my hand. "We're here."

I lean closer against her. "I can wait here," I just manage to say, just barely manage to say.

Zilla snorts. "There's nothing to be scared of. It's just a graveyard. There's no one here."

I peek up and see stone. First it is a wall, it has to be a wall, but then everything falls back into depth and no, it's row after row of headstones, all grey, some more or less straight but all weathered, chiselled and patterned with marks that mean nothing to me. In between them, the grass. Above us is the sky, and the sky is crossed with branches, and the trees are old, deep, dark. There are the birds, and the light, and the smell of earth and the noise on the street far away and muffled by these buildings. There's no one accusing me. There is no one.

"Let's find your fish." Zilla gives my hand a tug.

I patter after her, but my heart and my eyes are caught on every stone as we go past it. A person, another person, a soul, a soul, a soul. This is the feeling I don't know how to hold. The patterns on the headstones look like music, and they look like question marks. Every one is a person and there are too many of them to hold on to.

It's row on row on row, not neat, but labyrinthine, medieval; a dwarf forest of stone. Tall and short and tilted and fat and hunched and broken. There is a question that hangs over them, all of them, and it's a question for me, but I can't quite hear it to answer it. Zilla is walking and walking and I can't stop, not to ask or to explain.

And then Zilla says, "There it is! I see it."

I don't know how I have room left to feel more, but there's something particular for the prospect of the fish. I'm frightened. It's a wicked thing, I think, the thing that died, this fish. But the man killed it; he killed it with a single stroke and it did nothing to defend itself but cry holy words aloud, and too late. They put it to rest with relief, I remember, and with an amen for the rightness of it. Here is a place things were put right, I make myself remember.

My eyes are on the grass just in front of my feet because I'm afraid to see it. Zilla has stopped walking and drops my hand. "Well, here it is," she says.

As I lift my eyes, it is as if the monument drops slowly down into the grass from above. Just stones, first. Round stones piled together in a column, to about the height of my chest. And then a kind of stone table on top of that, and then—it's not frightening, the stone fish. It's arced like a letter U, tail to the sky, mouth to the sky. Its lips are opened wide as if to shout the words my grandmother said with such agony—but to me then it seems as if this is another fish, or perhaps the fish at another time, not at the hour of its death. It looks to me as if it's singing.

"There's nothing written, but this must be it," says Zilla. She walks around the stone fish, looking at the different sides of the monument. I just stand and stare. The moment is a flavour I can hold on my tongue and not have to swallow. I'm rinsed out inside, hollow and clean.

Zilla crosses her arms and looks around us. "I wish Papa could see us now," she says, more to herself than to me. It's hard to understand her sometimes. I am so glad our father can't see us. If Papa knew, I would be a coward again; I'd freeze up and be nothing.

"I'm going to walk around." My sister says it and stretches her ankles as she walks, one foot pointed straight in front of her, then the other. Away from me and into the garden of gravestones. I stay meanwhile by the fish. Whatever word is on its fat, gasping lips is a silent one, said forever—as if it's a word that only the fish knows, and God. And in this moment I feel that it's a joke between the two of them.

It's so easy to slip down onto my knees in the grass. My knees are bare and the ground is cold, damp, but not hard. I press my palms into the earth and watch the way the fish's stone column meets the earth, like a finger pressed hard into the ground, and the ground pushing back. I squeeze my own fingertips into the earth. I can get earth underneath my fingernails and in the lines on my fingertips. I can rub my knees green on the grass. I can take a part of it upon me, just a little bit.

Zilla, somewhere, is singing to herself, and the birds are singing and the earth is quiet.

A breeze in the trees.

And a bit of rain now beginning to fall, just a breath of it, a wet breath. This little boy I was is lying on the ground now, sinking into it. His eyes are closed, have been closed he doesn't know how long. He might be in bed. He might be dreaming.

Zilla shakes my jacket. "Get up, dummy. It's raining."

After pressing into the earth for so long, to sit up feels like floating. My front is muddied and greened, and my face must be too, my cheek on the side the earth pressed into me. Zilla just shakes her head and says, "You're a funny one."

The fish is exactly as it was, and this for some reason is the deepest comfort I can imagine. Nothing new but the spots of wet from the rain, speckling it darker and darker.

"Come on," says Zilla. "I'm freezing."

Though she makes me wipe my hand on the back of my short pants first, she takes my hand in hers and walks us through the rain, through the hospital lobby, out to the street. I drift beside her, watching my feet, not noticing the road or the people who pass. We stop beside a man roasting chestnuts in a steel barrel and Zilla pays him for a packet.

"The boy's going to be in trouble with his mama," says the chestnut vendor, from somewhere high above. I'm watching my knees, the way the mud is crusted on them, breaking and cracking and dark here, lighter there, like paint.

"I'll brush him off if I can. He's a little silly," says Zilla to the chestnut man, and he laughs.

Zilla gives me a chestnut and at first I only hold it, warming my hands. The day is cold and wet, after all, though I haven't felt it until now. There's a fire in the man's barrel, mainly charcoal, burning low. The same fire is in my chestnut, just enough of it. I press it hard between my hands and up against my chest.

Zilla says, "Eat it before it gets cold. I've got a whole bag."

And so I pull apart the shell with my thumbs, revealing the thing that looks like a little dried plum, or, in that moment, a shrivelled yellow heart, something long dead, and that makes my heart catch. I put it in my mouth as much to hide it as to taste it. It burns

30

me when I chew, but I don't mind, it's all warmth, and tastes like winter and potato and sweetness. There is a heat in the middle of me, a glowing coal.

Zilla is still talking to the chestnut man, and there's another gentleman, someone dressed in a good coat, with a scarf wrapped tight around his neck, smiling at her from a few feet away. I stand very close to my sister and as tall as I can manage. The heat is still there in the middle of me and I won't shy away while I have this fire inside me. It makes me into a stronger boy. It makes me into someone who doesn't run.

WHEN WE GET home, outside the building, Zilla does a good, fierce job beating the dirt off my clothes and my knees, and she wipes my face clean with her handkerchief. When we go inside, my mother is reading a letter on the sofa in the parlour, with her feet tucked up under her and her head propped against her knuckles, the light falling on her from the lamp on the wall making her face very beautiful. She doesn't look up right away as we walk in.

"Well, we're back," says Zilla to our mother, and our mother sighs and stretches one leg, like Babka's cat, still not quite looking at us.

"Oh, good. Make sure you wash up before supper."

She hasn't even seen the dirt on me, and this makes me feel suddenly as if she knows everything. Her un-smile, her soft cat-ness on the sofa is a power, a secret. I try to find the chestnut warmth in me. Zilla starts to press me out of the room, towards the stairs.

Then Mutti asks, "Where were you again, Zilla?"

And then I know, I know she knows. God! It's awful; it freezes my heart and pulls my forehead down.

But Zilla just says, "At the Prater, Mutti."

And my mother says, "Ah," and then nothing. And Zilla pushes her hands into my shoulder blades, *up, up*, because I've stopped walking on the stairs and she needs me to walk up, up. I find my feet, a thousand miles below me and heavy as lead, and lift the one, the other, up and up.

I go to my room, and under the soft light coming in through the window and the rain I curl up on my bed and close my eyes. I try to find in my heart the people across the canal. I can see them through rain but only barely, just barely. In the rain there is a fish swimming, laughing. There is a man who holds a bundle to his heart. There is the earth and the green grass and grey stone, and somewhere up above the clouds the sky is blue. And I am here in my own heart, pulling a shell back around the warmth in me.

I dream that night that everyone I ever knew is carved out of stone.

4

S O MUCH ONE DOES NOT WANT TO REMEMBER, AND YET, stirred up like mud in the riverbed, all of it comes back and stops me seeing clearly. I have felt this so often. But consider: I have felt also at times as if this might be a gift held out to me, something so prodigiously good I hardly dare receive it. And could it be that the way into some darker truths is through joy? I was a mud-covered child beside a fish's grave, but I was also a young man, and a young woman whose father first led me to my calling once wrote me a letter.

I haven't yet met my Anna when this happens; I'm about twenty, I think. I know her name because her father, who first saw me among the gravestones, sometimes mentions her.

(What a muddle this is, for I have so much left to explain, and I'm fitting the pieces as they come to hand. Wait, Josef; how did you become what you are—a graveyard keeper? And a man of faith? These matters still need to be set down plainly.)

Let me dwell a moment here, though—for before there is Anna's voice or her eyes or the bend of her small waist, there are her words on a sheet of paper her brother gives me:

Dear Josef Tobak,

My father likes you, and it's making me crazy.

Her brother Jakob Dükmann called to me near their father's shop: "Josef, my kid sister has some complaint with you," and passed this folded paper into my hand—and imagine it, I thought only, How can this girl be upset with me, she's never met me, as I tucked the page in my pocket and strode towards the canal to catch a tram. Now I read it while I ride the streetcar:

> *Don't you know what kind of ship he runs? A watertight one, Mr. Tobak—not the jolly sort, this man. And when I've committed some sin, do you know what he tells me? "That boy Tobak is so kind to me, and he is not even my flesh, but you . . ." And oh Mr. Tobak, the guilt, the guilt; he can spread it on thicker than butter. I can't stand it. It makes me tear my hair out. My father's daughter will be bald. Serves her right.*
>
> *And so: will you please say something rude to him, Mr. Tobak? For our household's sake, understand. It's either that or help me be more patient with him, but this is impossible, and after all you're so busy with work and the cemeteries and good-boy things like that. How I envy you your work! If I were a boy, would you take me as your apprentice? Forget it, actually—if I were a boy, I'd be halfway to New York by now.*
>
> *So please promise me one thing, Mr. Tobak: someday we must meet. I'm so sick of hearing about you, and I would like some argument besides, "I don't believe this person exists." What satisfaction I'd get to find out you were some oily sycophant, and that I was the deserving one all along.*

34

Until then, Mr. Tobak, I wish you rash judgment and offen-siveness. Be a rude fellow, please, and I'll be the sweet one; or else who knows what scene there will be when we meet. Don't even consider it, Mr. Tobak—I won't spend a moment's thought on it, I'm sure.

Yours in perfect sincerity,
Anna Dükmann

I miss my stop, I'll set that down; I'm twenty minutes late for work because of her letter. Oh, fool that I am, I don't dare write back; the idea, then, makes my heart beat wildly so that I nearly consider misunderstanding her cheek, taking her at her word and insulting her poor father for her supposed benefit.

It's foolishness, it's ridiculous; I haven't said a word about how I met these people, and I am getting so ahead of myself. Patience, Josef. Anna, dear heart: there is so much that is hard to set down, and I must concentrate, since I have set myself a task. But your words are part of it, and your mind is part of it; therefore it's not so silly to head down this road—because so little of our lives make sense apart from this, and despite this meandering I am trying to make sense, I promise you.

FIND A WAY down that road from our first path, then, Josef:

That same year I first hear from Anna Dükmann—around 1930, I imagine—there is an evening when I stand with Friedrich Zimmel on the balcony at the back of his parents' house in the nineteenth district, and he says to me, "I don't think I've ever had especially good justification for being alive."

This is Friedrich, then: he is taller than me, and broader, with dark, slicked hair and a tall forehead. He has a way of holding his mouth, I think unconsciously, so that his lips look soft and womanish. Tonight he is wearing a waistcoat over his white shirt, and his trousers are dark grey, expensively tailored in a way I wouldn't understand except for the fact that my clothes hang off me so oddly in comparison.

(This is all years before circumstances really try us, understand; years before any man, least of all myself, would call Friedrich *collaborator*, far less *murderer*. And forgive me if by setting down his darkness in this way I seem to suggest his guilt in advance. How can I say what I mean? That darkness is his innocence as much as it is his guilt, and that's all I can puzzle out now.)

But on the balcony that night, I don't say anything right away. It's possible he's had too much to drink. Behind us, beyond the glass doors, in the living room and throughout the house, Friedrich's and his mother and father's friends are laughing and talking and pouring drinks. Friedrich leans against the stone banister and looks out into the dark, at the apricot trees in the corner of the yard where it is almost completely black.

So I ask him, "Did you do something wrong?"

He shrugs and rubs his forehead. "No, that's not what I mean. It's just that . . . Well. A man wants his work to be meaningful, you understand?"

I scratch my wrist. It's very thin between my fingers—too thin, Babka would say. Babka is still alive, will still be alive even until I flee this city. I have trouble eating, sometimes. I get ill more often than a young man should.

"My father was certainly very grateful to have work after the war," I tell him, and it's true, though I don't think I've yet discussed it with Friedrich in such clear terms. It's understood that Friedrich was instrumental in keeping Papa employed when the economy was at its weakest. He did it for Zilla, I'm sure. But it's ridiculous. Zilla isn't interested in him; she's having an affair with a French painter (married, I believe, though I don't like to think about it), and the young women who would love to have Friedrich love them are probably lined up beyond the balcony doors, just there, a pane of glass away from us.

"I'm glad," he says, and he opens his mouth, wants to say more, but he doesn't. He stands straight and he stretches his arms. He turns towards the doors, and he looks as if he's about to walk back inside, but then he sets his drink down on the banister, and he swipes it off into the night as if flicking a bit of dirt off a tabletop. There's a shattering and a clinking on the stone patio below.

Friedrich stares after it a second or two, then says, "Oh, well."

He goes inside. I stand for a moment, and then I walk up to the banister and peer into the pool of light pouring onto the patio from the ground floor. Friedrich's glass is like a firework frozen on the stone, little shards of glass sparkling like stars. The night smells like earth and apricot blossoms, it's getting cold and a part of me is very much aware that I'm not at home here.

AND IT IS the same feeling, I think, on the night I meet Anna. It's New Year's Eve, 1932, and I am out with Zilla and her friends, for imitation-champagne toasts in the downtown streets and to visit the merchants, with their little stands, who sell the New Year's pigs made of tin or clay or wood.

But—think of it! how we'd meant to spend that night—I have to go back and re-examine the memory. (Considering it now, it seems almost portentous, in what way and when our paths intersect in life.) For Zilla and I had intended to meet with some Czechoslovakian cousins of ours who'd just moved to Vienna: my father's first cousin on his mother's side, her daughter Sarah Kostner, and Sarah's daughter, Lena.

Understand, my father was not close with them; he called them superstitious country folk and neglected to answer their letters. Mutti told Zilla our father had a bourgeois horror of Sarah's illegitimate daughter. Zilla saw it another way: "They're not assimilated," she told me. "They're like Babka. They embarrass him."

But these, we've learned, are proud cousins: sensing our judgment, Sarah Kostner now refuses to see us. Zilla, with her natural affinity for anyone who makes Papa nervous, has already penetrated these defences and made a friend of Sarah; but when I propose to go with her to spend New Year's Eve with the Kostners, we hear back, "No, thank you; my mother isn't well and Lena is just getting over a cold."

How it shames me, this answer. I feel all the barbed indignation of a single mother aimed at me, and it's too easy to believe I deserve it. But Zilla says, "Never mind, little Josef, you'll come out with my friends and have a wild time for once."

And I do dress for it, wool cap and scarf and jacket over my suit, and I walk along the old streets behind Zilla, who has her arm on that of a fellow I've never seen before. He's wearing imperial military dress in a size too small for his shoulders, which, because Zilla seems to put up with him, I can only assume is a joke. Friedrich is behind me, and has his arm around a shapely blond girl with a country accent whom I believe he is sleeping with but whose name I can never remember. There are others of Zilla's and Friedrich's friends with us too, but I find myself quiet tonight, and still a little ashamed. I listen to the way my feet crunch over refrozen slush. My mind replays a phrase of fiddle music, over and over, until I start to hum it to myself without thinking.

The air is sharp and thin, well below freezing, and the seasonal scents of chestnuts roasting in barrels and of hot spiced wine make this moment seem outside of time and eternal. Boys are lighting firecrackers on the side streets, snaps sounding sharp through the din and flavouring the air with hints of sulphur. People buy little model pigs at the stands by the roadside. Zilla searches every year for the most obscene figurines and makes her boyfriends buy them for her, and then she names the pigs after the men. It seems they always take it as a compliment in the moment.

And perhaps I would have stayed the whole night with them, drifting through the sounds and smells and into whichever apartment or club cupped the dregs of their laughing as the sky turned morning grey. I don't know what that other path would have been. But the fellow in the military coat finds a waxy-looking resin pig and hands it to Zilla. She starts when she first sees it, and this makes me pay attention—but then she throws back her head and laughs.

"You really know how to charm a girl, Franzi." Slaps his arm and makes as if to throw the figurine on the ground, and he cackles and snatches it.

"Let me buy it for you, ugly darling, let me buy it for you." He talks in a little-boy voice. It makes my blood boil. I know that Zilla despises him, as she always despises this kind of man, but she lets her admirers traipse around after her, making fools of themselves, as if it is the best kind of amusement she knows. I want to beat this fool, though, and make him stop laughing, make him kiss her feet through tears.

"My ugly, ugly darling," he coos, and she only laughs more, and they make hideous faces at each other. I see that Friedrich's blonde is trying to show him something, but his eyes are on Zilla and he looks as I feel, full of that static level rage that seems tranquil until the moment it explodes.

So I say, "What is it, Zilla?"

And, "Nothing," she says, "just a stupid pig."

The man behind the counter, the man selling the pigs, has a grin like a slug. Half his display is an open box, a case he can snap shut and thrust under the table, I know from years previous, if a police officer comes sniffing. He looks as if he's waiting for someone to catch his meaning, though he hasn't said anything.

Friedrich strides over to the pigs in the box, lifts one into the light.

"Oh, for God's sake," he says. "Worse and worse every year." But his girlfriend shrieks, and he half-grins at her sharp, strong country laugh.

"You're digging your own grave," Zilla tells this fellow, this Franzi, "but buy it if you must. If it's what you like."

"You know it's what I like," he says, and nudges her shoulder.

And now I expect Zilla to laugh, with and at this man so far beneath her, as she always does; but instead she glares at him for a moment, her face like flint.

I go over to the pig stand as Zilla is moving away from it, reach out towards a little figurine with Friedrich saying, behind me, "Don't bother; don't humour him, Josef"—but too late. I've got one in my hand. And of course it's pornographic, crude—I was expecting that: the creature's waxen trotter wrapped improbably round its little mushroom penis, eyes buggy in what I assume is meant to be ecstasy but which looks like rage. But beyond the pornographic aspect, it's not just a pig; it's a Turkish pig, or the stall man's vision, at least, of a Turkish pig, which means fez, moustache, black-lined eyes and red vest.

The stall man chortles to himself. "She liked one of these ones, over here."

At this point I know what it's going to be—because a stall keeper, in Vienna, at the cap of 1932, who sells masturbating Turkish pigs couldn't possibly fail to sell masturbating Jewish pigs. But it's more than that—and at the first one I almost want to laugh: another rage-faced hog, with a broad black hat and sidelocks, but this one is mounting a piggy bank from behind. The piggy bank's face is blithe and innocent, but there are cracks painted on its pink back end, cracks radiating from its assailant. I half-think, At least it's kind of clever; but then the fellow, this stall keeper, says, "No, these—these are even better."

He's showing me female pigs, half-female pigs, pig threesomes and pigs licking each other, all furious-looking, their Jewishness indicated by a yarmulke or (in cases of what must be laziness on the part of the sculptor) a Star of David painted on the rump. It's so absurdly juvenile, so completely unoriginal in its crudeness, that I glance up at the stall keeper and say, "And these sell?"

"Oh, certainly they sell," he says. "Who doesn't like them? Your friend, the little whore, you could tell: she's a Jew, but she wants it. Just like animals, you know? Fuck like pigs."

He starts to rearrange the creatures on the table. He's done paying attention to me.

And that feeling, now, as Friedrich is drifting away from me, even as he's calling, "Come on, Josef," and as Zilla finds something new to laugh at and as the night breathes cool on me: *Come!* But I can't do it. And certainly it's not the first time I've seen Vienna's ugly underbelly—so what, then? A finishedness, maybe; a tiredness, along with the anger. I've had enough.

Teenagers in the alley are screaming; the air is cold like peppermint. It's an hour before midnight. Enough, now.

As I'm walking away, Zilla calls, "Where are you going, Josef?"

"Just home, I think," I call back. "I'm tired."

They yell after me, "Happy New Year!"—and I raise a hand to them, but they won't miss me now, I know.

I am tired, and I do mean to go home, but so tired at first that I drift down the street past screaming women dangling off their men, people hanging out of bar doors, singing, and an accordion playing through one window, a trumpet through another.

When someone grabs my arm, my whole body tenses to shake him off and run—but then: "Tobak! Typical! You're the only fellow on the street who isn't smiling."

I turn towards Jakob Dükmann, this man, my friend. I take him by the hand. And, "Thank God," I say, "I thought you were going to murder me."

It makes him laugh. He slaps my arm. He invites me along with him: "Come back to my house," he says. His whole family's there, he tells me, and some friends too. "Vati will be glad to see you. You're his favourite son."

It's a joke, of course, but it changes the colour of the night. Tobias Dükmann is Jakob's father, and so different from my own father that it baffles me. From a distance and with a child's heart, I love Tobias Dükmann. And I love Jakob and his brother, and though I've hardly ever seen her, I love their mother, Ella, too.

Jakob adds: "My sister's there tonight. I'll let you dance with her, if you're good."

5

B ut wait—I must explain how Tobias Dükmann
came into my life. I told you that there was little religion
in our family, and this is true. Still, it's next to impossible to
escape it in Vienna, for better or for worse. And I do sometimes go
into synagogues, it's true, even as a boy—none of Papa's efforts can
prevent that. When my cousin Ben is thirteen, Oma and Opa keep
asking when his bar mitzvah will be, and my father finds it impossible to explain that he doesn't want us to attend. In the end he tells
them Zilla will find out, which of course she does immediately,
purely to make Papa crazy. On the day, I sit in the synagogue and
watch my older cousin who is for a moment like a creature turned
to gold and a pillar of song, and my ears seem to close off the rustling and breathing around me. I feel as if a conversation has begun;
but although I sense that I have met someone's eyes and smiled,
the first word is still hanging over us and I can't seem to remember
who it is I'm talking to.

Mutti's brother Tomas, my uncle, is not an especially pious
man, but he is good friends with the cantor at the Turkish synagogue, and he keeps kosher and observes the Sabbath and holy
days. He imports coffee and chocolate and runs a shop by the

canal; still, Papa can hardly stand to see him and tells Mutti he is a rat. Sometimes Tomas takes me to spend the day with him, and this is sometimes wonderful and sometimes terribly boring: it depends whether he is running errands in his buggy or stopping somewhere to drink with his friends, which usually lasts for hours and seems to let him forget I'm there.

Once, when I am eleven years old, Tomas takes me to the Turkish synagogue while he visits his friend. It's a sweltering day, the middle of summer, and the air inside is thick and still. He has left me alone in a pew while he and Mr. Zawady sit a ways away, talking quietly. The Turkish synagogue is beautiful inside, burnished gold. In the heat it seems the air itself is golden, and that this is what gives it weight. It strikes me for the first time then that a great deal of effort and money went into making this space, and still goes into keeping it up. And I think about how many seats there are around me, and how much space for people and how it is built to house a multitude—not for work and not for amusement, nor even simply for community, but for a community in prayer. For the first time I understand the fact that there are adults who sincerely believe in God.

I ought to be roasting in my skin, but the thought sends a chill through me. It seems ridiculous that Tomas and Mr. Zawady have not heard me think it, that they don't turn and stare at me. And then the fact that they don't, and that I'm still sitting here and that no one knows what has happened, makes me feel terribly small and alone. I peer all around me, at the ceiling and the walls and the pews and my own hands on the polished wood beside me. I am realizing something that I never realized before: that what the people who built this synagogue believed either is true or is not true. If it's not true, what a pity for them; but if it is true, and if a person could shuffle through his life never realizing it—well, pity wouldn't begin to account for it.

When Tomas is coming back towards me, I am still sitting in this new understanding, wide-eyed in it as I never am otherwise, except perhaps when I'm alone in the graveyard. Tomas is nearly beside me and I know that there is something I need to do before he speaks and a door shuts on this moment. And it seems then that I know what word has been hanging over me since that day at my cousin's bar mitzvah: it's what I have to say—it is, "I'm listening."

Tomas pats my shoulder as my mind says it and, like a switch, I feel my own sweat on my skin for the first time in what seems like hours.

At my own bar mitzvah, two years later (my mother's family having proven instrumental in overriding my father's disapproval), as I stand in front of a hundred faces who all look, for an instant, like candles flickering, there is a moment like the moment in the Turkish synagogue, but also different from it—a realization, both terrifying and wonderful, that in that earlier moment I had already decided what I believed.

AFTER THAT, WHEN I walk to the Seegasse cemetery (as I often do, no longer needing my sister to take me there by the hand), when I touch the gravestones and when I sit by the stone fish—in all those moments, this knowledge is a lamp and a hunger. I feel as if there is a direction I'm headed in now, but I don't yet know how to move my feet. I have not told anyone what I have become—a young man who believes in God—and I hold this secret inside me. This is the state I'm in when the Dükmann family first finds me, when I'm sixteen.

The two boys, one older than me and one younger, follow me when I leave the graveyard one day, run up after me and make me jump before I realize they're not looking for someone to punch. Chaim is a tall young man with a hard face and strong arms, and right away I defer to him; Jakob is small and grinning, healthier-looking than I am, but also more of a boy. Chaim introduces himself and his brother and then asks me if I would like to come to a meeting with them.

I suspect I know what kind of meeting he means. There are all kinds of youth movements in the second district, secular and religious, would-be militant and pacifist. I have never gone to any of their meetings, perhaps because of the many choices and a fear of choosing the wrong one. So I ask Chaim, "What group?"

He shakes his head. "Not a group," he says, "not like that. My father is having a meeting this afternoon at his shop. There's a Hebrew scholar from Poland in town. He's going to give an informal lecture."

"There will be food," Jakob adds.

I have a vision of a Polish scholar, a white-bearded man with hawkish eyes, quizzing me in Hebrew. "Thank you very much," I say, "but your father hasn't invited me."

"He told us to invite you," Chaim says. "He said, 'Go see if that young ghost of the Seegasse cemetery might be interested.'"

I suspect I go ghost-white when he says it. There are sometimes people in the cemetery when I visit, but I have always thought myself more or less invisible. That there may have been someone noticing me—observing me—fills me with a trespasser's guilt.

"I think he wants to meet you," Chaim says.

"But I'm not very interesting," I tell him. "Really, I'm not. And I don't know anything."

Jakob says, "More reason to come, then."

"You really ought to," says Chaim. "This isn't an everyday opportunity."

It's by some miracle of courage, I think, that I follow them, all the while thinking of excuses to leave suddenly. They talk mostly to each other, mostly about their personal concerns, names I don't recognize, schedules that sound important. Eventually, perhaps because this all seems so ridiculous and mysterious, I ask them, "Is your father a rabbi?"

They laugh, and Jakob says, "He's a tailor."

"But," Chaim says, in a quieter voice, "he's a very holy man."

I have never heard a teenaged boy say such a thing about his father, and it keeps me quiet, wondering, for the rest of the while we walk together.

We come to the tailor shop, a large-windowed shop on a street corner, with a suited mannequin in the display. Chaim holds the door open, and immediately there's the low grumble of male voices from the back room. We head towards the sound, and Jakob says, as we pass into the far room, "We brought him, Vati."

I will not remember in detail what the Polish scholar said in his lecture; he speaks mainly in Yiddish and about things I've never heard of before. All the same, it doesn't feel alien so much as deep, as if it were something I could fall into without completely understanding it, rather than something I had to think my way through—more like a river, perhaps, than an algebra problem.

I remember Tobias Dükmann, though. To me, as a sixteen-year-old, he is a strange new kind of man: one who smiles as much inwardly as outwardly, and who (above everything, and strangest of all) approaches every person here with the same quiet, steady attention. He seems older than my father, though perhaps it is because of his beard and glasses. Chaim introduces me by name, and Dükmann greets me with, "At last, young man," and grips my shoulders, smiling. He seats me by the wall, near the radiator, where I have a good view of everything and don't feel everyone's eyes on me.

Halfway through the lecture (which is indeed very informal, with this or that old fellow in the audience volunteering an anecdote or asking a question every few minutes), there's a knock on the door and a woman who must be Mrs. Dükmann enters, carrying a covered basket wafting scent that makes my mouth water. Dükmann stands and calls for an intermission, which the lecturer seems to welcome as much as anyone.

I eat with them—I hardly know, then, what it is, though I remember, I think, the squish of pastry. The people talk to me and I say Yes, and Pleased to meet you, and I'm Josef Tobak, I'm in school, and My father is an accountant. At one point Tobias Dükmann takes me by the arm and leads me to a corner, out of the way of the others, and he says, "What hope you give me, Tobak! What hope."

"Oh," is all I can say.

"Do you know," he goes on, "no one, unless he's mourning someone, looks the way you do in the cemetery. But even then— even the mourners, it's simpler: one soul, and you wish them back, or you wish you could have done more, you know, missed less. With you—ah. With you, Tobak."

He stares straight in my eyes, and I want to flinch. I want to look at the wall or his hairline or anywhere but back into his eyes. He says, "You didn't know those people, did you?"

"No," I say. "No, not one of them." Does he know how old the gravestones are?

"That's what I mean." I don't know yet that his eyes are always moist like that, and I think for a moment that he might weep. "But you don't look like a tourist. I wonder if you feel, sometimes, as if you're remembering all of them?"

I open my mouth to contradict him, but—nothing. Part of me thinks, It is something like that; but then again, not quite.

"Isn't it right—I ask myself this—isn't it right, in some sense, that we're all completely forgotten, eventually? By men, I mean. All but a few, the few of the few, who do something terrible or very, very good. It's right." He shrugs. "It keeps a man small, you see? It makes him mindful. 'Vanity of vanities!' But Tobak—" Now he leans into me, and I smell on his breath tobacco and his wife's cooking. "I persist in believing, you see, that there has to be some-one to bear the memory of us."

His "us" makes the corner of my lip twitch. I scratch the side of my head. "Yes, sir."

"I have seen," he says, "what happens when everyone forgets, and I'll show it to you. But it's more than that, you see. You know that, Josef." He is pleading for my yes, but I am still trying to understand what we're doing, the two of us, here in this corner. He goes on: "More than the stones, Josef, more than the grass and the trees, and more even than the bones—it's deeper than that, what's lost."

I try to mouth the yes he wants from me, but my mouth opens and shuts like the jaw of a fish. There is a hand on his sleeve now, and someone speaking to him—and that's all. Our conversation ends. He turns to walk back towards his friends, but at the last moment he reaches out towards me and he says, "I'll show you what I mean. This Sunday."

=

49

THERE IS THE rest of the evening, but it hardly matters; and the rest of the week, but it flies by without a thought. And on Sunday I meet with Tobias Dükmann in front of his shop. It's a white-grey day, overcast and cool; it smells like rain. The streets are quiet. He wears a dark wool coat and a black cap, and his beard reminds me of pipe smoke. We take the tram together, don't talk much, and then another tram into the nineteenth district. Then we walk.

As we get off the tram and as we are walking down Gymnasium-strasse, with the beech trees hanging over the fences and the drug-gist's sign shining clean and green, *Apotheker*, I say to him: "My friend lives near here," meaning Friedrich.

Dükmann smiles at me. "You have friends everywhere, I imagine."

"No, not at all." I'm not a popular boy, but not hated either—just unremarkable. "My sister has all the friends."

"She's a good girl, your sister?"

What am I meant to say to that? "She's lovely," I say, and then, because my heart and my pride are shouting it: "And she's good. A little wild. But good."

He asks me more about Zilla, and I answer as I think I should. This man, I imagine, would not approve of my sister's style of living. And yet: see the way his blue eyes shine. He is looking for the truth, I think, and perhaps he already knows it. I sense he does know it. He knows my mind all the way through. Why else would I be here?

A dribble of rain, and a bird singing—and in my heart, a tendril twining outwards.

The locked gate in the park is like this: heavy dark wood, framed in concrete, with shallow cobbled steps leading up to it. The steps are rubbed round with earth, and the wall on either side of the gate is brick and rises higher than my head towards grey sky, nearly to the lintel of the gate. Paved into the brick, into the top of the wall, are shards of broken glass. People in the park don't see this gate, I sense now: their eyes slide over it, and we, because we stand beside it, are invisible too.

Tobias Dükmann has a key in his pocket. He twists it in the lock and the metal grates, squeals as it gives. We slip through the gate into green.

The vines and the trees are deep and dark like water, the branches and the ivy draped over the stone. And of course the stone is cut, and you would see the angles and the words carved in, and sometimes the two carved hands—except that over everything, over all the stone and the earth and the walls and, yes, even over the sky: this green netted blanket of life, heavy and muting.

Dükmann beside me touches a stone with his foot, and it is a moment before I see the curl of script, just there, beside his toe. "Watch your step," he says.

Everywhere I step, I step on bodies. I am waiting for them to cry out; I feel at the base of my skull their wincing and the way the patient bones twist out from under my weight. As if the earth weren't enough heaviness. The stones are toppled this way and that, chipped and broken, with plaques held up by wire, hugged against pillars and to headstones, and all of it under the trees and the vines that are making this park theirs alone.

There are birds here, too—the little songbirds with high voices, invisible in the trees, and in this moment it does not feel impossible that the trees might themselves sing to one another here. Behind a thick-trunked, vine-choked chestnut I surprise a pheasant. As she flees, she raises her tail feathers a half second: flash of white down, flash of light.

Dükmann crouches in a hollow, nearly invisible in his dark coat under the shadows of trees. He touches the ground with his hand.

"Here, Josef," he says. "See what the rabbits and foxes dig up."

He holds it up and I think, A little stone: a little winged stone, yellow-brown. But as he places it in my hand, and I feel how it sits against my skin and how the dirt is rubbed into the hollows of it, I understand.

"You can't imagine how many bones there are, turned up around here." His hands are back in his pockets, but I can't take my eyes off the bone. A human vertebra—a man's, or a woman's? My mind's eye traces some absent back, the curve of a nineteenth-century spine under silk, skin and flesh; a person who turns to me to laugh, but I cannot see their face. Dükmann says, "You can't even be sure where the rest of the body is. Bones all mixed up in a heap. Dry bones." He laughs once when he says it, and he shakes his head at the ground.

He has told me about this cemetery, a nineteenth-century Jewish burial ground, though when I first stand here, in the mid-twenties, no new bodies have been buried for fifty years. This makes it a much newer cemetery than the one on Seegasse, but it feels older: no windows look onto it, no people see into it, and the trees grow broad and wild. The religious community, he said, looks after the grounds.

"But most of their families are forgetting," he told me on our way here. "Not many people still living knew the people buried here. Only a few come anymore. You have to really want to."

And now with this bone in my hand I ask him, "Do you want me to help look after it?"

Dükmann peers up through the trees, and he breathes out deep, and he says, "What do you want to do, Tobak?"

What do I want?

A little bird chips above my head. With a short, sharp stick I dig into the earth. It's wet, hard, cold soil and it doesn't break easily. I hear Dükmann wander off through brush and twigs as I pry at the ground. In five minutes I have a hole a bit deeper than my fist; in ten minutes, nearly twice that, but the earth gets harder, the deeper I go.

When it is nearly up to my elbow, I lay the bone at the bottom of the hole, and with both hands I bury it again, press the earth down firm. From behind me Dükmann says, quiet, "May His great Name be blessed forever and to all eternity, blessed," and I mouth the word, "Amen." I hear the pheasant chucking beyond the bushes, by the wall, and she sounds like the key in the locked gate.

WE TAKE THE tram home. This streetcar rattles around us. Neither of us speaks for a while.

"You needn't come more than once a month or so." He says it to me after the long pause. "There are other people who go. Just check for damage, pull some weeds if you can. Sometimes vandals sneak in, so if someone's made a mess, you just tell me."

I have my sleeves pulled down over my knuckles, so dirty are my hands, and I sense the woman across from me is pursing her lips at the sight of them.

"It's an old lock, so if the key doesn't work, we can oil it," he says.

And it's such a beautiful fact: this chink of metal he's given me, this cemetery key—how it rests in my pocket, little weight. In all my life I've never owned anything so beautiful.

AND SO, YEARS later, on a New Year's Eve, I walk with Dükmann's son towards his home. Jakob has orange-red hair and it peeks out from under the corners of his cap, glows bright like low-burning fire under the street lamps as we walk.

The building, when we reach it, is bright and merry, yellow light shining through the frost on the windows. There is music muffled by the windows and walls that just barely carries onto the street, and which is like a burst of laughter when we open the door. So it seems to me; and perhaps it is the contrast with what I've just left that makes it seem wonderful, but I am so grateful it hurts. Mrs. Dükmann meets us at the door and takes my coat, calls me "sad old fellow," and gives me a kiss.

Upstairs in her sitting room, there is an older man playing a fiddle and a young man on an accordion, and a thin middle-aged woman with thick glasses at the piano, her fingers popping over the keys like effervescence. Tobias Dükmann is laughing at them from the sofa, half-singing as if he remembers only the first two words of every line, and he has his arm around Chaim, who wears a half smile tonight. When Dükmann sees me, he pushes himself up with his cane and holds his arms out to me, embraces me and kisses my cheeks.

"Now we are all here," he says, and I laugh almost to hide my love. He sits me beside him on the sofa, on the opposite side from Chaim.

And I do wonder about the way I see them: would they glow so bright if I hadn't grown up so lonely? I don't know, I can't guess, and it doesn't matter. But I know that it opens a door, the state I'm in—that when the auburn-haired girl with a guitar comes in to sit next to the pianist on the bench, and she smiles, in that moment I'm molten, and I'm lost.

Chaim goes to her and for a wild moment I think, She's his girlfriend, and I'll have to kill him. But he drums on her head like a child with a toy and she bares her small, straight teeth at him. Beside me Tobias Dükmann leans in and says, "Make my son introduce you to little Anna."

When I stand beside the piano bench I feel my pulse in my ears, and I only smile at her, though Chaim says polite things about me, calls me "Vati's favourite."

She shakes her head and says, "No, I've decided Jakob's his favourite. Despite my history of complaints aimed at innocent bystanders." And then she smiles at me to acknowledge this as an old joke between us—her garnet eyes make me idiotic—and I feel I'm falling forward; I'm certain I'm going to lean in and kiss her. She says, "Don't take it too hard, Josef. You can join us runners-up."

Later we sit together on the couch, and when midnight comes, she kisses her father first, and then her mother and brothers, and then me. Perhaps she kisses another person after that, but I stand grinning by the door and watch the lights spin. She doesn't dance more with me than with any other man, but when her hand is on my shoulder, I feel like gold, solid all the way through. Her hair smells like apples. I want to kiss her so badly, I could scream.

When at three in the morning Jakob walks with me back towards my home, he says, "You like Anna, yeah?"

I blush and I say, "She's lovely. I thought once . . . I wondered if she had a bad opinion of me."

Jakob laughs. "That letter, huh? She's a funny kid." He whistles for a minute, and then he says, "You could take her out."

My heart catches. "I don't know if she—"

"Tobak," he says, "don't be an idiot."

I TAKE HER to the zoo. I buy her a Hungarian pastry and we look at the buffalo. It's terribly unromantic, I'm sure, and in the back of my mind a voice is saying, What must she think of you? What a joke you are! But she laughs, and she makes me laugh, and when she smiles at me I'm a balloon on a string.

Afterwards we sit in a café, and she makes circles on the table-top with the wet bottom of her coffee cup. "Next time," she says, "can you take me to your cemetery?"

(This girl, soft-cheeked and slender—how my mouth goes dry at her smile. Is it improper to write this? Forgive me: When she reaches back to pull on a jacket, my eyes are caught in the pooling of shade at the base of her neck, and the madman in me would lean in and drink from her. I settle for an arm around her waist and hope that she can't feel my trembling.)

Zilla teases me: "You've got a little Jewish girlfriend, Josef. Such a Josef Tobak kind of girl, so proper, such a sweet thing. Boring as hell, no doubt. At least Papa won't like her—there's something a little rebellious in you yet, I believe."

With Anna, the Währing cemetery is a different place. I feel I'm seeing everything through her eyes, and a part of me thinks, You haven't pulled those weeds! What must she think?

She doesn't say much, just touches stone, touches trees, runs her fingers along the top edge of the wall. She is wearing a brown hat and a dark green coat. When she crouches down to read an inscription, and her lips part as she reads, inwardly I see her stretching out on the fallen leaves, see the two of us making love then and there—but then I remember where we are, and I have to turn away.

She asks me later, "Do you love anyone alive as much as you love them?" And I can see, in her eyes, that she isn't teasing me—and the answer is so easy it makes me blush.

I know her almost a year before I dare to ask her father's permission to marry her, though I've known, I think, since that first New Year's Eve. And even then, he says it first: "Tobak! Aren't you ever going to marry my little Anna?" Yes, Mr. Dükmann. I am going to marry your little Anna, if she will have me.

I take her to the Augarten, near dusk, and we walk and we talk, and then we sit together on a bench and I ask myself the question, silent; and she with her eyes on the trees asks herself the question too. When I ask it aloud I'm almost tempted to apologize, but she peers up at me and she nods, and she says, "That would be perfect."

Her lips that evening taste like new wine, and her breath on my cheek is velvet. Her body tight against mine, and my heart bigger than my whole body.

6

THE WAY OUR STORY BEGINS, WE COULD BE ANYWHERE, Anna and I, and at any time. This is 1933, and for me that's what 1933 is: the year I fell in love with Anna. It is also the year, of course, that in Germany the National Socialist Party is declared the only legal party, but at the time this feels so unreal; I have to make myself remember it now.

Love makes my world huge in that it widens my heart, but at the same time it makes everything else smaller. Certainly there are evils in my own country even at this time. Certainly there are reasons to be wary. But where are the roots of my heart? In Anna, in her family, in Friedrich, in Zilla, in my parents, and in the Seegasse and Während cemeteries. They are rooted in a question of faith too, but that's less a ground for rooting and more a web netted over everything else. And anything that doesn't threaten these roots is in a way unreal to me.

This is his world, this man I was: In November of 1933 he's engaged, and meaning to marry very soon, as soon as can be. He lives with his parents (his mother's parents having passed away); he is looking for a cheap apartment. He is twenty-four years old and a low-level clerk in Geisman–Zimmel's accounts department, where his father has worked for years and years and still works, despite the ongoing financial crisis, though in a different office. The two don't talk much at work. They have not talked much in years.

The father, Daniel Tobak, is thinner, with a face drawn down and weathered. His doctor warns him about his blood pressure. After the Great War thousands lost their jobs; thousands became poor, and Vienna has not been since then the bright metropolis it was when his children were born. But Geisman–Zimmel did not flounder. By their fingernails Otto Geisman and Hans Zimmel clung to the eroding market. The factory stayed open, the offices stayed open and (though we can be almost certain it was because Hans Zimmel's son loved Daniel Tobak's daughter) Hans Zimmel told his chief accountant, Werner Nussbaum, that there would be work enough for that fellow Tobak, if perhaps at a reduced wage.

But the threat of poverty still hovers over Daniel Tobak, and the smoke-and-fish smell of the Leopoldstadt that greets him every evening as he steps off the tram is a species of curse. His skin takes on a grey tinge, around the lips and eyes especially.

Josef Tobak now is the kind of quiet, thin man one imagines dissolving away in the rain—except that there he is, in the rain, traeading among gravestones, picking up twigs and pulling weeds. He spends a good deal of time with Friedrich Zimmel, especially in between Friedrich's girlfriends, who tend to last about three weeks if they last overnight. With Anna in the picture now, he sees Friedrich less, though the man invites the couple over for almost weekly dinners in his apartment.

"You must read these things Josef likes," Friedrich tells Anna once, over his dining room table. "Poetry, mainly. I can barely follow it. Who's that girl you like, Josef?" Which for a moment makes Josef's head snap round towards him (Girl? How could you! No girl but this one!), but: "The poet—Henriette Something."

"Oh—Henriette Hardenberg," says Josef. "Yes, I like her poems very much."

Anna says, "You read woman poets! I approve of you more and more, Mr. Tobak."

And Friedrich beams with pleasure, peering between his two guests as if admiring the work of his hands.

In these days, too, Josef tries more than once to make amends with his Czechoslovakian cousins, but the word he hears always from Sarah Kostner is, "We can't see you, thank you, we're busy," and he does not feel he has the right to press the matter. He hears about them through Zilla. He wears this rejection like a garment under his shirt and imagines he deserves it. He does not bring it up with Anna.

What prevents Josef Tobak and Anna Dükmann from marrying as soon as they'd like is, first, Josef's income and, second, her father's health. Josef does not make much money in his current position, and until he thinks of providing a home for Anna it doesn't bother him. But when he considers the life he'd like to give her, and the possibility of a child, he tells her, "Wait three months, and I'll have a raise." He is content at Geisman–Zimmel, content among numbers and other people's money; the job isn't a vocation, to him, but something comfortable, something quiet and more or less useful: it feels as if he's helping to keep someone's walls from falling down.

(But he remembers, sometimes, that back when he was nineteen, when he was just starting work, Tobias Dükmann met him one day and said, "Have you considered the rabbinical academies?" And Josef for a moment felt a thrill of openness, carried that thrill into the Währing cemetery and walked it around for a while under the trees. But then in his mind a hundred strange faces asking impossible questions started to press in, and his heart went tight; the faces followed him home, and he lay awake hours in the dark. He woke the next morning with a sore throat, and told Dükmann that he did not think he was called to that life. The questions, ones no one had yet asked and ones he couldn't answer, bore down on him like the weight of packed earth. He had not put it that way to Dükmann, though: to the older man he'd said, "I like my work, and I need time for the cemeteries." And now that door stays closed, and he tries not to let himself look back at it.)

But Dükmann now is not well, and it's a pull on Anna, always. Her father has difficulties with his digestion. Jakob does some of the work at the shop, as does Dükmann's apprentice Albert, and Anna helps with the sewing. She stays home most evenings to help her mother look after her father. When Dükmann is very ill, Josef suspects his own presence only irritates Anna. She sleeps less, and though she doesn't become angry, she talks in a lower, level tone, and seems always to be tired.

TENSION, OF COURSE, in Austria as well—one starts to feel it, though it's impossible to know yet what one senses exactly. In February of 1934, members of the Austrian governing party's Home Guard invade the Hotel Schiff in Linz, which belongs to the leftist Social Democrat Party—like an act of civil war, it seems. For a day afterwards there's fighting even on the streets in Vienna. Blackouts and roadblocks, tension electric in the air, guns popping blocks away, and all parties except the ruling Christian Socials crushed down into ineffectiveness or into hiding. "Wait it out,"

Josef says to his hands when they shake, and most of his neighbours think it too. Two days later the chancellor orders the army to shell a new tenement house in the nineteenth district in Vienna, occupied mainly by unarmed workers and their families.

Zilla, in the middle of the night, tells Josef about it before the newspapers do—Zilla with her arm bruised and scraped, speaking fast and with a tightness in her voice he's rarely heard.

"I hate this country," she says to her brother, and she sucks a cut on her hand and rocks back and forth in her seat. "I hate these people. Liberality when it tastes nice, sure—but when they might have to think, when they might have to change, forget it."

In the nineteenth district the Karl-Marx-Hof stands shelled to pieces by our own army, gaping like a smashed mouth, teeth broken, and the families stand outside with still faces. Their clothes smell of ash.

In July of 1934, members of the illegal Austrian Nazi Party assassinate the Austrian chancellor, Engelbert Dollfuss. A radio cry goes out: *Rise up, National Socialists—the hour for coup is now!* But though pulses run rapid in the capital, and though there are fights in the provinces, and in Salzburg, still it fizzles out like a firework: conspirators jailed and executed, and the established Austrian brand of fascism under the Christian Socials reaffirmed. Josef, in his bedroom in the dark, prays without words, and he wonders as he watches himself: is this thanks, or is this pleading?

In September of that year, Josef Tobak gets a raise at work—a small one, but he holds the news close against his chest, carries it to Anna and brings up marriage again, half-frightened she's decided otherwise in the months that have passed. But Anna kisses him, and she leans into him, and she says, "Soon, so Vati can come."

They are married in November: November the sixth, a Tuesday, in the evening. Her father sits beside her mother, and they both weep; his father sits beside his mother, too, and though Daniel Tobak does nothing but stare straight ahead from the moment he walks into the synagogue until the moment he leaves it, Josef's mother slips her arm under her husband's, and she dabs her eyes on a handkerchief and says, louder than she means to, "Little Josef!"

Anna is beautiful as nighttime, beautiful as light. Her husband sees in her eyes a glow as if from candles in a dark room. She says, "My beloved is mine," and her voice is like warm honey.

On the first morning he wakes beside her, he finds her holding his hand in both of hers, uncurling his fingers against the sheets.

"I find I barely know what a man is like," she whispers, seeing him awake. "I'm figuring it out. This part is for blessings." She squeezes his hand. And then, kissing him: "Now! Bless me very well, dear husband."

(Ah! Blessings, be quiet, be secret—see my hand dance as I write it; let that be enough.)

THEY ARE MARRIED in November 1934, and in October of 1935, Tobias Dükmann dies. The first year of their marriage unfolds with this impending sadness hanging over it. The doctor has Dükmann shave his beard. Not until it's gone does Josef see how thin the man's face has become, how carved out it is, down almost to the bone. But Dükmann only laughs in his bed: "I look like a boy again. Ella will like it."

He talks to his sons quietly. He tries to talk peace to Chaim, who is angrier and warier every month, who has learned to use a gun. He talks seriousness and duty to Jakob, who even in his fear of death tries to laugh and to make his father laugh—and Dükmann does laugh; he is happy to laugh. To Josef he says, "If you are always the man you are today, Josef, I can fall asleep happy and dream good dreams."

When he dies, quietly, in his sleep, the burial society arranges his funeral while Anna and her family keep their vigil beside his bed. They bury him in the Zentralfriedhof, in the treeless Jewish section, and the earth thumping down onto the pine casket is almost like a heartbeat. Josef, with his arm around his wife who is so small today, so thin, feels suddenly that he could slide down into the earth with his father-in-law, and that it wouldn't be frightening: it would be home. He squeezes Anna closer to himself, anchors himself to her life with his eyes shut tight.

After the week of mourning at her mother's house, when Anna and Josef are home again, Anna cries and cries; for days she can't stop crying. She tells Josef one night, "When I finished school, he didn't let me go to university. He didn't think girls should go, and I was so angry at him. I blamed him for years and years, almost until the very end. I never told him."

Her husband takes in this new information, he lets it shock him silently, while he holds her at the kitchen table and rocks her and says, "You loved him so well, my darling."

She answers, "Oh, Josef, I tried."

It's in these months that Zilla meets Giorgio Repaci at one of Friedrich's parties, and Friedrich begins to regret forever whatever mad impulse had him introduce her to the Italian music professor. Zilla tells Josef about Giorgio the next day, how wrong he is about everything, and that she "certainly couldn't imagine putting up with that kind of man." But she talks on and on about his work, and his family, and his cream-coloured shirt and his brown jacket, and the way his black hair curls against his eyebrow, and the concerts he means to go see.

"But he's moving to Paris," Zilla tells her brother, "so I won't go to any concerts with him. That's that." At this statement her lips go tight, and she tugs at the cuffs of her sleeves, humming.

So Josef is not so surprised when, a month later, he gets a telegram from Zilla, from a train station in Frankfurt, saying she's heading to France with Giorgio: *Could not be helped*, she writes; *this poor fool loves me.* But he is surprised, and torn between laughter and a twinge of heartbreak, when, two weeks after that, he receives a card from his sister and Giorgio, announcing that they were married in Paris, with two new French friends as witnesses.

On that night Friedrich appears at Josef and Anna's door, weeping and almost blind drunk. Anna helps Josef lay him out on their sofa, tucked under an old pink quilt. He sobs until he vomits into a pot.

"I think they let people divorce in Paris," Friedrich tells Josef, "so maybe she didn't really mean it."

Anna gathers all the knives in the kitchen and tucks them into her underwear drawer in the bedroom. Josef sits beside Friedrich until he's snoring, and in the morning they all wake with headaches. Friedrich goes off to his father's country villa for a few weeks after that.

==

A COLD JANUARY, 1937. A cold and wet February, wet and muddy March, but the crocuses bloom in the graveyards, spikes of green and purple reaching up. A man loves his wife, and it is no remarkable thing; like a jeweller and a jewel, his love and her body, her love and his—but no journalist visits, no newspaper tells it. In July the papers tell, "Japan invades China," but not, "Already their child has been growing three months." They have known since May, and the whole world is being born, in the man's heart: the whole world stirring and growing and awakening, but not yet a thing you could take hold of, not yet something known.

The happiest summer, and the best autumn—though twice Anna seems seriously sick, and in each case her sudden fear sends the both of them, separately, into a world of silent, pleading prayer. The trouble passes, and the universe breathes deep again; it shines brighter, too. Anna names herself Flowerpot and Jam Jar, smiling and swaying as she walks. He calls her Little Melon. He kisses her neck, the soft pink place where it tilts into shoulder.

She tells him things he's never imagined: Somewhere in the smell of fish is the smell of German paper mills. The colour of sky in August makes her taste butter on her tongue. When she lies in bed with her eyes closed, the whole world tilts to the north, and she holds on to the sheets to stop herself rolling out. The tiny scar on his chin reminds her, for some reason, of bare trees, early spring.

On the last day of December, while on the streets the people pour wine and sing songs, and the men with the pig stalls set out clay pigs, wooden pigs, little resin pigs with painted faces, the woman is in a hospital bed, and the man waiting outside her door. All the roots of his heart are rearranged and knotted up in that one room. When he first sees the baby—little loaf of bread, raisin face—his heart sings a song he's never heard, a song with one high note that makes the world go quiet.

WE NAME HIM after Anna's father. It makes her cry, but it makes her happy, and she tells me it is like shutting a box she's kept open for years.

Sometimes I wish, years later, that there could have been a way to name him after everyone who ever lived, everyone who ever died. But then a part of me wonders—not how he'd write it out or remember it all—but whether anyone could ever carry so much history in them and bear it. Not for my son, I pray. For him: the things to come, every beautiful thing.

7

I AM IN LOVE, ABSURDLY IN LOVE, WITH MY WIFE AND WITH this little boy, and the rest of the country is like a paper model of the world. That there's all this politicking right now is ridiculous. The baby wakes us up in the middle of the night, every night, but despite the weariness this drapes over his parents, his cry aches like homesickness, pain drawn from love. I stand in the dark and rock Tobias, sing to him. He's a beautiful, strong baby, dark, with bright, searching eyes that very early on in his waking hours learn to lock on to things, lights and movement.

In the daytime I sit with them sometimes as Anna nurses him. She says her father never did that, that her mother thought men shouldn't see it, but our apartment is so small that to avoid her and the baby in these moments seems laughable. The intimacy between them and the peace they have in it—it strikes me that I will never know that with any child of mine, and I wonder if I know it even with Anna. Her face is so serious when she watches him, but so still, and with just the hint of a smile.

I don't see Friedrich often in those days, and this is perhaps to my discredit; Friedrich's father, Hans Zimmel, died around the same time that Anna's father did, and I know that he and his mother are grieving. But now Friedrich has, as well, his new life: his life as co-owner of his father's company, and his meetings with his business partner, Otto Geisman. So perhaps we would both like to see each other more; perhaps we both feel a little regret at the separation.

Still, I confess I have a hard time remembering that or anything outside our little family. Our radio stops working, but neither Anna nor I seem to mind, and I try only half-heartedly to fix it when Anna mentions she hasn't listened to the news in almost a week. Chaim comes sometimes, and he rocks Tobias for a little while, bumps him and pats him. But it isn't the baby he's thinking of, nor even really us. He wants to talk about Schuschnigg, the chancellor; about whether he will stand up to Hitler.

"Nobody wants them here," Anna says to him when we all sit at the table, and the baby is asleep against her shoulder. "The Party is still illegal, remember."

Her brother raps the table with his fingers and shakes his head. "You know they're not gone, Anna. Don't be naive. It's a thing balanced on a knife edge."

"It isn't so bad as that," I tell him. "You must have hope."

"The edge of a knife," he says again, and points at me. "You ask your upper-crust friends what they think. They wear the state crosses today, but in the back of their drawers they've got their Nazi arm bands folded and waiting."

"You really think they're the ones who want this?" Anna says. "You look at the parties in this country, and you look at their leaders. They've stood up and said they're not Germans. They know they wouldn't be allowed to make an about-face under Hitler if they've spoken against him in front of all the world."

"Not the party leaders, maybe. And maybe the rich have less to gain from it, though I maintain that they have a lot less to lose than you think. But the young folk, the workers—look at them. They don't care what party is illegal. They just want someone to blame."

"England and France would never let Hitler get away with taking Austria," I tell him. "If he's too greedy, he'll bring war to Germany. No one wants that, not even the National Socialists. They can't afford it."

"I'm not putting my faith in foreign gods," Chaim says, and there's that anger in him, the sort that made his father speak so soft and sad to him before he died. "Don't forget that you're vermin to them. Don't imagine Germany is so different from Austria. We have to look after our own now."

Anna sighs. "Oh, Chaim," she says. "Couldn't you keep this madness away from us till your nephew is out of diapers?"

And then he looks at her and smiles, shakes his head and takes Tobias in his arms.

ON THE TWELFTH of February I go for a walk in the Augarten park with Anna and Tobias, and we show the baby the trees and the sparrows. He drifts in and out of sleep in his pram, cocooned in knitting. His cheeks are red kisses, and a wisp of black hair curls down across his forehead from beneath his cap. Anna tucks her arm into mine and we watch two little boys kick a ball down the path.

On the twelfth of February too, Chancellor Schuschnigg meets with Hitler in Obersalzberg. Schuschnigg takes a Nazi sympathizer on as secretary of the interior, as a compromise. As if to permit a little leak will stop the dam from breaking, it seems then. And I think we all feel somehow, in those days, that perhaps this is really how one is meant to put things right.

And a few weeks later, on a day when Anna bleaches diapers

and I make shadow animals on the wall for the baby to watch, the Social Democrats try to throw their support behind Schuschnigg against Germany. He will not take it, not from them nor from any illegal party, whether on the left or the right. Zilla would have blamed him terribly—and probably, off in Paris, she still does. Chaim certainly blames him. But for me—to my discredit—it's another paper headline in a paper world, while in the world of flesh my son gurgles on the blanket spread out over the floor. The head of a dog on the wall with my hand, and the tail of a fish.

THE GRAFFITI IN those weeks is all *Kruckenkreuze*—the corporate state crosses under the Christian Socials—and the pamphlets handed out on the streets are for a "free, social, Christian" Austria. If the country is going to explode, I think then, it will explode in a fire of patriotism. Whoever is against these Austrian nationalists stays in the shadows. At my work, things continue as always. Sums and differences have a misleading constancy about them: though the economy seems crippled, the numbers that prove it stay calm and reasonable. I take consolation in that, and I remark on it to Lars Schreckenberger, who shares my office. He laughs. We can still laugh together then.

But then in March it is as if this thing that has stayed in the shadows starts to uncoil. The corporate state crosses are still spattered across buildings and streets, and yes, the Communist and socialist parties align themselves for once with the Christian Socials; but even so, while half the crowd shouts, "*Heil* Schuschnigg!" there is a gathering multitude on the opposite side of the Rotenturmstrasse screaming Nazi slogans. Where do they come from, I can't help but wonder, and how is it there can be so many?

Even fathers in love can't ignore the storm now, and I find myself to be one of those who stand on the side of a free Austria—literally, one side of the street. I am not a slogan-shouter; in fact, in the midst of this screaming, with the police keeping the two crowds from getting at one another, my throat is completely closed. The man next to me is shouting in Czech, and it makes the situation all the more unreal. On this corner there is a young priest all in black and men who seem to be the staff of a Communist printing press, shouting together at the young shaven-headed men across the street, and on the next corner there are four young blond women wearing dirndls, their hair up in braids, singing Austrian folk songs so loud and high that their music sounds like soldiers' song on the march.

But I am just a number in that crowd, I am one count added to the one side and subtracted from the other. I don't have a voice today and I have no words for which to use it—unless those were *Go home, everyone.* That's all I can think of wanting: peace, home, family. Everything the way it has always been.

I leave that crowd and I go walking, on through the streets, past shopfronts and churches and coffee shops, parks and statues of horses rearing beneath generals and emperors. The roar of the crowd on Rotenturmstrasse is still an echo in my ears, a ringing that doesn't fade but seems, in its persistence, to grow louder as I flee to quieter and quieter streets.

And now I have, without thinking (or without deciding, at least), come to the hospital entrance that lets onto the Seegasse cemetery. It sucks me through it like a gully guides a stream. The courtyard beyond smells of damp earth, and it makes my fingernails itch a moment as if I've been digging with my hands and the soil is trapped under them. The headstones are blank faces, but somehow more sympathetic than any face at the demonstrations.

So I walk in between them, touching one and then another. The feel of wet, cold stone is the same as it was when I was a boy, and a youth. New life comes into the world, the quiet seems to tell me, but you will be forever counting up and up, because the subtraction at the other end of life will never be un-birth. We go out a different door than the one we came in through.

There are sparrows in the trees here, too, and a red squirrel with ear tufts like exclamation marks bouncing from grass to tree trunk. And how can it be, I think, that anything could change, when these things are always the same? They will all calm down, I feel certain. The world will be a sane place again soon.

And now, winding around a row of stones so old the inscriptions on them are like half-finished thoughts, there in front of me is Simeon's stone fish. Its U-arched back, wide mouth, thick gills are a puzzle. If I dug beneath it, after all, would I find the bones of a fish?

The statue only seems to stare up at the sky, which is grey, and cold, and promises rain. I walk up to the monument and touch the mouth.

"You weren't a natural fish, really," I tell it.

The trees murmur in the breeze, and beyond the buildings around the cemetery there are children screaming at one another, that horrifying child-scream that means joy when it sounds like agony.

There is no sign, then, of what the next change will bring. There is the laughter and the scream, and I don't know which one is mad and which prophetic.

8

ON THE TWELFTH OF MARCH, 1938, THE GERMAN army advances over the Austrian border without firing a shot. When they reach the capital, the people of Vienna, we are told, throw flowers instead of stones at their invaders, and the church bells peal, and out of thin air swastika flags appear hanging out of windows and above parades of goose-stepping foreign soldiers. The crowds of shouting opponents from Rotenturmstrasse have dispersed down side streets and now they hide behind their anonymity, their ordinariness. There is no resistance. There is only cheering.

But before the parades and the speeches, before any of this has happened, on the morning of the day before the *Anschluss*, this man Josef Tobak hears a knock at the door of their flat. Anna is there with him, making coffee, and she opens the door to a blond boy, maybe twelve. He hands her an envelope. Josef feels his pockets for change, but the boy shakes his head. He would like a warm bun from their table, he says. Anna butters a *semmel*, wraps it in kitchen paper and tucks it into the boy's hands, and as he tromps off down the hall Josef says, "Clever scamp knows something about inflation."

Anna hands the envelope to Josef. "Nothing written on it," she says.

Josef turns it over in his hands before he slips a finger under the flap.

Anna says, "I hope it isn't Chaim in trouble."

Inside there's one folded sheet of paper and Josef tugs it out, unfolds it to reveal tall swoops of text.

"It's from Friedrich," he says. There isn't a signature—just those tall, loose pen-strokes like a familiar way of walking. He reads: *Stay home from work. As long as necessary. Danger for Jews, etc. Tell your family.*

Anna lays a hand on his arm as she reads over his shoulder and she says, as if it's an afterthought, "I wish you'd fixed the radio."

And now there is a tightness like barrel hoops around her husband's chest. He says, "Perhaps it isn't true." He imagines Zilla away in Paris, a little bit bored with her new friends. She sends a message to Friedrich; says, If you'd just play a little innocent trick on my baby brother . . . And Friedrich would do it, Josef thinks; he'd do it without a thought.

But Anna's cheek is against his arm now and she says, "I should tell my mother."

Josef breathes into her hair. She smells like flour. "Don't worry," he says. "I'll go."

Anna gets his coat for him ("And Chaim and Jakob too," she says. "They'll do something reckless"), and he stares out through the window. Are the streets quieter today? The windows darker?

She kisses him—"Don't try anything stupid, my love"—and he walks out into the streets with his collar up.

What is one meant to do, in such circumstances? Hurry, like this little man, through a maze of streets, so that one's hat almost flies into the gutter. What a simpleton he is. Yes, tell your brothers-in-law, Josef; only know these are types who don't heed warnings. Jakob and Chaim, in their apartment with two friends Josef barely knows (the one with the beard—Grigor, perhaps—and the one with bottle-green eyes), will tune their radio against the static. Mattresses on the floor in the far room, a stranger winding tefillin straps round his arm in the corner, and Chaim will tell Josef, Go home to your little mama. Leave us to our business. And he will, he'll leave them, our Josef, because he isn't the same kind of man they are.

So run on: run to Anna's mother, guarded against the cold in her old sister's home. And when she sees fear in a son-in-law's face, and says, "It's the baby, isn't it?" and is reaching for her coat, then tell her: We're all fine. For today, we're all fine. Only we must stay home. She'll listen. She will smile and take this man's hands in hers (which are rough and red with washing, see, though from afar they look small and fine). When he kisses her cheek, he will feel all the ages of his young wife in her.

And scurry to parents (who aren't at home, or who don't answer the door); bother the butcher for paper and pencil, and slip them a note under the door. (What might this accomplish, if they're already out? One can wonder later, behind a locked door.) The air grown heavier as the sun climbs higher, few neighbours out on these streets. So hurry then to a grandmother, to a little room that smells of hot milk and cats. She is only as high as Josef Tobak's elbow, and to her he can say, "Babka, I just came to tell you—" but, "Little Josef," she says in Yiddish, "you're so thin. Your wife doesn't cook?"

But after all, she understands, she listens, and she smiles and nods when he promises he'll bring the baby round to see her—only not today! Today, safety—and she obeys him. She makes the lock click loud in the door when he leaves her.

Home through empty streets. Over the sputters of radios in windows: ". . . the chancellor will not . . ." and ". . . a deadline within the next several . . ."

He gets back to his house and Anna lets him through the door with the baby in one arm. He says, "All done," and she says, "The coffee's old now, I'll have to make it fresh." Bolts the door as she says it.

This man spends an hour on his knees behind the radio that crackles and spits into their kitchen as Anna washes dishes and feeds the baby. In the end it's just a few connections that have come loose, but it's finicky work putting them right and by the time he's finished, Anna is peering out the window with the baby's tiny head against her shoulder. She says, "It's so still out there, Josef."

He tunes the radio, and for a long time they listen. Anna sits with her hand in his. Only Tobias thinks to cry out, now and then.

9

N O NATION THREATENS GERMANY WHEN OUR COUNTRY
is eaten up, as far as we hear; though of course our news is
German news. The whole of Austria is for the *Anschluss*:
that is the word in the papers, on the radio. There was meant to be
a plebiscite regarding the annexation; the chancellor called it before
the tanks crossed the border, meaning to demonstrate opposition
to a German takeover. But now it's been appropriated by the new
government, and in the booths on the tenth of April sit Nazi officers, ready to receive your ballot—to receive it, unfolded, into their
hands, in case of confusion, so that no one might accidentally check
the tiny *"Nein"* box when they meant the enormous *"Ja."*

Ninety-nine percent of the population is in favour of annexation, the ballot counters sing. See: this is how a civilized nation
works out peace.

And this man I was: what does he do? He falls sick. Not right
away—not quite at the same moment that Austria becomes the
German *Ostmark*, as if the thud of jackboots on Viennese cobble-
stones poisons his blood (though this too is a nice thought). First
he must lose his job, first he must see fear transfigure one of his
oldest friends—and then, perhaps, he can begin to fall apart.

It is as if, in basements and cupboards, in back alleys and places hidden from public view, the Austrian populace have had their annexation plans laid out for years: this is the only way Josef can explain it to himself. They are so at home in their German skins. The Monday after the country becomes German he loses his job.

"We can't extend work permits for resident aliens when so many German citizens remain unemployed," says his department boss, Urbrecht, when Josef comes into work on the fourteenth. They are standing beside his desk, he and this man: this fellow whose hound-dog jowls and square glasses have until this day seemed only comical—now, suddenly, they are grotesque. (Whether changed or unmasked, Josef cannot say.) Half his things have been cleared from his desk already.

"I can allow you a few minutes to pack up your things," says Urbrecht, "but after that I'll have to call security. You understand that this is my responsibility. I can't allow trespassing."

Josef leans on his hands, braced against the desk, and reads the word *owing* on a balance sheet over and over. Urbrecht begins to walk away, but then he turns. "Besides," he says, "you weren't in on Friday, and you didn't let anyone know."

Lars Schreckenberger, whose desk has sat beside Josef's these past five years, stares at his work: he is working on a sum. And when Josef whispers, "I didn't . . ."—then Lars coughs, wipes his mouth on his sleeve, and only after half a minute of silence glances up at Josef.

"Do you need help packing?" he asks, almost too quiet to hear. His face is white; he looks as if he might be ill.

"No," Josef says. He touches his hand to his forehead. He stands straight. "No. I'm fine. There isn't much to do."

When he walks down the hall towards the front door, his arms full of whatever notes seemed personal, and a photo of Anna in miniature, he hears footsteps behind him. Until he opens the door, he keeps his eyes focused ahead, but when he breathes in cool air from the street, he turns to look back, sees the security guard who has slowed upon seeing him exit, who watches him, expressionless, until the door closes behind him.

ANNA STARTLES HIM out of his silence with her outrage.

"Just because you missed work!" She has fastened on to this idea. "Half the city stayed in. Everyone knew what was going on. Besides, it was Friedrich who told you to stay home, wasn't it?"

Josef hasn't put down his papers yet; he holds them to his chest. "I . . . I think it was—"

"So there, you see? Just go to Friedrich, get it sorted out. He'll talk some sense into that old weasel." Her face red, her little body dense with energy. Josef lays the papers down on the table and kisses her cheek.

"Of course," he says. "You're right."

THE MAIN OFFICES of Geisman–Zimmel he finds uncontained, workers spilling into the street. They stand talking on the steps outside the main doors.

"I hope you're not here for your job," one man yells at Josef—a sharp-faced fellow in his forties, hatless and smoking a cigarette. "Don't bother," says this man. "They've killed you off. You don't exist."

A policeman at the door stands with his hand held out for identification papers. He's a Viennese policeman, true, but with accusation in his expression such as Josef can't remember seeing. Josef fumbles to find his papers. He has not often needed them before.

"You work here?" The policeman jerks his head towards the door.

"Not at these offices, but at the Strohgasse office, doing accounts—"

"Then you don't work here." The officer waves his hand. Dismissed, says the hand.

"I need to speak with Mr. Zimmel," Josef says. "Please, he knows me. It's important."

Now this hard-faced look—for staring down thieves, Josef thinks. "If it's about your job, you can forget it. Mr. Zimmel doesn't have time for any of you lot."

Josef tries to peer around this man's shoulders, but he moves to block the doorway.

"Can't you have someone call him?"

The policeman's hand is on his baton. "You really want to cause trouble, eh?"

He cannot be serious, Josef thinks. But he is: serious to the point of violence. Josef nods and backs away. Some of the men on the steps had turned to watch him, and now they raise their hands. "You see, you see," they say.

Josef will not hear; will turn their words, instead, as he walks away, into wind, into birds, into motorcar engines—the voice of the city that is the same as it was last week, last year, always.

THE AFTERNOONS IN the Währing cemetery, in these days, play out in peace while history gets its business done beyond the walls. Here, as always, I am at home in myself. Over the winter, dead branches have broken from the trees, fallen onto some of the head-stones, knocked a few over. And I think (on this day as every day) I should bring a saw, or an axe. The branch I take up is too large to lift, but I can drag it by one end. Up above me, the trees speak in birds' voices. On the high stone walls, the evergreen vines glisten; the squirrel with tufted ears skips from far away on my left to far away on my right.

Some of the headstones are made with a plaque set into the marker, and over time some of these plaques have fallen out. The headstones without plaques are little children without faces. Someone brought a spool of wire here some years before this, and many of these headstones have their faces held on with wire belts. When the wires rust, I replace them. I do a few that day, half for the feel of the wire biting my fingers and the weight of stone in my hands.

Around five o'clock, I head up the street towards Friedrich's house. It's a quiet street; it always is—no businesses, and the kinds of families who can pay someone to do their shopping. When I'm in sight of the house, I see a man walking out the front gate: a man in a hat and a dark coat. When he turns to shut the gate behind him, his arm band shows and I almost freeze in my steps. He's seen me. For an instant some part of me formed in grade school says *Run*.

But this man smiles and nods. And his hand stabs out and he chirps his salute as if he's saying, Beautiful day!

I've never saluted in my life, and my instinct is to bow, but I don't—and I manage to mimic this man, and to hiccup a "*Heil . . . !*" in a voice that would be mysterious to anyone who knew me.

Then, "Sorry," I say. (Sweat, suddenly; the horrible threat of laughter.) "It's new to me."

The man waves his hand. "Practise, practise, practise," he says.

"You are a German citizen now." He pats my arm before walking down to the corner where his car is parked. A young man in a military cap sits in the driver's seat. Through the reflection off the windshield I cannot make out the driver's expression. I turn through the gate and I don't look back again.

When Friedrich's butler, Kurtz, opens the door to my ring, he smiles at me for a moment and says, "Mr. Tobak, yes." But then his expression changes, almost as if someone has shouted his name. "Please wait here."

"Outside?" I've already taken off my hat.

Kurtz hesitates for a moment. "Come in and wait by the door," he says.

I stand running the brim of my hat between my fingers. In a minute the butler is back, beckoning me. "Mr. Zimmel will see you now," he says, and I cannot tell what his face is saying. I follow him up to Friedrich's sitting room.

Friedrich sits on his sofa with his hands open on his knees. He's pale, his face is damp; his brandy bottle is on the table in front of him, a little rocks glass beside it. When he hears us enter, he jumps up. "Josef," he says, "you really shouldn't have come."

"I had to. Urbrecht fired me today." I'll say it, I think; we'll hear each other, and if he has to deal with it later, I'll set a time.

Friedrich rubs his forehead and with the other hand beckons me over to sit beside him. "I'm sorry about that," he says. "Bad times for everyone, it seems."

A flush of anger under the skin. "Did you hear that? He fired me. Without reason. If I deserved it, I'd be ashamed to come to you, but I don't, and so . . . well, here I am. I have a wife and a child, Friedrich." I won't sit. Is he listening? He pours himself more brandy.

"Yes, I thought of that." Sucks his drink through his teeth, not looking at me. "Please, sit. This isn't a courtroom."

A chill, when he says that. But I do sit. "What do you mean," I say, "you thought of it?" I cough once. My chest is beginning to hurt. "You can't have known."

"Not about you specifically," Friedrich says. "But it was most of the company today. The managers would have heard over the weekend, or first thing this morning. They did what they thought right. I can't oversee every department."

"I don't understand." Is my voice calm? "They heard about what? And what's happened to most of the company?"

Friedrich swallows. He stares at the ceiling.

"Just, you know." He shrugs. "The whole National Socialist bit."

"Because we're German now, they fire Jews for no reason?"

He, refilling his glass again: "Well, you know. It's the company too. Because we've had to—we've had to make clear . . . our position. On these things."

A white blank in my mind, at these words. "What?"

"What do you expect me to do?" (This man gone ragged as he turns to me.) "They've got their war going. They wouldn't let us keep on making faucets and shower heads, would they? And—Jesus—do they let non-partisans head their munitions factories? Does that sound likely to you?"

"You joined the Party." I'm on my feet again; my hat is on my head. My throat is thick with cotton. "I see. I didn't— Well. If that's how it is, I'll go."

"Josef—please—"

"No, I'll go. You can't have me here. I understand."

And I've already turned to leave before he catches my shoulder.

"Josef." He looks now as if he might weep. "It's not like that. I'm not one of them."

I want to shove him back onto the sofa; I want to take a swing at his face. His sadness, his drunkenness, makes me by one turn despise him and by the next want to put my arms around him.

"And what about Geisman?" I ask.

Friedrich falls back on the couch. After a moment I sit beside him.

"Geisman's left the company," he says. "They're emigrating. The whole family. To London, I believe."

"Friedrich," I say, "he built the company with your father."

"I know that!" Spilling brandy on his shirt. "I know. But it was his choice. I had nothing to do with it. He told me months ago: 'If Germany invades, we're getting out.' He's made arrangements. They have money in England; they've been making transfers for a long time. They've got family too. So it's me in charge now." He wipes his nose on his shirt cuff. "Me and the board."

I stare at my hands. They're balled into fists, knuckles all bone.

"You could have stepped down too," I say—just loud enough for the two of us.

"No, Josef"—and now his voice is fierce again—"no, I couldn't. If it hadn't been me, they had someone else lined up—some shit in Munich, did the Führer a favour. Exemplary in all respects. No— this is the compromise. I am the compromise."

"The lesser evil."

His eyes glisten anew. "You don't really think that, do you?"

I can't look at him. This face saying, Pity me; tell me I did right. This same face fresh from simpering at a man who'd have spit on me, if he'd only known me. I can't look.

"Please." He says it with his hand on my shoulder. "Tell me you don't hate me. I couldn't—I couldn't bear it, Josef."

"I don't know where I'll work now." I speak down at my hands.

"Don't worry about that. I'll drop by tomorrow. We'll talk."

I swallow. "And the rest of the company?" I stop myself shrugging out from under his hand. "You'll drop by their houses too?"

"Josef—"

"Fine," I say. "Tomorrow."

He follows me to the hallway, where Kurtz is waiting—perhaps listening, I realize—and he says, "At least tell me you don't despise me."

I sigh. "I don't." It's true. "But I don't think I'd have believed you could be so cold."

He looks as if I've hit him. It strikes me then for the first time that my judgment of Friedrich is something that could keep him up at night.

"I'll see you tomorrow," I say, and Kurtz leads me to the door.

THE FOLLOWING MORNING arrives quiet and overcast, and I sit at our kitchen table while Anna rocks the baby in her arms. I find my mind saying, Enjoy this. The baby is asleep, but Anna still rocks him. She was singing a song I thought I recognized; now the song is nothing I know, just little noises.

"I can hold him, if you like," I say to her.

But she sings a lullaby. "I need to do something with my hands."

All our dishes are clean because of this, and the counters spotless, and the floor shining. I say to her, "Sit awhile."

"Not yet." Shaking her head at the sleeping baby. "Not yet, I couldn't stand it yet. Let me move a little longer."

"Maybe I'll make coffee."

"There are clean cups," she sings, "everywhere."

By the time the knock on the door comes, she is laying the baby down in another room, and I am pouring coffee. Then, *rap rap rap* on the door, and it makes me jump.

"It's Friedrich." His voice. I edge the door open, and he peers through.

"Just me," he says. "Really."

At the table across from him, until Anna comes back, I let my gaze rest like a dead weight on the Party arm band sewn to his jacket sleeve. He touches his hand to it. "Please, I don't like it any more than you do."

Anna knows, of course. She tilts her lips without parting them when she appears—this quiet smile for our friend. "Good to see you," she says.

He leans into her words as if starved. "And you! You look lovely, as always."

"I think Josef made coffee."

Friedrich's face is pale, sickish—perhaps a hangover, I suspect; and yet there's a part of me that is willing to allow, even now, that my friend is in a difficult position, and that he would like to put things right.

"You got here without trouble?" I ask.

"Yes, I think so." And such relief in his voice, now that I'm speaking to him, that it almost makes me ashamed. "I took the car downtown and then I walked. I tried to hurry through this part of town. I hope I didn't worry your neighbours."

I can't help but snort. "Of course you worried them," I tell him. "Unless they recognized you. Or perhaps especially, in that case."

"Something to eat, too, Friedrich?" Anna sets a roll down on a plate for him. I help her with coffee and Friedrich squirms for a moment at the table, alone.

When we sit, he says, "Josef, I'm going to get you a job."

"Oh." I sip my coffee. Friedrich grips his cup in both hands.

"Something out of the office," he says. "Perhaps with the art collections."

"Art collections?" Anna glances between us.

"That was a side project, wasn't it? Of your father's? And Geisman's?" Yes, he flinches at the name, but I can't stop myself and it's hard to feel sorry.

"They collected and sold paintings on the side," he tells Anna. "Quite a few very nice ones are still in the collection. I haven't seen all of them. But we need to get the records organized. Some of them need to be sold. For Geisman, actually." This he says to me. "I can hire you without going through anyone. I could even have you under a false name."

"I see."

"It'll pay the same as your old job. If I can find more, I'll pay you more. There will have to be a new round of hires anyway, the way they're letting half the company go. It won't attract notice. And if you need anything, you'll be able to let me know." He's speaking quickly, leaning forward, seeming to beg with his eyes: Say yes!

I take a drink from my cup as I think. We are all quiet. Then: "My father's job—"

"I don't—I can't hire everyone." Friedrich waves his hand. "Please, Josef. It's time your father retired, anyway."

"And his pension?" I want to say: Everyone's pension? Everyone's job?—but it's useless, I tell myself. Could it be that you're angry at the wrong person? I feel my mind ask. I don't know what answer to give it.

"I'll make sure his pension goes through," Friedrich says. "If I have to personally drop off a cheque each month—"

"Friedrich, you can't keep coming here. Not with the way things are now." Anna touches his arm. "If they know you spend time here, they'll ask questions. You'll lose your alibi."

The way he looks at her then—gratitude for her mercy, as though he were a man condemned—and I understand. *Alibi*, she said. You are the same man underneath, she means.

"You're right," he says. "I know. You're right. It will take some getting used to."

With the window closed, the noise from the street just makes it through to us—a car, a man calling to a friend. I want to say, You could have done better. And I want to tell him we would have stood beside him. If I asked him what Zilla would think—would that be too cruel? I think: But there are families now who can't buy bread. And again I think: But could he have saved them from this, even if he'd said no? I watch the inside of my coffee cup as I tilt it, and I don't say anything.

"I hope you will remember that we love you," Anna says to him.

And for a moment he seems about to cry, squeezes his eyes shut and touches his face with his hand. But then he says only, "Yes, I know." And forces a smile. "I can meet you tomorrow, Josef. I'll write down the address. Say, nine in the morning?"

When he leaves, I stand beside Anna at the sink, my hand on her lower back as she runs hot water for the dishes. Her hands move more slowly than they did this morning, less busily. And when she turns the faucet off, she says, "So you'll work for him?"

I watch the corner of her eye, her cheek, the near-invisible hairs that catch the light. "Don't you want me to?"

"Chaim won't speak to you."

I press my lips into her neck, against the collar of her blouse. "I don't have to do it."

"He'll probably have to fire you soon, anyway," Anna says, and starts wiping out a coffee cup. Then she adds, after she turns to kiss my forehead: "And I'll still talk to you."

=

In the first few days we hear stories of people driven into the canal in crowds, of beatings and murder on the street. Of others committing suicide. I don't want to believe that it is so bad already; or else, if it really is so, then I must imagine it will all blow over quickly and things will go back to the way they were. At the time, such a thought doesn't seem so foolish.

Meanwhile, I work on the art catalogue. The rooms where many of these works are kept make up a small rented office, a bit removed from the centre of town. No one else works here. A few of the paintings I like very much. A portrait of a girl and her baby brother, dressed in frills, neither of them smiling but both peering out at the painter with anxious looks that seem to demand explanation: Why are we sitting here? And another, a blurry kind of landscape, hills and a pond—smudge and mist and colour. It makes my eyes go unfocused; it makes me start to believe I can smell rain. Probably Zilla would like these, I think, and in the evenings I try to describe them to her in letters, and to Anna in our bed.

But very soon I'm ill—feverish, weak on my legs, mind dull—and I tell Friedrich I can't come in. He asks if he should send a doctor and I tell him, gently, that his survival instincts aren't very good (and perhaps this fact alone makes me forgive him more).

Anna leaves Tobias with her mother, in her house a few blocks away, while I'm home sick. It's a world of chicken broth and camomile tea in our house, with noises too loud and Anna's voice tinny to my ears. She's out often to feed Tobias, but the echoes seem never to cease. Once, I think I hear Chaim's voice in the kitchen and I call out, "You came after all!"—but I don't see him and Anna doesn't mention he was there. She brings home a compound from the apothecary. She says, later, "If you're not a little better tomorrow, I'll call the doctor."

The day after she says it, I am a bit better, as it turns out. I can sit up and speak normally, and though I feel weak and nauseated, the world around me looks and sounds the way it should. Anna feels my forehead and smiles. She says, "I'll have to pick up the baby soon. It'll break Mama's heart."

My clothes are damp and sticky. I change them and lie on the couch, stare out the window. "Have things improved at all?" I ask Anna.

She sits beside me, reading. "Things?"

"You know." I gesture at the grey spring sky. "Out there."

Anna puts down her book and feels my forehead. "Maybe I should call a doctor after all."

I feel my throat tighten. A swallow darts across the grey, too fast to be anything but a spot of black. I tell her, softly, "Well, I'm only hopeful."

10

THE THING THAT HAPPENS HAPPENS THIS WAY: SOME
weeks into the occupation, on a Saturday, a man walks from
the Leopoldstädter temple towards the little apartment
where his wife and his son are waiting. He is feeling a bit light-
headed from this fever he still hasn't kicked. His chest hurts. But
it is necessary, he feels, to try to frequent the synagogue as long
as one can, as long as they don't stop you and you're on your feet.
The effort of going in these times feels to him at once childish and
heroic, but many things in his life, he reflects, have made him feel
that way—the cemeteries, for one. He hasn't been to the Währing
cemetery this month. Perhaps later today, he thinks, or tomorrow.
Depending how the streets look.

He didn't allow Anna and Tobias to come with him today. Anna
didn't object this time. At other times, certainly, she's told him she
can't stay in. He doesn't like to think of her hurrying through the
streets to look after her mother, but she does it; nor of the baby
in his little pram in the park, vulnerable to the world, but on safer
days they take him anyway. They buy milk and bread and meat,
they pay their rent, and Anna sings songs to the baby, the same
ones her mother sang when she was young.

At the intersection with Wallensteinstrasse, a familiar face: here is Jakob Dükmann, reddish under his cap and handsome, young-looking in his coat. He is walking quickly towards Josef, and before he stops, he is saying already, "I wonder if you've heard from Chaim at all."

Josef pauses. "No," he says. "Have you asked Anna?"

Jakob has just come from asking her, he says. He shifts his weight, begins to whistle, and Josef says, "Wouldn't he be at a friend's house?"

Jakob clicks his tongue. "He heard something this morning about some shitheads bullying old women. I'm sure he went to find out. I meant to go with him. I was going to meet him at the bridge."

"And he didn't come," Josef says. His brother-in-law is tense, though his face is set. He peers over each of Josef's shoulders in turn, as if expecting to see someone farther down the street.

"I'll just keep looking," Jakob says. "He's probably nearby."

"He might have gone inside," Josef says.

"He might have."

But Jakob is leaning forward as if urging himself to go, and something at the back of Josef's mind prods him and makes him speak: "Why don't I go with you?"

Jakob meets his gaze, big-eyed. "You don't have to. Anna will be upset."

Josef shrugs, although already a wave of heat runs through him, saying, You're not quite well. "She'd be more upset if I let you go alone. She'd say you need a chaperone."

He grins, kicks the ground. "And you need a bodyguard."

And so they go together. The streets are quiet. Josef follows Jakob, lets him pick the route, and finds that in trailing him by a pace he can imagine that he really is only here as a chaperone, a looker-on keeping another man out of trouble.

But as they are about to turn towards the canal, a man comes around the corner in front of them and holds up his hand. Josef stops on instinct—a police officer, he thinks. This man has the confidence of authority and his clothes are a uniform. But Jakob hunches his shoulders and keeps walking, and Josef sees that this isn't an officer, but a man dressed in his Party uniform, red arm band sewn over his sleeve and a club in his hand.

This man yells at them to come clean up the mess they've made. Jakob yells back at him, "I haven't made any mess. Piss off."

He walks towards them now, this man, with his club raised, and Josef is hurrying to walk beside his brother-in-law so that Jakob won't crash alone into their accuser. But then from around the corner there comes a mob of men, some dressed as the first is, some in ordinary spring coats, and some drunk. They are pointing at the two of them. They are yelling at them to come clean up this mess.

"Just ignore them," Josef tries to tell Jakob—but it's pointless: the strangers grab Josef by the coat, grab Jakob by the coat, and though they try to shake them off, the strangers drag them back around the corner and into the street. One of them hits Josef on the shoulder—whether with a fist or with a club, he doesn't know. It sends a spasm of numbness through him so that he almost goes down on one knee. Jakob grabs him by the sleeve and they hold each other upright.

They are to scrub the last remaining Austrian nationalist graffiti off the streets and walls. Already there are two dozen men and women, young and old, on their hands and knees in the street, up to their elbows in lye solution and struggling to wash white crosses off the pavement. The crowd standing around them is men and boys, and a few young women too. The men dressed in the Party uniform have made themselves mob leaders, and they kick whoever stops scrubbing, or stand over them with a club. All of them retch hate: *Fucking Jews! Dogs! Scrub up your shit!* Josef is on his knees and scrubbing beside the others before he knows how it has happened. His hat has fallen off somewhere. He feels he is watching himself, that this Josef Tobak is another man, a man in a dream.

This man Josef starts to scrub in his coat sleeves but then stops to take off his coat, and the man with the club comes to kick him. Through a wave of nausea he manages to throw off his coat and roll up his shirt sleeves. There is a motherish-looking middle-aged woman kneeling beside him; her soft flesh jiggles as she moves, and her eyes are wide and fearful. Two men in the crowd are yelling obscenities at her, and Josef works to scrub faster, beside her—to help her, he thinks; to draw attention away from her, he hopes. The crowd only laughs, makes animalistic panting noises at them to the rhythm of their scrubbing. The woman beside Josef is crying. The paint does not come off easily. The lye rips bare skin raw before it makes the pavement clean.

Everything is slippery. Slime gets in through the skin. It covers everything, everyone: it's in the hate of the mob, it's in the loathing and fear and shame of the men and women on the ground, it's in their clothing and hair, and the taste of it is in their mouths, bitter.

It must be some loud voice in the crowd that suggests it, but the thought seems to come out of nowhere—the thought that these street cleaners should be shuttled on to the Prater grounds, now that the pavement is nearly clean. A few of the cleaners are given white paint and told to paint the shopfronts with new slogans.

The rest of them, Josef among them, are herded down the street towards the fairgrounds.

This movement forward happens on its own, it seems to Josef. Hands reach out now and again to catch him or to push him—hands of angels, hands of friends. The sky above him is strangely bright: now purple, now almost orange. He cannot feel his feet.

The mob herds them into a field, pushes them to their knees, and yells at them to eat the grass. Above the trees that ring the field, the Riesenrad Ferris wheel stands watching without yes and without no.

The young man beside him says he will not eat grass, and a boot strikes his ear, tears a red weal along his hairline. This white spring air is thick with slime, as if they are under water, and Josef is certain he will vomit; but the girl beside him cannot make herself swallow grass and so he has to show her, to make her feel less shame, that it can be done. Yes, we can eat grass. See? No problem. Just another vegetable.

Bitterness, bile in his throat, and the sky still this sickly winking colour. The Ferris wheel spins and reels. Josef's hands tingle like static on the radio. He tries to take another mouthful off the earth, wonders if he could not just sink into it, here, so low down. A fist is twisting harder and harder into his gut. His forehead drips sweat. The noises of the mob and of the girl vomiting in the grass are now so far away he can barely hear them.

And then it is as if someone has opened a hole in the back of his head and let all the feeling out. These colours flashing brilliant, fireworks sparking. He's on the grass, curled into a ball against the spike of sick in his middle.

He will never be able to remember what happens just then, up until the moment he feels the earth bucking beneath him, his head lolling this way and that. Jakob is kneeling over him, shaking him, face ripped with something like rage. Josef watches as if on a film reel as a man kicks Jakob in the ribs and tells him to get away.

But they are dispersing now, the mob. One or two glance back at the men and women who have fallen over in the grass. Some of these aren't moving and won't move; some are beginning to vomit green and yellow. Jakob crawls back to Josef and rolls him onto his side, speaks many strange words to him, asks a question again and again—but Josef cannot hear the question. He can't recall any words to answer with.

11

THERE WAS A TIME A BOY HIT ME ON THE SIDE OF THE head with a stick when we were young. I lay on the ground with no memory of falling and watched the boy's feet as he ran away, and for the next few days there were moments when I wasn't sure if things people said or things I saw were real or if I was imagining them. So it is like that again, for a while. The first time I come fully awake, I see that I am lying in a bed with white sheets and a green cover, in a room with peach-coloured walls, and I don't recognize it at all. This is a horror. I call out, in a voice that is hardly a voice, "*Hallo?*"

Footsteps on a staircase; the door opening. My fingers tight around the covers when Friedrich looks in.

"You're really awake," he says. "Yes, good. This is very good." He's wringing his hands. "How do you feel?"

"I don't know." I feel awful, is the truth, but I am only beginning to realize it—pain in my ribs and arms, sickness all through me. "What happened?"

He sits in a chair, a bit removed from my bed. "Jakob brought you to Anna, after the . . . incident. At the Prater." As he says it, I can't remember what he means, only flashes of colour, stabs of pain. "And she sent a boy to me, and I thought—I thought the hospital might not be safe. So I brought you back here. My doctor's been seeing to you."

So this is a room in his house. "How long ago?"

"Four days," he says. He's leaning forward; his forehead is tight.

"Four days! What must Anna think?"

"I've sent a message every day. The doctor will be back in an hour. No one else has been in here, and of course Anna couldn't bring the baby."

My chest hurts so that I must breathe slowly. I'm wearing someone else's pyjamas, too, I can tell. "I should go home," I say.

Friedrich snorts. "Out of the question."

"Really, you can't keep me. They'll find out I'm not—"

"It's not that." He shakes his head. "Don't worry about that. It's that you're under quarantine."

"What?" I want to sit, but all my bones are screaming. "For what?"

"Dr. Teuer says it's scarlet fever," he says. "I've hired a nurse. She's off until lunch. The staff haven't come up here. It wasn't hard to persuade them."

I say, "But you are here."

"Well." From the corner of my eye I see him tugging at his shirt cuffs. "My cousin had it when I was a boy, when we spent the summer at his parents' villa. I never got sick. Maybe I'm immune."

"But your visitors—"

"I told them my colleague from out of town is here and has come down with something awful. They've stayed away so far."

I cough, and the pain of it is awful enough that I have to close my eyes tight for a moment. I ask him, "Does the doctor think I'll be all right?"

"He might," says Friedrich, "now that you've woken up. You can ask him when he gets here." He stands. "Do you need anything? Water? An extra blanket?"

"Water, yes." Though I can't imagine how I'll drink it. As he turns towards the door, I say, "Friedrich—thank you. For all of this."

He pauses before he says, "Well—good, good." I can't see his face as he leaves.

My mother and father have left Vienna. This is one of the first things I understand. Friedrich tells me: to visit Zilla, perhaps to emigrate to France, if they can. Did they leave a message? I ask.

Friedrich reads a letter from my mother:

Dear Josef,

I wish this were a better goodbye; but never mind, I hope we'll see you again before long. What an embarrassment is this new administration! The Spanish Inquisition in proletarian uniform, as your father says. I wish you hadn't crossed them, Josef. It worried us terribly when we heard about what happened to you. You can't reason with these types. They're thugs. Still, like all thugs, they'll drive their movement into the dust before long. In the meantime, best to get out of the way.

Anna says you're in good hands and will be well soon. We wouldn't leave if we weren't confident about that. But after all, you have so many good friends in this city—more than your father and I ever had, perhaps. I know you feel at home here. We, meanwhile, are going to stay with Zilla and her husband in Paris. I hear he's a fine fellow, this Mr. Repaci. What a strange way to meet one's son-in-law! You and Zilla both flew the nest very early, I must say. Try not to forget your old parents.

I hope to see you very soon, little Josef, though I understand you have your wife and son to look after. Still, won't you consider joining us in Paris? I imagine you might like it.

Papa sends his love. He reminds me that his mother doesn't intend to join us. You might check in on her, when you're well.

They've closed up their apartment, Friedrich tells me. Their things are in storage. If they need me to try to ship things, they will send word. Friedrich says he doesn't think that will be possible, and I try not to wonder what that means.

"I wonder if they will have a telephone," I say to Friedrich. And I ask, "Did they see Anna before they went?"

"Yes, and the baby. They left the letter with her." Friedrich always looks tired now, but I cannot tell how much of what I see is from my sickness.

And so I begin to dream of leaving for Paris. Because it seems, suddenly, wise: like everyone who can read the signs of the times is doing this. Of course, I don't want to leave. I want to go home to my apartment in the Leopoldstadt and I want to go to work and to the cemeteries and to the synagogue and I want to live my life, just like that, troubling no one. In my own city.

But then this: I think I am dying. Some nights, the pain so desperate, the heat in my body making me sure I will never see or think clearly again—"Friedrich," I call out, "tell Anna they should go." Because they must, they must be safe. To me the gravestones are always here, teeth of the earth, in front of my eyes. And these become people, standing closer than they've ever stood—so close I can almost make out their faces. They are wrapped in wire and vine, these people, and it bites their arms as they stand with their hands pinned to their thighs. I want to cut their wires, trim back the vine, but I cannot; because aren't my arms, my hands, pinned as well by this wire that is beginning to rust, these vines coiling up from the earth—and the squeeze around my chest a vise, so that with every breath my lungs find less air?

"Oh my God, why don't you go!"

A man cries out into the night. But when the morning comes, I find myself alone.

THERE ARE NEW laws. Friedrich tells me about them in my long sickness. You need papers for everything—to cross the street, it seems, or to take a drink of water. Also, how the embassies are swamped: "The lines stretch around the block," my friend says. They wait outside all day for the chance to get a visa. More often than not, they're denied.

And I'm left to think about this, about what it means. I ask Friedrich to take a note, which I dictate: *Dear Anna*, I say, *it may be now that you ought to get out of Vienna. You know I can't join you yet, but I will. Perhaps Jakob will take you. Please let me know your plans. And please believe that I trust you in everything. Your Josef.* I see Friedrich add something to the note as he finishes, but he won't tell me what it is and I'm too tired to press him.

When Friedrich comes back with a reply, I can tell he doesn't want to read it to me, that he doesn't like it—and, my Lord, it must mean they're leaving. But he says, "They won't leave." He reads it to me: *We'll stay, thank you. Your Anna.* And now I don't know what to feel or think.

Friedrich says, "You should press them."

"I should press them," I repeat. My brain is a thick, hot fog and it takes me a moment to understand.

"Tell them to go," he says. "They can't afford to wait. Really, Josef. If you think it's bad now—" He trails off, staring at the wall. My bedside light is on and it throws shadows across one side of his face. "What I mean is that I hear things," he says. "And if I were you, I would make them leave."

"Friedrich," I say, "how can I make her leave?"

He shakes his head; he doesn't look at me. For a moment we are quiet together and the trees beyond the window seem to breathe in the wind.

He says, "I'll pay their way."

I peer at him from the bed. "You can't."

"Of course I can. Don't be ridiculous." His hands run over his face. "If you're worried about people finding out—well. They won't, is the first thing. I can handle this kind of business. But if they do—it's not a crime. It's what they want, really: the Jews gone. And if it's the money—" He laughs. "But of course you don't mean the money. I'm sick with money."

I feel strangely drunk—my bones fizzing; love and misery straight through me. I say, "Friedrich, I will pay everything I can—"

"Which is not enough," he says. "But I have enough."

Darling J,

What do you want me to do with these letters? Anyway, your handwriting is a little like you (small, not so neat, but lovely) and it makes me happy to have daily samples of it. Apologies if your son doesn't appreciate it as much just yet; he misses you so he's almost without words. (Though I think he may have said

"ma" on Tuesday. I'll write to you when I have confirmation.)
In the meantime: get better, my love, and come home quickly.
I don't mean to live without you in this mad old city.

Love from your A

Go, I TELL her; but over and over she writes me back, *We will stay.*

So THERE IS a day when Friedrich goes to her. The days hot by then—Lord, how this illness lingers. I lie in bed and realize, with my eyes on the ceiling, that he's really there with her. I think into the quiet: It is because he loves us.

When Friedrich gets home, I hear him downstairs awhile before he comes up to me. He arrives in my room holding a drink; he folds into the chair beside my bed.

"She wants to talk to you first," he says, and then all but finishes the drink in his hand—one long gulp.

"Oh." I sit a moment, thinking. "Before what?"

"Before they go." A sigh as he rubs his eye. "Before she *decides* to go, I suppose. But she's nearly there."

"What did you tell her?" I want to know, and I don't want to know—I want her to stay. I want them to be safe. Both at once, please!

"That things will get worse," he says. "I told her what I know. And what's rumoured. Perhaps I embellished things a bit, but I don't think—" He stops with a sound like a hiccup, but it could be his thought catching him all of a sudden by the throat. "I don't think I went to any kind of excess, given the circumstances."

I rub my chest. The rash around my middle, the thing the doctor pointed to, to say, "See, scarlet fever," is gone now, but my ribs
still ache and sometimes a flush of sweat still hits me, leaves me
parched. I ask him, "Did you frighten her?"

He shrugs. "As best I could," he says. "She's a brave little cat,
your Anna."

"I don't want her to be frightened."

"Yes, you do, Josef." His face is always sad now, if not angry.
"Frightened enough to run."

I roll my tongue in my mouth. "To run." I can't imagine running—my legs rubber, thin as beans. "That's what they want us
to do."

"Josef." He never raises his voice with me these days. "They
want you dead."

A MAN TALKS to his wife on his friend's telephone late in the evening. She is at a neighbour's house, borrowing their line. There is
no breeze tonight, no rain. Beyond the windows, only quiet.

Is Tobias there?

                              No, he's with my mother.

Ah. I was hoping to hear him.

                              I'm sorry, love. He's
                              asleep now, anyway.

Well.

So. You've thought.

> Friedrich gave us a lot to
> think about.

I'm sorry, Anna.

> Do you think it's all true?

All . . . ?

> What he told us. Or
> did he just want to scare
> me?

I have to admit, I don't know
exactly what he told you.

> I think it was mostly a
> lie. Or his worst fears, at
> least. Nothing he knows
> for certain.

He's worried. I know that.

> If it's true—if any part of
> it's true . . .

You'll have to leave. I know.

I mean that *you* have
to leave too. Have you
thought of that?

What are you going
to do?

I'd have to get well first.

You might not have time.

I wouldn't be allowed on
any ship in this state.

Oh, God, a ship!

I just mean—

No, you're right.

We have to go far away,
I think.

Friedrich seems to think
it's best.

But you have to join us.

Josef?

I will.   Josef—

I promise I will, darling.

                                           All right. I believe you.
                                           Good.

Have you thought about
where you'll go?

                                           Well, I would like to go
                                           to America or Canada.
                                           But I don't know anyone
                                           there, and it's next to
                                           impossible to get a visa.

Perhaps Friedrich knows someone. He'll help you.

                                           I know he will. But it's
                                           really very hard, Josef.
                                           You haven't seen it. And
                                           it's in the news, always—
                                           that these countries
                                           are full with refugees,
                                           and they're done with
                                           it. They won't take any
                                           more. It pleases these
                                           people very much, you
                                           know, to see that no one

wants us. They're prac-
tically singing.

Anna, you must be hopeful.

Josef, honestly. I love
you, darling, but you're
very strange about these
things.

So you'll go, then.

Yes, if we can.
As soon as we can.

I'm glad.

Are you glad?

Anna—what would you like
me to say?

No, it's not that.

Please don't cry, love.

It's just a cold.

Mama won't come
with us.

Did you tell her—   But she wants us to go.

Oh. Well. That's good, I think.

                                     And you will come soon.

I will come very soon.

                                     Yes. And then won't we
                                     all be terribly happy!

It may still be that everything
will be all right, darling.

                                     And it may be that we'll
                                     come home soon.

We will come back home
soon.

                                     I wonder, though, Josef.
                                     Will we want to?

I think we will always want
to, love.

12

CAN'T IMAGINE, AT THIS POINT, HOW HARD IT WILL BE FOR Anna and Tobias to get a visa. I think, Of all applicants, a woman and a baby—surely they would have it easiest? But it isn't so. And the ships fill up, and the weeks go by, and people in the embassy lineups are arrested for loitering, or assembling publicly, or anything else the police care to charge them with. Anna tells me that Jakob has been arrested, and charged, and sent to a labour camp—not yet an absolute terror. He comes back, after two weeks, a little thinner, and with a tan.

And then Friedrich comes to me one day and says: "I think I've found something."

I sit in the chair in my room, a little removed from the window to avoid the drafts, with a blanket over my legs, reading a biography of Schiller. I feel about a hundred years old. Friedrich sits on the edge of the bed.

"Where?" I ask him.

"You're not going to like it," he says, "but it's a real option, and I think they should take it."

He tells me then, and I look out the window, through light filtered past peach-coloured drapes. A word that means to me "the ends of the earth"—that's what it is. The other side of the universe.

"Shanghai." I try it out in my mouth. "China."

"I know," Friedrich says, "it's hard to imagine. But they'll take people. With almost no conditions. And there are advantages to being so far away."

I peer at him awhile, into the light in his eyes, still clear in these days. And I say, "No Nazis in China."

13

A T THE WESTBAHNHOF A MAN CALLS OUT, "THIS IS
the five o'clock," through steam, and Friedrich carries
Anna's bags, one in each hand. I watch. He won't let me
lift them—"The contagion," he says, and "The baby"; and if I
don't press him, it's in part because I know I'm not strong enough
to carry a bag. But there is my Anna: she watches me. She holds
my little son on her arm, and I can hold this; I can hold on to this
moment after this long while spent apart.

When Friedrich first told her about China, near midnight, sitting in her mother's front room, he told me she was quiet a full four
minutes. He wanted to talk into that silence, he said, but he sensed
that she needed it. At last she said, "Josef thinks we should go?"

"He agrees with me," Friedrich told her. And then another
long silence, and the dark of the house listening to them breathe.

"Tell me about Shanghai," she said. "How the people live there."

And Friedrich did his best, I think. It was what he thought he
knew—word from friends or friends of friends who'd travelled east
on business; stories from magazines, from his childhood, from a
dream. A great crowded city, he told her. Wide rivers. A snaking
riddle of a language, to his ears. Beautiful dark-haired women in

silk dresses. But plenty of English and French too, all scented and spiced with imperial sensibility; the Europeans came to carry it back west. And White Russian refugees, he tells her. Jews, probably. Possibly it wouldn't feel too different from Vienna, in places. Perhaps, he suggested, she'd feel right at home.

He knew, it was true, that Shanghai was an occupied city; he'd read bits and pieces about the brutality of the Japanese towards the Chinese. Anna had no doubt read about it too, he understood. But there were no Nuremberg laws in China, after all. And it was a city that would receive them.

She looked, he said, like a sergeant in the army—the way her face hardened and showed nothing. But she told me later that it was a war to her, this proposition. Because Shanghai was a terrible nothing—so far outside Europe, so far from home. Everything she'd ever heard about it sounded strange. She had no friends there. And to go alone, with a baby—but what was the alternative?

When she asked this of Friedrich, he said, "This won't be your home for long, Anna." And what did he mean by that? Her mind filled in the possibilities. Homeless. Without rights. And without friends—could it ever come to that? Surely not everyone would leave. Here, she knew the language. She could introduce herself, she could ask for work. She knew what kind of work people did. Could she pass for a Gentile? Was that the only problem?

"Anna." She told me his voice was so tired, but he pleaded. "For your son's sake, please. Get out of Europe. Go as far as you can."

And now we stand with trains hooting and hissing around us, these trains bound for everywhere and this train bound for Italy, which is where my wife and my son will go. The ship will meet them at Genoa. For a long, long while it will steam away east, into strange oceans, dragging its trail of foam like a spool of thread winding out from my heart.

The men in square-shouldered coats, the women with curled hair like little golden wings around their faces—all of Vienna surrounds us, and my wife says to me, "Smile for me before I go, Josef." She is smiling for me, beautiful. And I do smile. I say, "This is the start of a very big adventure." And she smiles a different smile, and she whispers it, my words, into Tobias's little ear: *The start of a very big adventure.*

"And you will write to me," I say, "every day, won't you?"

"Won't we, Tobias?"—and the baby makes a cooing noise, his eyes focused on Anna's shoulder.

An old couple brushes past us, carrying their lunch of smoked meat and dumplings, feeding us home with the smell of it. It is all, for an instant, so ordinary. Could it be that we imagined everything dangerous?

But I know: because it wasn't Friedrich's visit that convinced Anna to go. He left that evening after she said, "I will have to think about this." When he got home, I heard him moving through the house, but he didn't come up to my room. The night spent itself slowly, made me think I was getting sick again. I watched the little window come alive through shades of blue-violet and gold in the hours before I could expect Friedrich to wake up.

In the Leopoldstadt, Anna looked after her mother and the baby. She did not want to leave. She saw more reason to stay: her mother needed help, her husband could not travel, and all her family were here. When her mother asked her what Friedrich had suggested, she first said—too quickly, almost angry: "Nothing." But then later, when she said, "China, Mama"—she began to cry, and her mother held her.

Ella Dükmann said to her then: "Don't be afraid to go, Anna." And told her that now was a time to be brave. It was better to go if she could. Ella herself would not go: "I'll stay here till they lay me down beside your old father," she said. "I am so old. But the two of you should make a new life while you can."

Through all this, though, Anna could not see herself leaving. She thought, We can wait until Josef is better, at least. We should all go together.

And this she thought until two mornings later, when she woke to the sound of people gathered on the street—and saw, when she opened the front door, the crowd of men who were carrying her mother's neighbour and his son into their home. Both were dead: the man, a little older than she was, and the eleven-year-old boy. And the people who watched didn't wail or cry, but were silent. Their hands and their clothes had turned red. They were all so solemn, so calm, that Anna—as she might at a family gathering—felt herself compelled to call out: "Do you need help?"

One of the men wiped his forehead with the back of his hand, painted it with blood. "You could bring some clean cloths."

When she brought a pile of clean linens over to them, joined them in the kitchen—the two bodies laid out on benches, the table pushed against the wall—she asked what had happened. At first no one said anything, just cleaned and wrapped the bodies. The mashed and crushed faces of the man and his son, shapeless as old footballs, they covered. At length a man said to Anna, "They were walking through the park, I think."

She swallowed before she said, "What will the police do?"

And this man answered, "Nothing more to these two, at least, I pray."

At home, a half-hour later, she was sick in the bathroom for a long time. When her mother awoke, they sat in the front room together. Somehow, this morning, the baby slept on. Ella held her daughter's hand, prayed faintly through just-parted lips. After a long while she said to Anna, "I want you to take my grandson away from here."

I heard from Anna in a note that evening, and by phone that night. They would go on the next ship, if they could. I said to her, "Don't be afraid." And I said also, "I will come to you soon."

FRIEDRICH NOW IS telling her that the train will leave shortly. Still I haven't kissed her: I'm afraid of hurting her, or the baby, in this last moment of contact. Really, I'm not meant to be out of the house; the doctor wants me quarantined another two weeks, but today Friedrich did not even ask if I wanted to come with him to the train station—just helped me with my coat, let me lean on his arm down the stairs and to his car.

He drove us today. Earlier, he paid for Anna's berth on a ship. "At the end of all your letters, he wrote that he'd pay for everything," Anna told me on the phone. And I knew by the gentleness in her voice that she was asking me: forgive him, now, once and for all. But I forgave him months ago. I am now nothing but helpless with gratitude.

But in this moment I could forget it, because I don't want them to go.

Anna smiles at me. "It's time, Josef."

Can I breathe, can I speak—but I do, and I say, "All right, my love." I ask if she has everything she needs—ticket, money, passport. She and Friedrich both check, and all is well.

Friedrich turns away—to give us privacy, I realize, and now I must make myself understand the moment has come. This brief widening of my life, this time spent with this woman, is ending. It wells up through my chest—can I speak? No, not now. My Anna, my love—I can't say it; I only hold her eyes with mine.

She shifts the baby onto one arm. She kisses the fingers of her brown leather glove, a sweet, long kiss. Presses the kiss, her fingers, to my cheek. My hand to her hand. Anna, don't go: every part but my tongue will say it. But she only slides her fingers out of the glove, leaves me holding it against my skin.

"We'll see you soon, Josef," she says.

"Soon." I cough. And then, from some unstopped well of grief: "There will never be anyone but you, Anna."

And she—mercy—leans through this space between us and kisses my lips. Our son's hand finds my shirt collar. Coal burning as we breathe. She leans away. I am still kissing her, bending into her, but she has to step away and to Friedrich, who takes her two bags to the compartment for her.

When Friedrich appears again, without the bags, he kisses Anna on the cheek. She puts her arm around his neck and draws him down to kiss his lips, gentle. They both smile, and are sad. But Friedrich comes towards me, hands in his pockets, and Anna does not.

Anna has the baby propped against her chest so that he's looking away from me. His black hair grows in all directions like cotton fluff. She stands watching me as if waiting for something.

But—as the world is jostling me side to side, as the men and women pass with bags and children and trunks and with their hats pulled low—what can I give her? Steam hisses out above us, away down the platform, up into nothing. My back is straight, yes, but I doubt I could speak; not to save my life, not even if someone were to hold a pistol to my head. But she only sees me staring with this hard, straight face, because this face can't hold the feeling I have.

There is the train hissing, whistling, and the conductor shouting and people nudging past each other and the police, here and there, terrible as sharks, and there is Friedrich's hand on my shoulder because, at last, Anna is turning from me. She watches as long as she can, but then she is gone, heading up the steps.

And in the small moment after she turns, there are the baby's eyes; he has his hand in his mouth and he's watching an old man's hat. He sucks his hand and he watches the hat and he rises up the steps in my wife's arms, little life—and then they're gone.

The train whistles. A door closes.

My life snaps to; it's a dream that's over. The world is small again.

14

MOMENT OF LIGHT WHEN ANNA'S POSTCARD ARRIVES from Italy:

Beautiful start to our vacation: nothing but sunshine since the border, and the customs man made friends with Baby. The mountains were just like I knew they would be, but more so. I miss them already.

We wish you were here with all our little hearts. Feel better soon, sad fellow.

Love always,
Your A

It knocks the wind out of me, imagining them at the border. All my prayers have been aimed towards this. I've heard such terrible stories—the way they search people, the shame of it—but see, Anna did get through. I wonder, staring out the window of my bedroom at the view that's been, for some time now, the whole outside world for me, how much she leaves out of her writing. And then I think: of course she must leave things out. She is better at this than I am—better at surviving.

I fold in on myself with prayer: *Let me live,* my heart says; *for them, if nothing else. Let me not be a fool.*

15

B UT SEE THIS, TOBAK: THAT IS NOT ALL. SET IT DOWN
plainly, every piece, or else it won't hold together.
There—I have set myself a task. I will see it done right.
I have not written everything I ought to about that time.

IT'S AROUND THE same time, early autumn, perhaps, that
Friedrich receives at his house a letter from Paris, addressed to me.
He does not open it himself, but carries it rather to his friend who
sits shrivelled and preoccupied in one of his guest rooms.

When he hands it to me, he has not fetched himself a drink, as
he usually would before coming upstairs. He sets the envelope in
my hands and says, "From your sister, I suppose."

The return address and the penmanship are hers, indeed. I sit
up in my armchair as he sits on the bed across from me, and I realize it would not occur to him to leave me in privacy with this letter.

"I could have some funds transferred to Paris," he says. And
adds, as I read without looking up or responding: "I'm glad she
knew she could write to you here."

It is not so simple, though, what my sister is asking—not simple, and not so quickly resolved, when (all these years later) I recall it. But when I first read her letter, I don't, can't, know that—and the matter does not seem so ominous, after all:

Dear little J,

—Zilla writes by hand, tight, angled loops.

I hope very much that you're being well looked after chez Frédéric, and that your wife finds it in her to forgive you for this long separation. I hope it's not unreasonable for me to write to you; I realize I've been a bad, bad correspondent, but you understand that very little in me can remain backwards-facing. (Paris is not so awful. One or two thinking people, at least. You ought to come join us here.)

But your dreadful old city is still chasing me, dear J. Do you remember our cousin Sarah K? I doubt you do—she insisted on spurning you lot, of course, after Papa turned up his nose at her. I can hardly blame her.

All this to preface my real purpose: Mrs. K has fallen on hard times. (As have we all, you will say.) Her employer has let her go. The standard idiotic reason, in addition to which, it would seem, she has only a Czechoslovakian passport. It makes one vulnerable, I understand. When last she wrote to me, she seemed almost in despair. She didn't dare ask for help, and I didn't dare offer any. But here I am writing to you, little J. To be precise, I am hoping you might mention this to our old friend FZ. It may be he has among his affairs some little position, currently neglected, which a sharp and responsible (if perhaps humourless) kind of lady might fill, one who has a mother and daughter to feed.

She has her pride, but I suspect she will not be too choosy.

I do hope FZ is willing to hear out this request if you put it to him reasonably. I appreciate that he serves new masters now and it may be that I don't know any longer who I am talking about. And yet there you are with him, little J, and as best I know he hasn't turned you out on your ear or had his cook bake you into a pie. It may be he will understand. It may be he'll remember our friendship and help a cousin of ours for our sake. I do hope so. With that hope, I've noted Mrs. K's current address on the reverse of this page. You might write to her if something can be arranged.

Mutti and Papa send their love, insofar as they know how. They are adjusting as best they can to their new home. I heard Papa speaking French the other day and was almost impressed by his accent. Who knows? He may be home at last in France, our old Austrian assimilator.

Get well fast, dummy.

Z

"I suspect I know a good lawyer in Paris, if she needs one," Friedrich says as I finish, leaning in towards me as if he might read the letter through my eyes.

"I think you could help her," I say to him. "But she's asking on our cousin's behalf."

"Oh." Something in his eyes flickers, shrinks, recovers. "What is it, then?"

I tell him, and he takes the letter from me, reads it tight-jawed. "I know it isn't easy," I tell him as he reads. "Perhaps it isn't clear to them in Paris how much things have changed."

"Never mind all that." He folds the letter, folds it again, slips it into his pocket, and I almost reach out to stop him (this slip of my family, something flying away from me as he takes it to himself), but then think: After all, he needs her address more than I do. "Well, I have no one looking after the paintings just now, after all. Good luck that you got sick, then."

"Oh." And it does seem, for a moment, almost like good luck. "So you can manage it?"

"It isn't so complicated." (If he's angry, is it at me?) "It's a little matter. I couldn't say that it's sustainable. But yes, fine, I can find an old mother an odd job or two."

"I'll write to Zilla right away. That's marvellous," I tell my friend. "She'll be grateful, I'm sure."

"Why shouldn't I write to her myself? And why, for that matter, shouldn't she write to me? This is nonsense. She knows me better than that."

I want to tell him, It's not so simple, but my throat is all prickles, and I can only sputter as he strides out through the door with this piece of my sister he can't let me keep.

AND IT IS a thing one can almost forget in the midst of this madness, for don't I have a hundred and one prayers to offer for my wife and my child, and isn't this business some triviality in the midst of it—but it isn't quite so, understand. I can't effect a single movement in the world, and yet here is something that was offered to me, was asked of me. And have I carried it out? It surfaces in my mind and I pray.

═══

A DAY THREE weeks later when Friedrich brings me another letter from my sister in Paris.

"But I did write to your cousin," he tells me as he hands me the letter—not sitting, this time, but pacing in front of me. "If she didn't receive it—Perhaps I could have done more. But I did use the address . . . Ah, I might have found someone who knew better—"

But I am not listening to him; I am with someone I know well in a faraway room, talking quietly:

Dear J,

The trail of correspondence in this mad case defies belief. Since I last wrote to you, you talked (I presume) to F; he wrote to our cousin Sarah K; she has written to me, and now I write again to you! J, our mutual friend has underestimated how disturbing it might be for the persecuted Mrs. K to receive an offer of work from someone in F's position. I did tell her he was an old friend; I told her he was looking after you, but she will not reply to him. She asks why you could not write to her, if you were so well looked-after. She wonders what will become of her, of her daughter, if they are known to someone like F.

Will you do something to look after this situation, little brother? I imagine that even if she could speak with you, hear from you what kind of person F is, she would be more willing to trust. (I have told her what I think, but she protests—perhaps wisely; who can say—that I knew our friend only before the annexation.) Would it put you very much in danger, little brother? Would it put her in danger? I'm not certain how contagious you're meant to be.

You might write back to me. I realize it seems I have forgotten you—writing only when I need something from you, terrible

Z—but it isn't so. I worry about all of you. I wish you would get out of Vienna. I wish you would go anywhere. Forget it all, everybody you care about, and be selfish, be safe, so I can sleep easy. Consider it, little J.

Until then, I judge you to be an old-fashioned idiot. I invite you to prove me wrong.

Z

"Oh, Friedrich," I say to him, "you frightened her."

It isn't exactly like that, I'll later learn; Sarah Kostner isn't so easy to frighten. Cautious, even suspicious, but it will be some time yet before fear in fact directs her actions.

But my friend stares at me like a hunted creature, so I must tell him what the letter says. (I do not tell him all, note—I won't give up this letter to him. That paragraph at the end, the softest declaration from Zilla I can remember, such that I strain even to fit her voice to the words—this he won't take from me, won't even read.)

"You can't just write to her like that." In this instance I would like him to defer to me, grant that I might understand better—and yet to stand against him, after these months, is impossible.

"And still Zilla won't write to me. Why will she not write to me? My help is still welcome, of course. Look after her brother, certainly—find work for this or that old bat on request . . . but correspond with her? Unthinkable!"

"Friedrich—" A dozen things I would like to say, and all of them true, and none of which would appease him—and then at last some little light shining up out of the rubble, and I can hand it to him: "She's a married woman, Friedrich. This changes things. She can't simply carry on a correspondence with you as before."

The pacing stops. One can see it, the trail left by the ache that runs through him, departing his forehead and running down to his gut. He holds one hand against his chest. But, "No," he says. "I see that. I see."

Now he sits on the bed, curled forward as if to mirror me, and rests his face in his hands.

"It's all right. I forget myself, that's all. Forgive me." All of this, quiet. "It's no one's fault but mine. I introduced her to him. And I never . . . I didn't ever really . . . Well." Sitting straighter, breathing deep: "He was bold, and I wasn't. There. It's done now."

"I'm sorry, Friedrich," is all I can say.

A pause before he says, "So she thinks you should speak to this woman."

"I'll write to her now," I tell him. "It might be enough."

So I WRITE to Sarah Kostner. (Clear offers, gentle words.) I think: My family failed you before; my father wanted nothing to do with you—and here I am asking you to trust me. Will my word be enough? How hard it is to build confidence through an exchange of letters. I write at the end of the message:

> *Could we meet, I wonder? My sister dearly loves you, and I've regretted for many years that there remained this rift between us. I feel responsible. Only I cannot leave this house. I understand that you might be reluctant to visit this address. Is there some arrangement that could be made?*

AND AFTER I send it: nothing. A whole week.

—UNTIL (ON A Thursday, cold) her letter:

*It is indeed hard to trust, Mr. Tobak. But circumstances are what
they are. I begin to understand it.*
    So be it.
    It shall be arranged. I will meet you.

AUTUMN HARDENING INTO frost the morning I finally meet my
cousin. It makes better sense for me to wait by the old servants'
entrance than have someone else answer the door for her: in the
time it would take me to wheeze my way down the stairs to her,
she would bolt, I imagine—besides all of which, a part of me is well
aware, it's the height of imprudence to let one such as her and one
such as me meet in Friedrich's house.

In the delirium I feel on wobbling down these stairs, the world
is not quite real. This fool of a man who imagines he might have a
civil conversation with his relation in their oppressor's doorway—
does he see himself clearly? Does he dream himself rational?

The doorway at the base of these narrow stairs is painted white,
and a little window looks into the lane between the house and the
tall spiked fence. Branches hang over it. Here there's no chair to
sit in and so I've folded down to perch on the stairs. Just that strip
of the outdoors visible from this angle, but it's different from what
one can see from the upstairs window and so it comes to me as
unfamiliar, like a different country.

There is a bird that keeps swooping by, fleck of ink. And is it that
it has repeatedly swooped by, as it seems to me, or that I imagined it?
Shade wavers on walls. My stomach lifts and falls like the surface of a
lake. The whole house sways, or perhaps it is my breathing.

When a dark coat passes at last in front of the window, at first it's only more birds, and when the knock comes, it comes through water. Though I'm six feet from the door, she must knock twice before it reaches me. And then at last—wobble to my feet, totter to the lock.

She is sharp, thin, so serious, her hard, slender face turned up to look at me. Right away she says: "Mr. Tobak, yes?"

"That's right," I tell her. "And you are Mrs. Kostner?"

"Sarah Kostner." She stands with hands folded in front of her, clips her words and barely blinks. "I shouldn't stay long."

"Yes." (This wooziness one can't shake but must speak through.)

"I'll get straight to the point. I appreciate your hesitation to accept help from Mr. Zimmel. But it's good you've met me here. He isn't what he seems to be in public, I promise you. These are strange times indeed, but—"

"You don't seem well, Mr. Tobak," she interrupts.

It makes me cough, the way she says it. "Pardon me. I'm recovering from illness. But no longer contagious, they assure me." I smile at her, but her face is a wall.

"It doesn't bode well." She peers down the narrow lane, both ways.

"Mrs. Kostner—Sarah," I say (though taming my own pulse that rushes at her words), "it was Mr. Zimmel who helped me when I was sick." More coughing. Oh, Lord—there is a Josef Tobak apart from me, half-delirious, and he is laughing at this. Still, one must try to speak. "I would have fared so much worse. I might be dead."

"I understand you," she says. Calm but hard, this woman. No part of her yet has yielded. "But I understand, too, what these men are made of. A bit of shame, perhaps, at the way they must now treat their old friends. But it passes, you see. It doesn't overwhelm them. And when their masters call on them to demonstrate their position, there won't be any question, Mr. Tobak. They'll make an example of individuals like us."

The birds dart overhead. My throat itches. It's hard to speak.

"If you had only my word, you'd be quite wise to say this. Quite wise. But recall that my sister, who's always been a friend to you—she recommends this too."

She clicks her tongue. "Away in Paris, yes. Zilla barely understands, of course. Besides which, she doesn't see— It's different when one has a child. It's different when it isn't just one's own life being risked."

"Ah—but see, I understand that." I reach out, touch her shoulder, and I can tell that she isn't certain about this touch, but I need it as much to steady myself as to reassure her. "I have a child. Even now, my wife and my son are entrusted, in a sense, to Mr. Zimmel. And he has been very good. And they will be very safe." (Very safe—speak it aloud.) "And if my child had been sick and in need of care, as I am now, I'd have been afraid." Swallow, and then say it truthfully: "But I would have been so grateful to have Mr. Zimmel's help. I would have accepted it."

"Easy enough to say," she says, eyeing me from that low angle.

"I can't make you trust him," I tell her. "But my conscience will be troubled if I don't insist on this. Here is a man who means you no harm. He wants, indeed, to prove himself worthy of my sister's trust." (And here's betrayal, I think, but I must say it.) "He's in love with Zilla, in fact. Did she tell you? He always has been. It doesn't matter that she's married. Not for your sake but for hers, certainly, he'll keep being a man he imagines she could love."

She stares at me a moment. "But he's already joined the Party."

"So now it's all the more vital." It's hard to make myself understood. A part of me doesn't see my friend as worthy of this defence, but another part seems to have rehearsed the words well. "You see? To show himself, and show her, that it's all just a ruse. Everything since this annexation, for Mr. Zimmel, has been a reckoning. And he's been trustworthy. He remembers his friends. He remembers himself."

She takes a sharp breath. "I don't believe the real tests have come yet, for their type."

"Sarah," I say, "it's simply a job he's offering you. Take it. Disappear if he seems unworthy of trust. Unless he cares about you to protect you, you're no one to him. He wouldn't track you down."

Sarah Kostner stares into my eyes a moment. "I don't imagine you know what you're suggesting, Mr. Tobak," she says at last. "No doubt you've suffered. But you don't see. I have no rights. And it's not simply that I've been dismissed more than once in these past months. I've learned that I open myself to blackmail. My last employer—I cleaned for him, a doctor with a small office, but after the first week he stopped paying me. I was afraid to bring it up. This man—he'd mention my mother and my daughter every time he spoke to me. And he'd refer to our home by its address." She watches my face as she says it. I don't know what she sees. "I won't tell you what else he suggested to me. It doesn't bear repeating. Men are— Well. You understand, perhaps, Mr. Tobak."

Do I? I would like not to. I rub my eyes.

She says: "I had to get out of that in a hurry. And to a new apartment, on top of everything. Though of course no one will rent to me." She laughs once, without humour. "Thank the Lord, I found another flat by a miracle, from a friend who was leaving town. She slipped out without giving her landlord notice, told us to move in quietly and keep paying the rent. No one's said anything yet. But it's only a matter of time, Mr. Tobak. And if I don't have the rent money next week, I—"

Her throat seems to close mid-sentence, and only now does she look away from me. Though my own voice is like gravel, I say: "You've come here as a last resort. I understand."

After a pause—"I wonder if it's not simply a gesture of defeat."

"Sarah," I say—gently, as I hope a stranger might speak to Anna in her exile, "Mr. Zimmel invented this position for me. He doesn't need to take advantage of anyone. He only wants to help. And since I got sick, and I can't work— Well. Here is something that seems almost readied for you in advance."

A long, narrow-eyed look she gives me then. "You're a religious man, Mr. Tobak?"

Even in these days, a moment's hesitation. "I am, yes."

"Then tell me once, for certain," she says, "knowing that more than one person's safety may hang in the balance, and that I'm your flesh and blood, and a mother without a husband to protect her, besides—can you vouch for this man's honour?"

I tell her, "I can. I do." It is simple to say. It's true.

She peers at me awhile. We've been speaking quietly, and the laneway is quiet, and the birds and the leaves make their small noises. I will need to sit soon, but until this woman leaves, it seems to me I must be someone steady.

"Very well," she says at last. "I will write to him."

I nod, and smile, and kiss her cheeks before she goes, and as she disappears from sight down the back laneway, checking over her shoulders as she walks, I feel myself touched by something weighty and golden. *Look here, sad fellow*, says this feeling. *You aren't gone just yet; there is still a work or two of good you might accomplish in this life.*

With the door closed again, I sit a long while on the stairs, breathing slow.

SHE WRITES TO my friend. He hires her right away. I barely hear about Sarah Kostner in the time that remains for me in this city—but it is a matter Friedrich can write about to Zilla, and it's a light I can hold in myself.

You have changed something, I can tell my sad heart, when still no letter has come from Anna, when I lie coughing in the dark. *Someone in your family, at least, is safer, thanks to you.*

Circumstances will let me cherish this thought a long while.

16

N THE LAST DAYS OF OCTOBER, A LETTER FROM ANNA
arrives:

Dear friend,

Hello from China! I hope this letter makes it to you, and quickly. I imagine you must be concerned for us after such a long silence. Rest assured that our cruise went as smoothly as could be hoped. We made friends on the ship with an old Swedish couple who used to work as diplomats: they practically adopted Baby, but at the last moment I suggested his father might object. Among the ship's staff were a few very nice young Italian men, and they were of course keen to hear all my stories about my Austrian husband who'd be joining me very soon.

We arrived in Shanghai a week ago. Disembarking was a little funny and I'll have to tell you about it sometime, once I'm confident in the postal system. (It will take some paper.) They've got a nice little group of people here who spend all their time helping new arrivals, and these people led us to a perfectly snug little room in the French Concession. I'm sure you'll agree when

*you see it: local charm aplenty! I've got some flowers on the sill
now, and if Baby doesn't eat them, they'll keep me happy through
the rest of the week.*

*We wish you were here. Rest well (but not too long). Please
be confident that you have all our love.*

Josef writes two copies of his reply, then copies it out another
two times, directs two to each of the addresses Anna has given him.
When Friedrich goes out to mail them, Josef reads and rereads his
wife's letter. How she writes as if strangers might open and read
it—and strangers likely did read it, he thinks. Now in every line he
can find her sadness hidden between words.

Josef himself is sick again—not as before, with fever, but a con-
tinual cough and a weakness in his limbs. He can't deny it, though
he tries, and Friedrich has him stay in his room. The thought of a
ship sends his mind reeling—he watches the ceiling and sighs. If
such are the conditions of escape, he starts to think . . . But it's a
thought he has trouble finishing.

(How awful to set it down: in those days I'm consoled by the
thought that my wife could raise a child quite capably as a widow.)

THINGS WE CANNOT yet know, here in Vienna: that miles away,
where Germany's border meets Poland, the misery of refugees
denied flight in either direction will leave a refugee's son in Paris
so afflicted and hopeless as to enter the office of a German diplomat with a gun. A rose of blood on the wall of the embassy—but
on the Polish border, and throughout Germany, there won't be
any pity. November of 1938 will spill out: graffiti, blood, a galaxy
of shattered glass.

====

On a Wednesday night, November the ninth, Friedrich comes into Josef's room and says, "I'm going to have to rethink things. It's chaos out there."

Josef in his armchair looks up from his book, a Russian story, one with a sad romance. (The hero seems ready to die in Italy.)

"The news on Monday," Friedrich tells him, "was that a Polish Jew in Paris murdered a German diplomat in his office."

Josef can only grip his book. "Oh."

"Yes! Damned foolish boy. What did he think would come of it? What—" Friedrich holds the back of his hand to his lips as he regards the wall a moment. "He wanted the world's attention. He didn't think. It's inevitable now—Goebbels all but ordered a pogrom throughout Germany."

An alarm sounding against Josef's ribs. And there is Anna's mother's face, and Jakob's and Chaim's before his eyes, and his cousins', and every one of his neighbours, his friends—so, "What should we do?" he asks.

Friedrich sits on the edge of Josef's bed. "I don't know," he says. "I have to think."

"I should warn my family," Josef says, mostly to himself.

But, "How do you plan to do that, Josef?" Pain or anger in Friedrich's eyes. "You wouldn't make it across the canal."

"I don't know. I don't know what else to do."

"It's never enough." Friedrich says it, quiet. "Never mind trespassing through a political minefield, getting impossible tickets, impossible papers. It's nothing." He stands.

Josef stands with him. "Please. I haven't asked for anything."

"Of course not. You've never had to, have you? I've made sure of that," he says. "We act as if the world still worked the way our minds do, but it doesn't." His forehead hardens as he speaks. "Perhaps it never did."

Through the window comes the sound of a car accelerating. A man shouts.

Friedrich says, "It'll be out of my hands soon." And then he is gone.

Recall: Anna did not tremble when she left the station, all but alone. And all the way to China—did she cry? And yet here is Josef Tobak, shivering like a branch in the wind.

Oh, Lord—he begins to pray, but he has no other words, just his heart between his two thin hands. He offers it up, in case it should mean anything.

WHEN FRIEDRICH GETS home, so many hours later, Josef Tobak sits awake in his bed. From the rooms below comes the sound of slow footsteps. A mind can trace this other's movement through the house: from the sitting room, where footsteps pause awhile (the door of the liquor cabinet clicking shut, perhaps), to the back room, which looks over a garden now invisible in the night, to the foot of the staircase, and then heavily, heavily, up so many stairs.

When Friedrich passes by the open doorway to Josef's room, he is a shadow in a dark hall, but Josef himself sits lit by a bedside light. And so the shadow pauses, seeing him.

"Still awake," says Friedrich. Josef does not reply, and in a moment Friedrich joins him, sits in the armchair across from the bed, legs stretched out before him. A crystal rocks glass rests in his palm. He runs a thumb along an angle of cut glass.

"I hope nothing happened to you," Josef says to him.

His smile at his hands, and the glow from the bedside lamp throws shadows across both their faces, finding the corners of things. "Nothing at all, Josef," he says.

Josef sits still; he is working up the energy to make himself speak, but then Friedrich kicks off one of his shoes. He picks it up from the floor and with his handkerchief over his fingers pries something from the sole: a tiny shard of glass.

"Careful," Josef says.

"It's fine."

"It didn't cut you?"

Friedrich sets it on the bedside table. "No."

Laid so upon the little table, under an electric light bulb glowing yellow gold, this fragment of glass wounds almost upon sight. Josef feels it in himself. But Friedrich sits there staring down into the drink he's holding, and what can Josef do? He knows nothing.

(Lord, forgive me that I can't give a first-hand account of these evils, that through some mad twist of fate the man I was is safe in the home of a National Socialist during Vienna's Kristallnacht. It will be so long before he can take it all in. Understand that in this pogrom, across the city, thousands of men and women will be arrested and sent to the labour camps, and twenty-seven killed, and every one of the synagogues set alight and left to burn. The Turkish synagogue, where, it seems to me, I first saw myself as a creature in the presence of God, was in my youth so lovingly adorned through the craft and bounty of a whole community. Now, in my mind's eye, I see that gold flowing molten as if in a furnace, and little flakes of it flying upwards with the smoke to hang like stars above the Leopoldstadt. I know the stones cannot cry out, but Lord, I'm still answering to them.)

These two men are silent for so many minutes that Josef is certain Friedrich has fallen asleep, or passed out from drink or secret injury—but his eyes are still half-open, the light dimly shows. He is watching the wall, Josef thinks, or the curtains; or else looking at nothing, listening for the wind outside. Josef's own eyelids are weighted down by exhaustion.

After a very long time, Friedrich says, "After all, there's not much one can do in such situations."

Josef Tobak tries to swallow, tries to reply; but now Friedrich looks at him and says, "Lucky you're safe up here, then." And pats the bedspread, smiles for a moment.

In the minutes that follow, in the quiet of this space, Friedrich Zimmel falls asleep and Josef Tobak comes wide awake. From the table beside him, a tiny artifact of violence gleams mute and cold. The bedspread beneath him is becoming unbearable, warmth from the radiator unbearable.

Whatever it means—this pogrom—people must be frightened. What did Friedrich see? Whom did he meet? Josef hardly dares hope anything. Does it matter what he might hope? One can go on forever hoping for an outcome, after all, without lifting a finger to bring it about. He thinks at last of the face of a woman, thin, hardened strength, that peered up at him from the old servants' entrance, and he told her, with hope framed as certainty, that she'd be safe.

Most of Josef's things are in a little case by the closet door, ready to be taken up at any moment. The few things left to pack he gathers now, folds them, and stows them in a case. While his friend sits sleeping, he puts on his shoes; his coat too, and hat. Opens the case, unfolds the scarf, and hangs it round his neck. And now his throat begins to itch and twitch, as if it's been waiting for an excuse to cause trouble. In the bathroom across the hallway he draws a cup of water and drinks it. When he sets the cup down, he stands listening a moment. Not a sound from his bedroom. The whole house quiet.

Does he believe he'll get far? This is a fine thing to ask—and it is unlikely Josef could answer. Already when he reaches the second floor he's wheezing, and all the way down the long staircase to the front door he slides his shoulder along the wall to stay upright. He lets himself start coughing once he's almost at the door, when surely Friedrich won't hear him; but once he begins, he can't stop. Ugly, brutal coughs—he opens the front door to take his noisiness out of this building, but then he must sit on the front step. Sit . . . ? All but collapse, then. This fit sends his vision swirling.

No lights to be seen in the windows of the houses, and the trees lining the street are black against a sky of ash. Across the street and in front of another great old house, a street lamp sends a star through the dark. Josef rests his head on his suitcase.

To get to the second district tonight, to anyone he loves, is out of the question. It strikes him, then, that the Währing cemetery is not far from here. A comfortable walk to one in good health. The fragment of shattered glass is lodged in his mind; a smashed and trampled Währing gravestone seems carved out by this thought. An angry mob might, he thinks, attack the dead as well as the living.

But his skin is clammy, throat raw—he will not be able to walk down the street alone, he understands. So what is there to do?

I will tell Friedrich I can't stay any longer, he thinks. Or I'll tell him I'll take my chances on a train alone. Or I'll say, I forgive you for everything, I more than forgive you—treat me as your Party says you should, but I will continue to think well of you. Or . . . But he wonders, could he say all this? Would he mean it? Watches the shine of the street lamp through the trees. And thinks, Friedrich would not do anything truly evil. Not even if I told him all that, not even if he were afraid for his life. For my sister's sake, if not mine—he would remember himself, he would be (not a hero, but) human.

Breath slowing, and the weight of the suitcase in my lap a solidness that brings me back to myself—here I am, despite everything. The autumn air disperses my coughing into cold white clouds. I think of my cousin whom I convinced to trust against her instincts, and I think of my sister in Paris, she with her Italian husband, happy. And how it hurt Friedrich. It shouldn't matter, I think. (Now, when I sit up straight, the coughing comes intermittently.) But what does it take, I wonder, to change a person's heart? And how much change do you need before it matters?

This old house behind me is a friend sitting silent in sleep. Maybe I will have to go back inside, I think. In front of that house across the street, that street lamp still glows and it might be that someone else is thankful for this same light, perhaps coming home, perhaps sitting at their window in a dark room.

When Friedrich stirs, a couple of hours on, I haven't found it in myself to move, but sit on this step, suitcase in my lap. At last I hear footsteps behind the door. He hasn't turned a light on, but in the grey morning light filtering in through frosted glass, I must be visible to him. A few seconds before he pushes the door open and I turn to look at him. He and I stare at each other a long moment.

I wait while he steps out to me. I'm too tired to stand.

He says, "You gave me quite a fright."

"I'm sorry." My voice like that of an old man, it seems to me.

"I thought you'd disappeared."

I sit still. I'm working up the energy to make myself speak, but then he clears his throat and sits beside me. Leans back on his elbows, gestures to his crossed legs stretched out towards the street. "Mother would have something to say about this," he quips.

And again I prime myself to speak, but he reaches his hand out and taps the suitcase with his knuckles. He doesn't remark; he goes, "Hmm," and looks back out at the street.

So this is the way we are: two mismatched men, sitting side by side on concrete steps, the trees above us lightening in the first pale hours of the day. After a very long time Friedrich says to this beleaguered Josef, "You're not leaving this morning, I hope."

That small coal of heat, glowing—and, "I don't know," this Josef says. "I was thinking of it. But perhaps not yet, if you say so."

Friedrich pats Josef's shoulder with one heavy hand. "Good. Because I have new papers for you. And a new destination. Our good luck they never . . ." A pause. "Anyway, best not to dwell on these things. The man who last had them won't need them anymore, is all." A chill, then sudden heat. (A spirit that races to claim Josef.) But Friedrich says, "You'll go to New York, if I can manage it."

"New York!" He can barely whisper, but covers his mouth as if the neighbours might have heard him.

"I know what you're going to say," Friedrich begins, "and it's true, it's very far from Anna and Tobias. But I have no confidence whatsoever you'd survive the trip to Shanghai. And besides all that, you can recover in America, and then you can send for them. How would that be?" He's looking at Josef, who can only stare. "You won't be foolish enough to turn it down."

Josef coughs, and then: "The person these papers belonged to . . ."

"Ah! Tobak." Friedrich waves a hand. "I had nothing to do with what happened to him. You have my word. It's just . . . circum- stance and luck in sorry times. Really. You take advantage of what luck hands you, if you've got any brains at all."

Josef swallows. "New York." The star of lamplight through branches growing smaller and fainter as he says it.

"Sunday, we'll leave." Friedrich breathes deep, glancing behind him. "Lord! What an awful house to have to live in, all alone."

Josef says, "Friedrich, if ever, someday, I can help you—please tell me. I'll do it."

"Well." Friedrich stretches his back against the steps. "There's a kind word after a wicked night."

A few moments more, and Friedrich will help Josef upstairs, as far as the sitting room, where Josef's coughing will make them both stop and rest on the sofa. Later, Josef will wake in this spot with his suitcase still on his lap, and Friedrich slouched sideways across the sofa's armrest, head towards the window. The man's face so much younger in sleep—Josef will think it as he drapes his jacket over his friend. The climb to his room will be hard and slow but his mind strangely quiet, and when he gets to his room, he will fall asleep in his clothes and dream of nothing.

17

I T'S POSSIBLE THERE WERE OTHER WAYS A VIENNESE JEW could get to America after Kristallnacht, but I can barely understand or believe the one that worked for me. These things I know: without false papers, I would have been dead. Without the portfolio of artwork, I would have had no story for the customs agents. If Friedrich had not gone with me as far as my ship, I might have gone dumb with fear, or forgotten how I was meant to answer questions, or I might have simply passed out from exhaustion and been picked up by the police. (And that, certainly, would have been the end.) And if he hadn't arranged things in New York, I'd have been sent back, like somebody else's mail.

In November of 1938, through the fog of a reawakened sickness, this much is clear to me: the man who is travelling answers to Josef Bauer. He is employed by Friedrich Zimmel as an art dealer, and he is going to America with a set of paintings and sketches he will sell to buyers in New York and Philadelphia. (Where the real Josef Bauer might be, and why his passport is now in my pocket, is not a question I dare ask Friedrich—but the face in the passport photo is very much like mine, I think, so perhaps it's a fake.) Sometimes this man will feel faint from standing too long with his little bag in his hand (far less than any emigrant would carry, surely) and the two great black portfolios leaning against his hip. Every time the customs officers open these, Josef must be sure to say, "Careful, careful!" as if the greater risk is that the art might suffer damage, rather than that he not be allowed through.

On the day he leaves Vienna, they drive past the Währing park. The walls of the cemetery are just barely visible from the road. But on the bricks (and how much is in Josef's swimming mind, he doesn't know) there are paint marks like the wings of white birds and black birds, flocks flying beyond the branches—it takes him a moment to understand what it is.

"Yes, it's been that way awhile now." Friedrich barely glances out the window when Josef mentions it. "I was a little surprised. I didn't think many people knew it was a Jewish graveyard."

The driver calls back to them, "I think a lot of people were fairly scandalized, sir. Imagine it! In this neighbourhood."

A swell of solidarity as Josef thinks the man is talking about the vandalism, the painted swastikas, but then the driver says to Friedrich: "Perhaps you'll have it torn down, sir."

Friedrich taps his fingers to his chin. In his car, on the street, he wears his Party arm band without any semblance of shame. He says, "Hmm," as the park disappears behind them. And then, "Perhaps."

Josef sits without speaking, tries not to think, all the rest of the way to the Westbahnhof.

He's wearing new clothes, bought by Friedrich in town. With this fine cloth rubbing against him, he does not feel like himself. The sky is November-dark, and the streets wear the smash and smear of the nights previous: a word of hate on a storefront, white stars painted in condemnation. (He thinks: It isn't a mark of shame, but see how determined they are to make it one.)

And for a moment his mind cries out (as his hand presses hard into the padded black door), I have no right to be here. Why is not my home smashed in, why am I not among the dead or missing?— as if I had the right to rise above this. For he isn't any better, this Josef Tobak-Bauer, than the most ordinary man, and yet he is the one in this long black Benz, planning his way to America. Get out, his mind cries. Throw your lot in with those who have more right than you to escape, but who must stay.

But now another part of his mind, the part that sounds sometimes like Anna, pipes in: If you were trapped, and any of your neighbours had the chance you have, is there anything you wouldn't do to help him take it? And Josef knows how he would feel, even in his heartbreak: that a part of himself, however small, were escaping with that person. Now how many such pieces, he wonders, can I stand to carry with me?

All around the English embassy, the lineup of mothers with children winds like a tail around the feet of a cat. The driver calls back, "See that, sir. I wish they'd grant them visas, after all. Though of course they won't."

Friedrich answers, "Save everybody a lot of trouble."

"It just goes to show, sir." The driver seems to shrug. Josef wonders what this man's name is, and is he from Vienna? His whole life, Josef wonders, has this man lived among neighbours he hated, and said nothing?

At the station, the air grinds with machinery. Josef carries his bag and the portfolios—he will pretend he has strength enough for this, rather than leave his hands free: for every police or military officer they meet salutes them, and Josef has this excuse to keep his arms down.

When a porter comes to take the portfolios, Josef snaps, "No,

I'll carry those. You take this." Hands the man his suitcase even as his nerves crest a surge of terror. The porter nods and takes the suitcase—not suspicious, Josef sees; nervous, in fact, and keen not to offend. Josef prays: *If there is a chance I might survive this, help me not to squander it.*

They find their compartment. This fraudulent art dealer sits facing away from the engine. He lets his eyes close for a moment, and he touches his chest, the place where his passport and tickets are folded inside his coat, in the pocket against his heart. Miraculously there.

The first test passes without incident: the conductor takes their tickets and doesn't remark, does not even let his eyes linger on Josef. He says, "Thank you, Mr. Bauer," in the same crisp, professional tone that he uses for, "Thank you, Mr. Zimmel." The train is already leaving the city. They are entering vineyards and farmland, browned with the coming winter—but broad and open in a way that feels strange to Josef: boundaries falling away, shelter shrinking into the horizon.

Friedrich stretches his legs out into the space between their seats. Josef tucks his own feet back underneath him.

It is best, indeed, that Josef isn't in charge of this business. He would hide from everyone, he wouldn't eat. But Friedrich tells him, after an hour, that they'll get coffee in the dining car. And though Josef is half-certain he'll be ill, he perceives that eating might be ordinary behaviour.

In the dining car, they aren't made to wait, but are led to a little table by a window right away, a table with a white tablecloth swaying like a girl's skirt to the rhythm of the tracks sweeping along beneath them. The waiter bends low when he talks to them, and speaks mainly to Friedrich. Today they have a Hungarian goulash, he tells them: very hot, very nice. With a white beer, perfect. But Friedrich says, "Just coffee, I think. And two apple strudels." The waiter walks backwards a few strides before hurrying off.

Outside, hills. Lakes winking silver-grey between banks of black forest. White caps of mountains in the far distance, receding as the train snakes north.

Friedrich doesn't look out the window. He is smiling off over Josef's shoulder. Josef turns to see: he is watching two young women. They're with their friends or family (older people, at least); they lean into each other and whisper between giggles.

The waiter comes with coffee and pastry, sets these down with a steady hand, and the china rattles only a little, a gentle tinkling that seems meant to infuse a meal with excitement. Josef eats it but can't taste it. He cannot recall if he's wiped his lips, and so does it over and over, like a cat.

Soon the waiter appears again with a note. "From the young ladies," he says, as he hands it to Friedrich, who opens it and smiles a little.

"Yes, very well." He folds the note and says to Josef, "If you'll excuse me just a moment."

What can he say? For already Friedrich is standing, is stepping across the carriage to the table where the two young women are smiling at him (their family dispersed or banished)—and Josef is alone.

The window blurs into impressionism. Josef's stomach writhes. The waiter clears Friedrich's place and says, "All is well, sir?" and Josef says, "The coffee is nice." (For what else can he say, this Josef?)

"From Avignon, lovely," is the first thing he hears Friedrich say, behind him. They are talking about Europe. Politics. The girls have finished university. (There are still universities. Young people still attend them.)

Murmuring and murmuring, minutes of it. And one of the girls says, "My father says Hitler might try to invade France."

At a table across the carriage from the girls, a frightened little man feels his guts churn in his belly. Flashes of colour before his eyes. France! he thinks. No, no—a safe place!

But then there is Friedrich: "The Führer seeks only to reunify the Germanic race into one nation. France has no part in that."

A woman's voice asks, "And what did you think, when the Führer drove into your city?"

And before Friedrich can reply, the other girl jumps in: "Why, Marie, didn't you hear how the Austrians welcomed him? They threw flowers."

A rain of petals. Josef's vision is swimming with strange colours. He cannot see. A thrill of horror—it occurs to him that he might actually faint. He leans onto his elbows and fixes a smile on his lips.

Friedrich is saying, "Thank God there was no real combat." And then someone is saying another thing, and another voice (whose?) says, "Trout, mustard"—but that doesn't make sense, Josef decides; it must have been something else. Or else nothing. Are they still talking?

"I love Schiller." A woman's voice.

And now composers zinging through the air to his ears— Mozart, Schubert, Brahms. "Beethoven was booted out of every inn in Vienna." "That fish, as big as his arm." Josef hears it from a country away. Or doesn't hear it; it doesn't matter. He smiles, he smiles, and he thinks: Do not let this hysteria become a laugh now, you poor fool.

Friedrich has stood up—Josef hears how the dishes rattle a little as he pushes his chair back. And now he has come, he is talking to Josef: "A stroll through the locomotive countryside, Mr. Bauer?"

"Ah." Josef makes as if to look out the window, but it's all the same, it's all smears of flashing light. He listens for what his mouth might say. "I'm going to sit and finish my coffee. You go ahead without me."

A second of hesitation before Friedrich says, "You're sure?"

"Yes." Josef's voice almost merry. "Yes, I'm enjoying the view."

When there is nothing but the barely-noise of other diners, tables away, and the rattle of the tracks beneath them, Josef thinks: I'm trapped. He can't stand, he cannot get back to his compartment like this. He could cry for help—but that, he thinks, would be disaster. Why are you blind? they'd ask. Because I'm terrified, his answer ought to be, and though he wouldn't say it, some doctor called in from a second-class car would pronounce him so. Deathly afraid. Of what? Of being discovered a Jew, this doctor would say, and a fraud, and a refugee. Then wouldn't they press Aspirin into his hand, pat him on the shoulder and push him off into the waiting arms of the Gestapo at the next station—oh, yes, and then to a prison camp, some deep black pit behind barbed wire.

There is a fish swimming through his mind—laughing and swimming after a hook made of light. To the rhythm of the rattling car, rows of coloured blocks stream past him, each one crying out with its strange, inaudible scream. He sees by the marks on them, at last, that they're gravestones, and a cemetery is spilling out of the sky. These cemetery walls around him, he thinks—it's simply that I can't see over them, that's all. There is a light over the wall, sparkling off shards of glass, and the voice of the fox crying *Shema Ysrael* into the ear of a dead fish.

His head bumps against the glass of the window and he shakes his head. You are a man on a train, says his memory, and you are sitting at a table, still alive.

Just in time, this thought, because the next voice he hears is one from a table across the aisle.

"Pardon me, but you're travelling with Mr. Zimmel, aren't you?"

A male voice. Josef turns to nod at this person. (Never mind that there is only a dull grey shape the size of a man.)

"Not a friend of his, though?"

What to make of this? But Josef finds he can say, "Not as such—an employee. I'm handling some artwork of his." Regrets this immediately: Say less, say less, he thinks.

The stranger laughs. "Don't tell me he's a painter."

"Not at all. A collector."

"Ah! Naturally. Excellent opportunities for a collector these days."

Otto Geisman's family comes to mind, but Josef sets them aside to say, "Quite good, I'd say, although Mr. Zimmel is currently intent on selling some of his works."

The man grunts. "A little odd," he says. "I imagine the market's saturated. This was on your advice?"

"No," Josef answers, and swallows, and adds, "Although certainly one can find excellent opportunities, if one looks in the right places."

"The right places?"

"Abroad," Josef says. "America." (Dear Lord, free me from this.)

"Ah." (The voice lower now, and the words coming slow.) "You have passage to America, then."

Sickness bubbling up, but he mustn't show it—must smile, must nod, must pick up a coffee cup and pretend to drink from it.

"Pardon me, but what was your name again?" this grey shadow asks.

Josef thinks, I don't have to tell him, I can call a waiter right now; but instead he answers: "Bauer."

"Bauer. Hmm. I know some Bauers in Vienna. Perhaps you're related to them."

Josef shrugs, shakes his head. "I don't live in Vienna. I live in—" A pause so short, surely no one can detect it, to recall the address inscribed on his false papers. "Klosterneuburg."

"Ah, I see. I'd have imagined an art dealer would like his base in Vienna. But what do I know of these things?"

"It's not a difficult commute," Josef tells him. "I like the quiet." Says this last part a little more harshly than he typically would; hopes this stranger might take the hint.

Indeed, there is a moment of quiet—cups against saucers; the rattling of the train—but then:

"If you'll forgive me," the man says (seeming to lean towards Josef), "you don't seem like the type a man like Friedrich Zimmel would usually hire."

"I'm sure I don't know what you mean."

"I imagine he has a great deal of concern for his public image." Creak of a chair as this person leans farther across the aisle. "The Party has its standards, after all."

"I beg your pardon." Josef, possessed of assertiveness born of panic, turns to him one last time—eyes squinting, for he can't make them focus—and exclaims, "That's an exceedingly presumptuous insinuation, and I've nothing else to add to this conversation."

A harsh laugh at this. And the next voice he hears is Friedrich's. "You're still here! This is taking it a bit far, I think."

Josef sighs deep. He beckons his friend to bring his face closer. When he feels Friedrich right there, above him, he says in a whisper: "I can't see."

A pause. "What do you mean?"

"I mean I can't see anything. I don't know why."

"Your glasses? Is something wrong?" The urgency, the strange sternness—Josef feels his glasses leave his face, and then they're back.

"No, that does nothing."

When Friedrich damns him, he does it very quietly. "Follow me back to the compartment. You can't stay here."

"Is there something the matter, gentlemen?" The grey stranger again.

"Certainly not," Josef snaps.

Friedrich grips his arm and adds, "We're fine, thank you."

"I've been talking to your employee," the man says, "and I must admit I'm a little concerned about him."

"He's quite all right," Friedrich says, but there is now a subtle note of fierceness to his tone.

"Are you certain? I can come with you. I've got a little medical training. I'll look at him in your compartment."

"There's not the least need for that," Friedrich tells him, and pulls up on Josef's arm.

With his other arm, Josef pushes himself up from the chair. You only have to last a few cars' lengths, he tells his legs.

"These trains are a revelation, aren't they, but the clientele not much better than they ever were." Friedrich says it: not unnaturally loud, but plainly. Josef smiles and makes his feet begin to move in Friedrich's direction. His fingers splayed a little, at hip level, in case of chairs or tables on the way.

And now here is Friedrich's hand, heavy on his shoulder. The voice low: "Try not to look too helpless. No idiot's going to believe I hired a blind art dealer."

Josef smiles and nods. If I knock into something, he says to himself, it's clumsiness. That's all.

From behind them, the stranger calls, "Perhaps I'll ask an attendant to come check on you." And though Josef feels the blood drain from his face, he smiles, and he treads steadily after his friend's footfalls.

Now they are out of the dining car—the waiter's voice fading behind them: "Thank you, sirs."

And now they are walking down a straight aisle: through this car, into the next. Friedrich is saying, "You know how it is with these Romanians, eh?" The door of a compartment is sliding open. A hand grabs him by the arm and pulls him through it, while he grins, terrified, at nothing.

The door closes. The sound of blinds being lowered. Hands on his shoulders. "All right, rest here." Josef lets himself be guided onto the bank of chairs. He sits and folds his body sideways across the adjacent seat. The armrests press into his ribs.

"Better?"

"I'll rest a minute," Josef says. "It should be fine." Of course it will be fine. Just a moment of faintness. All is not lost, he says to himself.

And he is better, he realizes; the blood is flowing back into his head; already he feels less strange. He becomes aware of a low murmur from Friedrich's direction. He asks, "Are you saying something?"

"I'm praying to Saint Lucy," Friedrich snaps.

A silence before Josef says, "I didn't think you were very religious."

Friedrich says, "Everyone's religious in these situations."

The sounds beyond the window sound almost normal, almost like a train. Josef opens his eyes. The light sways a little across his vision, but it's real. He breathes deep. His thoughts find their chorus again: Slow breaths; don't cough.

"Friedrich," he says. "That man in the dining car—"

"What did you say to him?"

"Nothing—barely anything. But he said I didn't look like I belonged with you."

Muttering, Friedrich stands, opens the compartment door, waves at someone—an attendant, Josef realizes, though mercifully he and Josef are invisible to each other. Friedrich whispers with this person for a minute.

When the door closes and Friedrich takes a seat, he says, "That's taken care of."

A lump hard as a nut in Josef's throat. "But what if he tells them to investigate me?"

Friedrich snorts, "That won't be an issue," and takes up the newspaper he'd laid on the seat beside him.

They are quiet for some time before Josef says, perhaps without consideration: "I wish you hadn't gone off with those women."

Almost a laugh, the sound his friend makes. But then there is silence, and then he says: "They just wanted to know about . . . you know. Politics, and all that."

But his words trail off into smallness. Josef peers at him: that boy-like shame. In Josef's eyes, this man flickers blue and purple.

Friedrich says, "Perhaps it was a mistake. It won't happen again."

Josef says, "You're very good to me, my friend."

"Josef." Friedrich sighs. "Get some rest."

=

Josef Tobak wakes from sleep to find Friedrich whispering once again with a railway attendant.

"... so it won't be a problem," this young man says, standing in the doorway of their compartment with his hands folded behind his back.

"Naturally. I appreciate your taking it so seriously."

"Of course." A discreet smile; a nod. He touches the brim of his cap with one gloved hand. "Just call if you need anything further, Mr. Zimmel." And he's gone, the door sliding shut behind him.

"What was that?" Josef asks.

"They took that strange person off the train," Friedrich says. He's stroking his chin, his eyes not quite meeting Josef's. He clears his throat. "It seems there was a problem with his papers, after all that."

What had arisen first in Josef as a swell of relief now begins to sink as doubt. "Oh." And then: "Friedrich, you don't think . . ."

"What? That he's a criminal of some kind? Certainly I think that. Glad I told someone. He'd have come after us for blackmail." But Friedrich is still not looking at him, Josef notes. For a while they both turn to watch out the window. The shadows of trees and hillsides are leaning into afternoon angles.

"Still," Josef says. "It's what someone would have said of me."

"Josef, there's no doubt in my mind he was an opportunist of some kind." Annoyance in Friedrich's tone, but it softens to something meant to reassure when he says, "And besides, if he was a refugee, he was a damned idiotic one, making trouble like that."

But it only swells in Josef, this feeling, so that he sees spots throbbing in the air and feels almost faint. He can't reply. He turns to the window; he holds a hand over his eyes; he prays, *Forgive me, forgive me.*

18

A DANCE ACROSS OBSOLETE BORDERS, AT PASSAU; INTO what used to be a foreign land; transfer at Frankfurt. All the way towards the port at Hamburg, carrying suitcases, carrying art—he doesn't go blind again, our Josef Bauer. At Frankfurt, he watches himself huff as a security officer flips through sketches. And when they pick up Josef's tickets in Hamburg, the agent says, "You're a friend of Mr. Zimmel, then?"

Josef shrugs. "An employee."

"You know, they don't like Nazis so much in America."

"Perhaps not," he finds he can say, "but they know art."

The agent laughs. "They have money, you mean." He stamps Josef's passport, waves him through. "Best of luck to you, then."

At Hamburg, they stay in a hotel. The next day Josef's ship sails for New York City. Josef cannot make himself believe it. Surely there will be someone to stop him. Surely they'll turn him around, send him back to Vienna. Surely, he thinks, Friedrich can't leave him now.

AND NOW I can see this man as myself, lying on this hotel bed—and Friedrich on the other side of the room, in his own bed, staring up at the same ceiling, a bedside lamp still glowing between us. I am thinking: But even if they let you board, it isn't over yet. They could turn you around once you surrender yourself in America. Friedrich says he has a contact, but what if it's no good? Well, then—back home, and that's the end of you.

The simplicity of the whole thing makes me strangely calm. Chances are things will fail—but until they do, keep acting as if they won't.

I ask Friedrich, "Do you mind if I pray?"

Friedrich breathes in sharp, as if waking from a half sleep. "Not aloud. What if somebody hears you?"

"I'd like to, though."

"Be quiet as a mouse, then," Friedrich says. "If I can hear you, perhaps they can hear you in the next room over too." He rolls over. "Remember that, when you're on the ship."

I haven't got my prayer book, of course, nor anything I might have had in the old days. I can unfold a fringed scarf and drape it like a shawl. I can pray in whisper—words remembered. *Blessed are you, Lord*, I say. And think: *It's true, amen.*

The hotel air smells of cigarettes and soap and, from the cracked-open window, a salty ocean cold. It occurs to me: this is my last night in Europe for who knows how long. To this kind of thought, a person must close his eyes. *He causes the wind to blow and the rain to fall*—it's so, I think.

In the dark, when I lie back down in my bed, Friedrich says, "Did you pray for me too?"

And I find myself startled—not only because of the question's intimacy, but because it hadn't occurred to me. I say, though, and mean it: "I pray always in thanksgiving for you."

Friedrich says nothing for a moment, and then: "Try to remember me, when you're away."

A swelling in my heart; a coal fanned to glowing. "Don't worry about that, Friedrich. Really."

AND WHEN, ON the pier the next day with his portfolios at his hip, this man I was shakes his friend's hand, Friedrich says, "Well, you haven't fainted, at least," and Josef makes himself smile.

"I've been meaning to ask you, Friedrich—and please don't misunderstand me, I know you're under terrible pressure—but please, don't let them tear down the Währing cemetery."

Friedrich looks at Josef awhile, then off down the pier, at the grey sea that heaves beneath a grey sky. "I won't bring it up," he says at last. And then he turns to Josef to add, "I suspect it will still be there when you come back."

And though he smiles, Josef thinks, with a start: So, that is the future! A return to Vienna. Someday, he thinks—if there is a time after the Reich, if his country is free again. And how could this be? Impossible to know, but there it is: like a range of mountains in the far distance, a boundary to this greyish place of fleeing, even if for now it remains abstract. Josef thinks: First, my family. But then, someday: home.

PART II

1

THE OCEAN I CROSS FROM EUROPE IS A BLACK ARC FROM sunrise to sunset. In my cabin, where I lie green with sick, I fix on the image of Leviathan asleep in the sea beneath us, pitching us up and down with his snoring.

I have also an image of children running on the deck, their mother calling after them. They stand near the prow, and the horizon beyond them lifts and falls, lifts and falls.

And also, a dream of a drowned man: his white puckered flesh, the wounds of fishes' mouths around his eyes. He walks towards me and I wake suddenly, slick with my own cold sweat.

THEN THIS: THE port at New York, customs officials and immigration officers and all manner of officiated chaos. Children with tags and parents craning their necks like birds. Memories of papers handed over to a man at a desk, of dull panic, of a language I can't speak, green walls, a European fellow beside me on a bench saying (I think), "They don't always like the way we smell."

Then an American stranger, Rudy Steiner, who appears at my side and knows my name; he is a fat, chuckling angel from God.

He commands, I nod; I speak, he translates. My name is Tobak again, he tells me. Germans want to kill me: that's all I need to say. I say a few words and he translates them into foreign eloquence, adds gestures and pitiful expressions. Immigration officials glance back and forth between us and tap their pencils.

Once, Steiner says to me, still chuckling, as if it's all a tricky sports match: "I thought you were a goner there. That agent's had it up to here with refugee claimants." He makes a gesture at throat level as he says it. And then he nudges me in the side and says, "But Mr. Tobak has friends in high places!"

Next—what I believe is quarantine: a brick building and a chain-link fence; people stacked close in bunks. I listen to the chatter, but as origins slip farther from central Europe the conversation, to my ears, becomes babbling.

There is for a time a Russian named Lev, who talks to me for hours. Always he starts a sentence in rough German but by the end of it has slipped into Russian, and I lose all sense of his meaning. He makes shapes with his long brown fingers when he talks; his eyes are wide and black with revelation. In a day or so he's gone. I don't know where.

Then: my name called out, papers signed and stamped, congratulations from Steiner in German; my bags handed to me, my portfolios from the train, and all plastered with stickers I can't read.

Winter air; a car; Steiner driving. The name of a Jewish host family with cousins in Germany (and Steiner so proud to have found them for me). Buildings higher than I thought possible (am I dreaming again? is this sickness?), and the roads like rivers cutting through deep canyons, and bridges, and the names Manhattan, Long Island, Brooklyn, Queens. Friedrich Zimmel's name as well is held out once or twice by Steiner like a pledge, but at this I can only nod.

Grey water beneath the bridge. The sudden thought: That water reaches as far as Europe.

Cars, carts, bicycles. Boys in the street chasing a ball. Houses smaller and farther apart as we drive. Trees. Quiet.

At last: a two-storey house, painted brown. A woman and a man step out, waving. They are both roundish, dark-haired, kind-looking.

"That is Mr. and Mrs. Schwartz," Steiner says as the engine chokes into silence. "Their German is okay. You can say hello to them."

The woman, Mrs. Schwartz, smiles. She comes down the steps that lead from her door, she walks up to me, says, "Welcome, Mr. Tobak!" in beautiful, English-sounding German.

I explode into tears; there's no helping it.

But she hugs me, and Mr. Schwartz comes and pats me on the back. He says, "You are very welcome, very welcome," and Steiner chuckles. He is saying, "Well, well, well."

They tell me I'm thin, and that their cousin, a doctor, will be by. They lay their soft hands on my shoulders. They say, "Thank the Lord, thank the Lord."

Mr. Schwartz says, "This will make the young folks grateful for what they have in America!" and Steiner says, "Yes, yes."

A brown American house folds me into its warmth. I can't know, then, that for eight years I will have to make-believe that this is home.

2

T HERE BEGINS THIS COMMERCE IN LETTERS.

Dear Josef,

writes my wife.

You'll be shocked to hear that this letter stood the chance of never being written. I must confess that the villain in this drama is your son. Did you know that paper is considered a delicacy in Shanghai? I didn't, but Tobias knew better and indulged in perhaps five or six pages' worth before I reminded him that he'd need to save some room for dessert. I think I saved about three sheets; the rest are no doubt becoming a slightly larger little boy.

Is she feeding herself? She tells me:

I was feeling perfectly incompetent until I saw the neighbour trying to turn a coat for her grown-up son. Aha! I remembered— yes, I know how to turn coats. I had it done for her by the following evening and she brought us dinner as payment (nothing

166

paper-based, thankfully). It made me happy: I feel like my father is still looking after us, even now. Mr. Aizenberg in the next house is a tailor with some good clients, and he said he might have work for me. Maybe he'll send patterns, and then Tobias can help me go over them.

Does she think of me? She writes:

Here, we have old buildings, but not too old—ours at home are older. It's very loud and busy, but we stay in such a small part of town that the city feels tight and small to me. Really, it goes on for miles and miles—who knows? Perhaps it goes on forever, and somewhere becomes Vienna and New York too. Maybe there's a streetcar route that would take you here. We could meet for lunch. I'll make you chicken soup.

And my son? Yes, my son—she tells me:

Tobias is as tall as the hem of my blue skirt when we're both standing (and I haven't let it down at all). He weighs about as much as a sack of potatoes (not a big one, a medium-sized one). His favourite word is "Spinne," which does not bode well, if you ask me. We had a spider making a big web in the window and he watched it for hours; now every little crawling thing is die Spinne.

I tell him about his Vati every day. Sometimes he points to people in the street and says, "Vati," and sometimes he calls his toy mouse "Vati" when he's playing. It's ridiculous for a person to cry as much as I want to cry, so I give myself about fifteen minutes every afternoon while Tobias is napping and that just about does it.

And his son signs a scribble, loops that set a father's heart awhirl.

These pages come from across the world. So a man in a quiet home, in a country not at war, writes to his love:

There are parts of Manhattan where the buildings are so many times taller than the streets are wide that you almost never see the sun. Then again, there are neighbourhoods on Long Island where the houses are far apart and there are trees in between, and there are cemeteries and parks and gardens. There are the richest people in the world, driving cars like you wouldn't believe, and buying clothes and jewellery that are probably just the sort of shiny whiteness your cinemas show. There are parts of the city so slashed by poverty that one can hardly believe this is really America: the children are like refugees of a long war. There's also a Chinatown in Manhattan, and I have gone there a few times and tried to imagine that it's like where my family lives. Is it, I wonder? Someday I'll take you there and you can tell me.

I haven't been quite well the whole time I've been here. I begin to see this illness as a chronic companion—weakness in my nerves or shortness of breath; I'm not sure what to call it, but it won't leave me. There are so many kind doctors among my hosts' friends that I'm quite over-diagnosed. I'm so fortunate to be among people who speak German. You know my Yiddish isn't very good, and even if I thought I might understand a few words of English, people here speak it so quickly that I might as well be deaf for all I understand. But I have learned a few good phrases, so I can ask for directions to the train or a telephone if I get lost. And if I am getting lost, then I must be exploring, and if I'm exploring, then I must not be too sick.

I wish that streetcar you imagined were real. I would spend everything I have to be where you are, Anna. I don't have anything, really, but I would spend the nothing I have and I would work my way there, serving coffee to tourists or scrubbing the windowpanes. I hope you wouldn't be ashamed of me, covered in soot or coffee-stained. Would you kiss me when you saw me? Would you recognize me? I will be the unwashed fellow at the station who is hugging your son.

He draws a cat for his son—pencilled soft and blunt-faced, eating tuna from a can. Means it all as consolation. But then, in his weakness, this refugee tells his wife:

I can't explain how much I miss you. This sickness, the situation, all of it is enough to drive me completely mad; still, the Lord let it happen, and so I must believe He has some intention for us. I try to believe this, and difficult as it is, it helps to think that your father certainly would have believed it. Someday before too long, my love, we will be back together and this whole ridiculous period of time will be as if it were nothing. And when that happens—I won't describe what I'll do, because it will make your neighbours blush if they find this paper lying around.

He goes on like this, working for Herschel Schwartz's firm—accounts, sums (such things as have no language)—and meanwhile hoping and writing his letters, from the autumn of his arrival to the autumn three years later. He pays his hosts from his salary, he saves what's left, and they don't let him speak of leaving. In September before the first year is up, Germany invades Poland, and now half the world is at war (and it's good, they all say, it's good: at last someone does something). The next summer, Germany invades France, and then he must stay home sick several days. He writes a letter to Paris that won't receive an answer. But Giorgio will look after them, he tells himself.

Two of the teenaged nieces want to learn German, and he tutors them three evenings a week for an hour at a time, teaches them (besides "How do you do" and "When will the next train leave for Graz?") to drink strong coffee with whipped cream and to read German poetry aloud. The girls swoon over Rilke, and wonder between themselves, in private, if this foreigner is flirting with them. (He isn't, but he imagines sometimes that if he teaches them well enough, these American-born girls might remember Vienna.)

But then it is December of 1941, and his last letter from Anna is almost a month old. He wakes up on the morning of the seventh to find Herschel and Edith Schwartz conferring in hushed voices beside the radio, and Herschel's friend Leon sitting at the breakfast table and tutting to anyone who will listen. The newspaper is on the table, and Josef picks it up before anyone thinks to warn him.

If he didn't know English well enough by now, the size of the headlines would have spoken to him—or perhaps the photograph of an aircraft carrier, American, burning into nothing might have explained everything. But it is a simple fact, a faraway fact but so suddenly close, because Japanese-occupied China was not, in the end, far enough away from Europe.

He sits staring down at this table as if blind as Herschel explains that it's a good thing, it's good; that this spells the end for Hitler and that the war in Europe is about to turn. But, for this horrible moment, he would trade it all, all of Europe, everyone, for a woman and a little boy in Shanghai whom he has suddenly, today, failed utterly to protect.

3

Anna:

Tell me you are all right. I don't know what to think. I never imagined as many airplanes could exist as I see in the newspapers. Sometimes it seems there will be no one left at the end of this. But I mustn't think that way; after all, I know you are being brave. You're always brave, my Anna. Keep being brave. Find a way to live through this, and tell Tobias I want him to look after you. He will be brave to protect you, I know he will. But he must also be sensible.

The Lord bless and protect you both, my loves. I am troubling Him constantly to look after you, so He can't pretend to forget, not for a second, no matter what calamities are happening in the world. He's numbered the stars in the heavens, they say, and so I suppose He has done for the hairs on your head, my darling. I wish I had thought to do that. I regret everything I don't know about you.

The war does not turn so fast as they had hoped, and there is the draft now, though it does not affect the Schwartz family so personally, right away, as it does others. Herschel is too old, and Josef himself too ill. He is called in to an office in Manhattan, once, for a long interview—he is an enemy alien here, say the men in suits—but the refugee claim is a strong one, and this thin, quiet man staring through spectacles at them is no threat to the United States, they deem. He is sent home with new papers, stamped and signed, to be renewed each month.

The girls stop coming for German lessons. German is right out.

F—

Have you heard from A? From Z? Or anyone? Send word of any kind, please.

J

Darling,

I pray that this one will make it to you. I won't say a thing about the war, and maybe that will help. I will just say that I miss our baby's soft little head and his breath that smells like bread, and it hurts to think that that baby doesn't exist anymore but that there's a wild and thoughtful little boy for me to love, instead. Tell him I do love him, though I don't know him. I have kept a space in my heart for him, so big and so liberal, that he can't possibly outgrow it in any dimension of his personality. As soon as I meet him I will nestle it more closely around him, his real self. Oh my love, I do try to do this.

Sometimes I wonder whether there might be some kind gentleman in Shanghai who wants to look after you and Tobias, who would take you in and have you for his own. What would I do? What could I say? It makes my breath stop, just thinking about it. My mouth goes dry. But Anna, I mean this: if things are terrible, if you are desperate, I will forgive you anything. Only please live.

But my love! Please, if you can, please wait for me. There will never be anyone else for me.

There is snow outside my window. Is there ever snow where you are? Tell me anything, but please write.

Here, the man Josef is lost in a dream. He wanders up and down and through his life, and the neighbourhood children tolerate him when he comes up to them and pats their heads and asks their ages.

"Five years old," says a boy, and the man says, "My son also is five years old!" And he gives the boy a penny, and the other boys say, "I'm five too," or, "I just turned six," and penny, penny, penny from his pocket to each boy. They laugh at all his misused words and hold their fingers up as rings around their eyes, peer at him through the holes; but he likes to see them laugh, and he laughs too. They get tired out by the way he clasps his hands and looks at them with that strange, starved intensity. They run off shouting down the street. The soles of their shoes in the sun flash up like the tails of deer.

He has a pile of old letters in his room beside his bed, and every night he reads them before he sleeps. The pile is not so big as he would wish it, but not so small that he has yet memorized every word. Sometimes he falls asleep before the last page, and the papers are scattered across his bed in the morning like fallen leaves. Sometimes he reads them through and cannot sleep, and then reads them through again and then lies staring at the ceiling, or out the window at the flat grey sky with so very few stars—he could number them on two hands, the stars of New York.

He works on Schwartz's numbers, day by day, tallies and figures and papers spread across his desk at the office, with rulers and tables and with ink on his fingers. He works and he squints, and he works when he is weary and when he feels ill. Sometimes, though—once or twice a month, perhaps—for a few days he is too sick to go in to work. He stays in bed and he cannot read. He holds on to handfuls of bedding. Edith Schwartz brings him his soup in bed, and shakes her head as she leaves his room. But on the days he is well, he works hard.

Dear Zilla, Mutti, Papa—

If I don't hear from you, I'll assume you've escaped Paris and gone somewhere better—England, maybe, though no place in Europe seems quite safe. Dear Zilla, I love you, and if I can do anything to help you and Giorgio to get out of danger, please find a way to tell me.

Josef also prays during this time. He isn't a holy man, he is no mystic, and it does not come easily to him, this communion with God. God is a great white silence, he feels, and the certainty he felt as a youth is just a memory now. When he is praying, there is a space in him that reaches back forever, to the first moment he knew himself, and then again forward into that blankness.

And in the midst of that: Anna, Tobias, like a seal on his heart, and like a weight around his neck. When he prays, their faces are light and oil, painted colour and calligraphy behind his eyes; but it isn't how he wants them. He wants them, flesh and blood, fingernails and knit stockings, here, in his arms.

4

DURING THESE YEARS HE THINKS ALSO, IT'S TRUE, OF Friedrich Zimmel. In Josef's mind are two pictures of his friend, and either one could keep him up at night.

In the first, a man Josef used to know, having saluted for too many years, forgets himself in the maelstrom of propaganda and becomes exactly who he is pretending to be. How proud this man must be of his factory, manufacturing his Party's munitions. How it must disgust him, if he remembers it, to think he wasted so many years pining after a Jewish girl and supporting her feeble brother. They ask him for information on the Jewish community in Vienna and he gives it to them. He remembers, perhaps, a Czechoslovakian woman whose safety he deigned to care about awhile. He can send them after her. Josef imagines he gets some satisfaction from it. He says a word, and they're taken: power like that. And meanwhile his compatriots are pleased to help him forget who he was.

The Währing cemetery he tears down, of course.

The other picture: A red band tightens round his arm like a blood pressure cuff, so he tears it off. I can't support this, he says—though he can't say it to many. Once they see he's serious: To prison with you, to the prison camps; or perhaps right away he's hanged. His former workers who thought they might go to him if in peril are suddenly without answers. Without his protection, a Czechoslovakian woman and her family are rooted out and deported. Who is left to speak a word or sign a paper or find money for food or lodging or escape? Vienna is a desert of unsympathy.

The Währing cemetery, naturally, they tear down.

AND FORGIVE ME, forgive me as I can't forgive myself, that the cemetery merits inclusion in this; for still, every time I think of it, after the thought of every person makes me faint with helplessness, this quiet green space with broken stones sinks heavy into my heart. This feels already like mourning. The rest of it brings panic; the graveyard makes me weep.

All my clothes ought to be torn, I know this. But it's all mystery during those years, you see. How strange to set it down and live it all again. Recall it: I didn't know then that a man like Friedrich could find or lose himself in a thousand ways, not two.

5

S NOW, AND RAIN, AND HOT SUN, AND COUSINS AND
neighbours off to war; aunts and nieces to the factories; blue
stars and gold in the windows, a blood star worn in the heart,
invisible, and two bright stars over China and so many, so small,
blinking over Europe. This is how the world goes.

A man comes to them from Montreal, from Canada. His name
is Samuel Grubler; he is Schwartz's cousin, according to some for-
mula. He's in New York for business, but Josef could not say what
this might be. When the family sits at the table together, they talk
about the news and of family who are or are not accounted for.
Grubler is young; he has a daughter just Tobias's age, or a few years
older. He was almost in the navy, he tells them. He appeared for
training, but before they could ship him over, they discovered his
secret: he could not move his right hand.

Schwartz laughs when he hears this. "You didn't last through a
day of training, if that's the case. How could you even get drafted?"

"Look!" Grubler holds both his hands up high. They look normal, Josef sees. Grubler picks up his knife with his hand and it's
fine, it's fine—except that if you look closely, how the fingers aren't
really clasped, and the knife rests balanced on his middle finger.

"Perhaps it didn't take them so long," he says. "But I thought, if I could go over, I could do some good."

"You could endanger someone's life, you mean, with hands like that," Edith Schwartz says. "Better to stay at home and work from here. Make the things we can send overseas."

"Ah." Samuel Grubler shrugs and looks down into his dinner. Josef's heart moves out towards him: this picture of his safer self.

Later, they sit together on the front steps. The evening hangs indigo above the trees. Samuel Grubler pops the joints on his paralyzed hand, pulling the fingers one by one.

"You ever come to Montreal?" Grubler asks.

"No," Josef says. "I haven't really left New York."

"Well, you come visit, when you can," he tells Josef. "Maybe it's not so different from this place, compared to where you're from, but it's a different flavour. And people speak French!"

Josef listens to the pop, pop, pop of the man's fingers. "I can speak a little French," he says. "Not so well, but my English isn't great either."

"It's fine." Grubler waves his good hand. "Everybody's an immigrant here."

Josef stuffs his hands into his pockets. Still the evenings aren't warm, this time of year. It's early in May.

"Were you born in Canada?" he asks.

"No, I was born in a little town near Hamburg. But my family moved to Canada when I was three. I don't remember Germany." He sighs. "I'm glad. I'm ashamed of it!"

Josef's heart twists. "Not everyone over there is a Nazi," he says. Grubler gives him a look that says, Let's not kid ourselves. Josef says: "I think of my country, and it confuses me too. But think of all those people who are suffering! They're Austrians too."

"The Jews, you mean," Grubler says. "But will they still want to be Austrian, after all of this?"

Josef stares across the street. The twilight blurs the trees and doorways into shadow. "I don't know," he says. "I don't know anything."

Grubler sits and chews this thought for a while, popping his fingers. He says, "You have a little boy, then."

"Yes," says Josef, "his name is Tobias. He is seven years old."

The other man nods. "He's with his mother?"

"In Shanghai. Yes. We had to leave Vienna separately."

"Ah." A noise of compassion, and Josef knows he doesn't have to explain further. Grubler asks, "Do you have a photo of them?"

"Anna sent me one when Tobias was two." Josef has it in his wallet, folded in his pocket: the little boy on his mother's lap, big dark eyes shining at a photographer, not quite smiling but with a readiness to smile. And Anna is quiet humour, smallness and light—that gentleness! How much of that warmth did she give, at the time, for me?—Josef has wondered it daily.

Grubler takes the photo and nods at it. "Very handsome. Very beautiful family," he says. "But this must be old."

"This is from—yes, four years ago." Josef sighs. Receives the photo back and tucks it into the wallet in a practised way that stops the corners from bending. "I haven't had anything from them since the war in the Pacific started."

Grubler peers at him awhile after he says it. Josef knows that in the space between them hangs all the possibility this statement entails. He turns his face away and towards the end of the street, where a gang of children are playing tag. Their shadows are living creatures in the twilight.

Grubler coughs. "My little Sarah," he says, "is nine, and she can't talk about anything but horses."

A smile he can't help—and Josef tilts his ear back to this man. "You have a horse?" he asks.

"Lord, no! We live in the city. She hardly even sees them, except in her books. We stop and look at the horse-drawn carts whenever they go by, and she tells me everything about each one of the horses: how big he is in hands, what his colour is called, everything. And she makes things up too, like his name and his favourite food and the sort of friends he has." Grubler's cheeks are red and his good hand clasps his bad. "You know, I think, if I had a bit of money, there is nothing in the world that would make me happier than to get her one of her own."

Josef smiles—thinks of another Sarah, the one in Austria, and her daughter. "There were horses everywhere when I was a boy," he says. "I hardly ever thought about them. Perhaps sometimes in the rain or the snow, or if they were pulling a very heavy cart, I pitied them."

Samuel Grubler laughs. "Yes, it was the same with me."

And Josef would like to say, My son talks about airplanes, or, He reads his comic books over and over, or anything like that, specific and individual—but he doesn't know.

Night comes, and the children at the end of the street disappear into houses. Josef and Samuel Grubler sit awhile in the new quiet, through the dark, before turning back to the house, and to sleep.

THE NEXT DAY, the war in Europe ends.

Josef is in Schwartz's office, working on the accounts, when it comes over the radio: unconditional surrender of all the German forces. All these people around him shouting, hugging, running into the streets. Someone has put a drink in his hand, someone is singing. A moment ago they were huddled around the radio; now they are out on the street, and people are hugging strangers, waving bright American flags. A woman in her doorway collapses altogether; Josef thinks, without knowing if it's true, Now her son will come home.

The man at the corner store is handing every person he sees an ice cream cone. Boys weave their bicycles through the crowds; they let their bells sing out.

Josef meanwhile does not know what sort of face he is wearing. A string tied to his heart is vibrating, a violin string, or a fishing line.

Today the air is alive, today even grief is sweetened with joy. He cannot find the words to ask his questions. So he puts the questions away. He sings instead, in English, with strangers: Bring them home, bring them home!

6

GRUBLER LEAVES FOR CANADA THAT AFTERNOON. He says, laughing, "I wish I could have been home for this! Oh, my heart, my girls!" He dances to the car; he swings his suitcase in wide arcs.

When for a moment the house is quiet—the Schwartzes visiting neighbours—Josef sits and thinks about Shanghai. The war in the Pacific has not ended. Josef thinks, They can have no hope, the Japanese. Perhaps it will be tomorrow. Perhaps it will be in a week. Perhaps in two. And when could one hope to hear word from China? He makes the calculations in his head, makes them more generous as he considers the administrative chaos that would follow the end of hostilities. His hope stretches out from him to follow the projected date.

Of course it is possible too that the Japanese forces will become more terrible, more violent; they might take everything down with them. Or the Allies might pound them too hard, Josef thinks; there could be more civilian casualties.

And now he stops thinking of this. If you have to think, pray, says his mind, and he bends his head a moment to let his longing speak.

THE FIRST TIME there are photographs in *Life* magazine—it could be Victory in Europe has not even been declared before it happens—Josef finds Mrs. Schwartz and her friend huddled over a copy of it, whispering—and when they see him, they fold it and pull it aside. "No, no—don't look at this right now, Mr. Tobak. Wait a little while, have a drink."

He feels his face go white. Theirs are almost sick-looking and his first thought is: *Shanghai!* "Please show me," he says, holding out his hand. "I must see it."

"Sit down first, sit down." Mrs. Schwartz pulls out a chair for him and he settles into it with his knees already starting to tremble. "It's about the camps, Josef. They printed pictures."

He thinks: Camps in China? But then realizes, with his stomach shrunk suddenly to the size of a pea, that they mean Europe.

"The prison camps," he says.

"And worse," says this friend of Mrs. Schwartz. "You see, they just meant to kill everyone. Really, kill them!"

"Show me the pictures."

(It isn't as if I hadn't heard, like everyone, that things were much worse in the camps than they had been in 1938, or that there was torture and murder and sadism and hate. Over the weeks since the beginning of April, with more and more of Europe coming out from under the Nazi heel, we heard stories. But always I thought: This is an exaggeration, of course. This information is second-hand, and they already hate the Germans, so of course the story comes out this way.)

And now this man I was, safe in New York, sits looking at a picture of the bodies laid out in a row beside the road, and he is very calm, peering at one indistinct face after another and trying to see if he recognizes any of them. When the faces become too little and grainy to make out, he starts back at the beginning of the row, to be sure.

"The journalist says that's not the worst of it, either," says this woman.

"Hilda, be quiet awhile," says Mrs. Schwartz.

At some point that day, he looks up to find a bowl of lukewarm soup by his elbow and doesn't know how it got there. But it doesn't matter, he thinks. He goes back to the pictures. When he looks up again, someone has taken the soup away.

IN THE LONG heat of the last day of July, and with warplanes still flying over the Pacific, there comes a letter from Vienna. From Friedrich Zimmel, in fact. Mrs. Schwartz wears a wide-eyed expression when she hands it to Josef in the kitchen, as if she doesn't know whether to rejoice or curse with him. He receives the envelope and sits with it awhile; he runs his fingers over the address, the strange stamp.

After he opens it, while he's reading it, Schwartz and his friends come into the kitchen. Tom and Jens. Josef knows them, though he doesn't look up—and they pour coffee from the pot on the stove and talk to each other.

Jens asks, over his coffee, "What's that letter, Tobak?"

Josef swallows and glances up. "It just came from Vienna."

"From who?" Tom picks up the envelope. They all look at it.

"Aha! From your Nazi friend!"

"What's he want now?"

"Probably some help getting out of trouble, eh?"

"Here's what I would do," says Tom. "I'd shit in a box and send it back, airmail."

Jens waves his hand. "Ah, it wouldn't clear customs."

"Anyway, a bomb is better."

"That must be a shock, Josef," is all Herschel Schwartz says. Josef looks up at him, and nods, and goes back to reading.

"I wish they'd round them all up," says Jens, "and shoot them."

"And then what?" says Schwartz. "Then half of Europe's dead. That's what you want?"

"He probably was at these camps himself, your damned patron," Jens says to Josef.

Josef leans farther over the letter, forehead crinkled, and he tells them: "He says he hid a Jewish girl in his house. My cousin. She survived the purges."

They gather around behind him, trying to peer down at the pages, but Josef hunches so deeply into the text they can't see past him.

"Maybe there were others like that," says Schwartz, quiet.

"Probably he kept her for his amusement," says Tom, but Jens hits his arm.

Jens says, "If it's true, then Herschel is right: there might have been others."

"And meanwhile, this man perpetuated their horrors by churning out weapons. Who knows if the war would have ended sooner, if he hadn't?"

"It doesn't work like that. They would have replaced him."

"But why shouldn't they all have refused? It takes a willing population, that's what I'm saying."

"I don't know, I don't know." Schwartz rubs his forehead. "Anyway, he helped Josef and his family, and now this girl—who knows what else he might have done?"

Josef has left them to their discussion. He reads; he tries to pull together this sudden truth.

Josef:

You will be surprised to receive this letter, I suspect. I write to you from Vienna, from my same old house: as of yesterday, it's now part of the American-occupied quarter. I am thankful—the Soviet occupation was something I will not soon forget, though I would like to. But it seems impossible that my house should still be standing, and that I should be writing to you at all! Dear Josef, I hope with all my heart that this will reach you. Please reply, if it does.

I don't know what you've heard about us and our situation. There was a great deal of bombing, and then when the Soviets came there was fighting in the streets. The factory was hit in the campaigns over the winter, and there was then some suggestion of my leaving the city, but I found a way around that. Then in the last days of fighting I was nearly conscripted (how desperate they were, Josef—they were enlisting everyone; it was a death sentence), but it was chaos by then and I gambled on the hunch that I had a better chance hiding out here as a deserter than being ground to mincemeat in the retreat. I was right: the Soviets took the city almost the next day.

I must tell you that there has been a Jewish girl staying hidden in my house these past several years: your relation Lena Kostner, Mrs. Sarah Kostner's daughter. She is now nineteen. I was worried about her, as some in the second wave of Soviet soldiers were said to be raping Austrian women. When they came to my house they didn't find her, but they beat me and took me to jail. There they beat me further, but I was not surprised, really. I was happy they did not kill me. When the Russian officer came to question me he was lenient and let me send a message back to my home, where Lena could find it. Later some American officers questioned me, and let me take them to see my house: when they met Lena she told them about how she hid there for so many years, and these officers took this as a sign of good faith and let me stay in my home. What I told them about you, and about Anna and the others, was also helpful. Still, they watch me carefully. They can arrest me any time they like, and that is, I know, as it should be.

Lena has left. It is what I expected; she hasn't been outside the house these six years. Her mother, alas, was deported, and I harbour no hope that she lived. Lena is staying with some American Red Cross nurses, who seem very kind. She talks about emigrating. I will try to help her, if I can. I don't know if I will be allowed, but for now I am hopeful.

There was also, at the beginning of the war, some business I had with visas for other Jews—that fact helped me too. I suppose it was much like the situation with you and Anna. (Though I never escorted anyone to his ship again, it's true.) Anyway, the occupiers know it now, and it makes them sympathetic.

It is very, very difficult to get anything in this city and the black market is thriving. Food is scarce, and very bad. German money is worth basically nothing. The Soviet soldiers more or less stripped my house so now I have very little to trade with. I don't think I'll starve; still, it's distressing.

I decided to write to you immediately in case you were planning on coming back right away. I would say to you: wait awhile. Wait until the supply chains have improved, until there is food to be had and more of the roads are made safe. I have been thinking of going to my father's old villa in the western countryside, if I am allowed; perhaps conditions are better there. I will write to you and you can plan to join me when you get word. Please write to let me know how long you can wait, and when Anna and Tobias might join you.

As for me, I will wait. I know there are those who say I should be shot in the street; perhaps this will happen, but perhaps not. Someone (one of these occupiers, it doesn't matter who) said within my hearing that I had better kill myself. It is funny he says this, for the idea has so often come into my mind, but here I am. I am sure the same could be said for many other people. But I will tell you, don't worry over me (though you might pray for me): I am content in thinking that you, and Anna, and Tobias, and Lena were able to get out, and that I might see you again before long.

Please send word regarding your plans, and send any news at all. It would be good to hear about something outside this country.

With the utmost respect and brotherly feeling,
Friedrich Zimmel

Josef reads this letter over and over. He lets Schwartz read it when his friends have left, and Schwartz takes his glasses off upon finishing it—says, "Well!" and seems to sum up Josef's feelings, confused as they are. Schwartz asks him, after a long pause, "Is it possible he doesn't know about what was happening in Germany and Poland?"

Josef says, "It was likely happening in Austria too." And then he says, "And no, it isn't possible, I don't think."

"And no word . . . no word of your sister, then, or your parents."

Josef swallows. "It would seem not."

Schwartz takes up the letter again and sets his glasses back on his nose. "He seems fairly certain you'll return, this Mr. Zimmel."

"Yes." Josef can't find his voice. He wonders, How much of this news has reached Shanghai? Any of it?—and sees his wife and child alive, brave, resisting, awaiting the end of war. And then in the same moment sees them dead, buried, bombed and burned to nothing.

"There, there," says Schwartz, and he pats Josef on the shoulder while this man folds forward over the table, his face in his hands.

7

LOW CLOUDS, SUMMER 1945, IN THE PORT CITY OF Shanghai—my mind paints the city and a figure of a woman. She walks through the restricted sector, a place I've never seen. The sidewalk is uneven, and to either side of her huddle two- and three-storey buildings, one-room apartments. What the air smells like in that neighborhood—I have to imagine it: garbage and raw sewage, but also hot oil, like our home, and salt water.

The woman I carry in this vision is small—petite under the richest of circumstances but here also whittled down by poverty. She wears a European style of ladies' hat; she carries a worn leather bag in both hands. Her shoes are down at the heel, but she steps across the pavement with purpose.

Twice that morning the air-raid sirens have blown, but there were no bombs; now the day is hot, and the streets clang only with voices, footsteps and carts.

Every window of every building is blacked over inside: shallow glass set like false eyes on this narrow street. Now and then comes a Japanese guard strolling by on foot patrol, gun or club at his hip; more often, through the heat, comes a Shanghainese woman or man, striding quickly, perhaps weighed down with a sack slung over their back. These latter meet the gaze of the woman on the sidewalk with a look rather like that of the blacked-over windows, and she returns this gaze in kind. There's no animosity among them, I imagine. Each is only busy surviving.

The clouds hang so low in this summer heat that they won't see the planes, and the pilots won't see them. The people on the streets will hear later, if they live, that the bombing raid was aimed at a radio tower. Meanwhile the whistle of bombs comes at first almost thoughtful and unthreatening, like a memory one can't quite place.

The world cracks. The woman on the sidewalk has time only to throw herself down against the wall of a building. Explosions not as sound but as a punch in the head, and then only ringing as of a strange dream.

—But see, I can't know whether this woman in my mind is Anna, nor if she survives. Some woman is caught in an Allied bombing in Shanghai. Some woman dies. See your heart, Tobak, and the twist in its love—for you'd praise the Lord in knowing your wife lived, even if it meant another woman were dead in her place.

On August 6, when the bomb falls on Hiroshima, I am walking in the field near the cemetery and praying. Here the summer has roasted the earth brown; just these few patches of thirsty grass are left. In Vienna, in the Währing cemetery, there was this same unevenness in the soil, and the sense of fingers reaching up to push back. And it didn't frighten me. I wanted only to reach down in comfort. To say, No, I have not forgotten you. Yes, you still are. I don't know what or who you are, but you are, still.

In this air: the smell of flush green leaves and brown hot earth. The sun presses down on me at an evening angle from the west. And the question comes into me, as if through the light—the question of what lonesomeness becomes, and where we go, if this living person walking on uneven ground and reaching down in love forgets, or stops caring, or is gone.

As I walk home, a part of me holds the question and turns it over and over like a smooth stone. But another part begins already to turn the Währing dead—these strange faces who have followed me since I was a youth—into an old mother and father, and a sister, and Anna, and a little boy, seven years old. I imagine them on the opposite pole of the earth, their weight pressing down, and the earth beneath my feet rising just a little in response. I will reach down, I think, through everything, to them.

And here, so far from any of that, I can believe for a moment that the net sum of it all might be hope. Consider Lena Kostner, my cousin whom Friedrich protected. So she lived! And so, I can tell my younger self, you did right, you helped to save her—you made her mother trust him. Through grief for Sarah Kostner I can be thankful for Lena. These are little victories, true, but they don't come undone.

It's a warm-drunk swell of hope in my heart, outgrowing the hollow of grief to say: Isn't it possible that the world will not go on killing itself forever? Isn't it possible that having seen the worst of hatred and evil, we will cover our mouths, we will cover our heads in ashes, and we will turn back towards something better? The sun is almost gone, the sky is purple, and the trees reach up to God— and I have forgotten who I am; I could be someone happy.

When I stamp the dust from my feet into the mat at the Schwartzes' front door, I hear Edith say: "There is Josef at the door; now be sensitive." They're a gaggle of grown-ups with peering, half-ashamed child faces, clumped in a U around the radio.

This man I was then does not know what an atomic bomb might be, but he recognizes the shock that threatens to make an empire surrender. He will never remember the exact words he hears over the radio this evening, just the sudden quiet understanding that arrives in him. He goes to the back doors of the house, looks out at the garden in the dark. Behind him, an electric voice crackles away in English; somewhere on the next block, there are men and women shouting in the streets that the world is not what it was half an hour ago.

8

Anna, Tobias, loves:

May this letter find you—may it find you alive and well! My Lord, everything in me prays it. I am here in New York still. I will do whatever I can to help you and join you. Won't you write and tell me what you need? I will do everything in my power. I will do anything.

And to the city that raised him and spat him out, he also can write:

How strange, how good, to hear from you at last, dear Friedrich. I thank God that you are alive, and that you remember us. And you protected little Lena! You give me hope; if only everyone had done as you did. Perhaps there were others like you. I pray there were.

Please, if you can, let me know where I can reach Lena Kostner. I would like to write to her. I wonder if she has any other family at all, if her mother really is gone.

I have to ask you: do you know what has become of our family and friends? Have you heard from Zilla, or my parents, or Anna's mother or brothers? Do you know how many people from Vienna were taken to these horrific Nazi camps? Friedrich, I know it must pain you to think about it, but I beg you, as a dear friend: please tell me everything you know. I am trying to get in touch with everyone, but I don't know how long that will take.

My friend, is it possible we have all come out on the other side of this ordeal? Have we survived? I pray it might be true— it seems impossible that it could be over at last. I know it's too much to hope that everyone I love is all right, but the thought of seeing any of you again is so beautiful.

He writes also to Paris, but there comes no word. And in time, as autumn sets in, a new letter comes from Vienna:

Dear Josef,

Your letter arrived just this morning. You console and you disturb me. I am so glad you are alive, and that you still love me. All the rest is agony, Josef! I wish you didn't admire me: please, hate me rather than say you admire me.

You don't know what you ask when you ask me about your family. It's so hard to know yet what happened to anyone. Perhaps things will become clear in the next few months. Zilla wrote to me maybe once after France surrendered. It is conceivable that she and your parents are still alive, but I confess that for a long time I have mourned them all as dead. No—I have to correct that: perhaps it has not yet really been mourning—I did not want to face the fullness of that feeling. Even now I don't think I can. But it is very, very hard to hope that anyone escaped. Please forgive me for writing this, Josef, but I don't want to mislead you. Still, it's possible they were among the few who survived.

I'm grateful that these occupiers judge me mercifully: they believe I joined the Party under duress—I hope you would agree that this is true. They are happy that I didn't give Lena up to the police, and that I helped you. And a lot of neighbours whom I never heard of before have started to say that they supported me because they knew I wasn't really a brute at heart. Could this be true? I have trouble believing anything good, Josef. I wish you were here, despite everything.

Regarding Lena: I'll see about putting you in touch with her, but I don't know that she'll be receptive. I don't think she likes to remember her old life. I believe it hurts her.

I will wait for your next letter. I will try to contact people and get more news for you. These things, I think, will be enough to guard me from the worst kind of thoughts.

An envelope arrives back from Paris, and it is marked only: *Return to sender: Not at this address.*

Dear Ella,

he writes to Anna's mother (for what is there to do but write).

Please write back immediately if this reaches you, and let me know if you need help, or money, or anything. I wish I could write with news of your daughter and grandson, but I haven't heard from Anna yet; still, please don't be afraid—the mail is slow, and China is such a long way away.

It would be so good to hear from you. It would be so good to know you are all right. I pray that you are, and that Chaim and Jakob also are safe. I miss you all terribly.

To an embassy in Paris, and to friends he fears may not remember him. He writes until his fingers seize and the wall behind his eyes rises dark.

IT'S A WEDNESDAY, early in the autumn, raining, when he gets home to Edith Schwartz waiting at the door: this look of strained exhilaration on her face, or is it fear? She is holding the mail in her hands. She says, "Josef, it's for you," in such reverent tones that his mind seems to hear the words echo off stone walls. He holds out his hands, and he receives the two envelopes, says, "Thank you, Edith."

He moves into the living room, and he sits down on the low sofa, before he lets himself look at the return addresses. And see, both of these letters, from China:

Josef! Dear Josef—

I'm writing this in a hurry to let you know we're alive, we're together, we're all right. I cried when I saw your letter, and Tobias said, "He's dead!" He didn't understand when I told him you were alive and you'd written to us; he said I should laugh. So we laughed, and we danced a little. Now I'm writing this in a great hurry so I can get it into the mail today. Tobias will mail it for me.

A better letter is on its way, don't worry. But I hope this will put your mind a little at ease. I know we will be dancing for the next month at least.

With all my love,
Anna

PS: Tobias adds the following:

Dear Vati,
We read your letter today and I was very happy. Please send
another one soon. How is America? Please draw for me another
picture of a cat. I love you.

Tobias

Dear Josef,

Now that I have sent our first message off in such a rush, let me
take a bit of time to let you know how we are. Your letter finally
reached us at our second apartment in Shanghai: we've made do
here these past few years; it's small and rough, but by now it feels
very much like home.

The Japanese soldiers were awful when they were here. I
don't want to write about that today; I will tell you about it
someday, when we're together, when I feel very safe and far
from all this. (Don't worry, though: the two of us weren't
attacked, specifically.) Also, there was bombing; but again, we
were all right. It's a very crowded and poor little ghetto they've
crowded us into these last few years, but overall I think the
Shanghainese had it worse than we did, and it makes me very
sad to think of it.

There are American soldiers everywhere, and they're very
friendly and happy, for the most part; it's like they're on holiday,

now that the war is over. Tobias and some of his friends like to follow them around.

How should I describe how things have been? I suppose we've been very poor, I suppose things have been hard—but then again, as I said, there are so many Chinese families who were poorer than us, and after all, we survived. There were long periods of time when I'd be so tense with fear of not having enough for Tobias and me, but then after a few weeks I'd realize we'd had a little to eat every day, and Tobias didn't really know the difference, and it was like coming up for air after a long time under water.

Tobias often surprises me. He knows much more Shanghainese than I do (I know practically nothing, admittedly); he talks with some of the street vendors, which made me very nervous at first. Most of the other European children stick with their own kind. Not that Tobias hasn't made friends at school—actually, I think he is fairly well liked. Then again, at home he has a very cruel mother, so perhaps he's been careful to find allies out in the world.

My darling, I don't want to frighten you, but I must admit that your little boy has seen some very hard things. It is not unheard of for people who die in the street to be left out for a little while, if no one comes to get them, so more than once he's come across these bodies. Perhaps this has happened more times than I know. And as I said, the Japanese soldiers were sometimes very cruel to the locals—I don't know exactly how much he witnessed of this, or how much he remembers. (People have been beaten to death, I know, and horrible things done to women.) I hope he's been spared seeing it, but he wouldn't tell me, I don't think: he's very protective, and he doesn't like to upset me with bad stories. Perhaps someday he will understand that leaving it to my imagination is much worse.

I will write again very soon. My Josef, I miss you, and I love you, and I want to assure you that as lonely as I've sometimes been, there's never been another man to take your place in my heart. I will live now for the day when I'll see you again. I owe you about seven years' worth of tenderness, and I mean to repay it in full.

I'll let Tobias sign off at the bottom of the page again. We are both so happy you're well. All our love to your friends in New York, and especially to you, Mr. Tobak.

Love from your Anna

PS: Dear Vati,
I found a brown dog today. I wanted to take him home but there is not enough space. My friend Fayvel tried to chase the dog with a stick but I made him stop. Then the dog barked very loud and a man came out of his staircase and said GO AWAY and we laughed. It was very funny. I am happy you are alive and my teacher gave me a new pencil. Please send drawings but I am sorry if it was rude for me to ask for them so soon. When will I meet you? I love you.

Tobias Tobak

Already these pages are softening under his fingerprints and the tears he can't keep from falling on them. The sudden spasms of laughter that bubble out of him like shaken champagne make

Edith Schwartz peer in on him, wringing her hands. He can't make the words, "It's all right!" but the look on his face, his tears and his beatitude, make her cry out and embrace him.

"See, there is still happiness in the world," she says, wiping her eyes, and Josef kisses her cheek.

The whole evening he spends filling pages and pages with drawings of cats.

9

L ATE DECEMBER: HERSCHEL SCHWARTZ AND I SIT BY
the window at a deli in the city. Under Schwartz's nose his
moustache twitches, just a little, and a bead of coffee above
his lip catches the light like amber. He speaks to me in German,
quietly.

"I think I can understand this need to go back," he says.

"It's foolish. But I won't have any peace until I do."

Taxis slip and honk through the slush outside. A young man at
a table near us tells the girl across from him, "She's got nothing on
you, Bets, she's all gristle," and the girl says, with strange tenderness, "Well, she's got nice teeth."

Schwartz takes a napkin and dabs his moustache. He says, "It's
a brave choice. It's the choice of love."

"I hardly feel I have a choice."

"Ah, but I mean—" He swirls the air with his left hand, looking for the words. "One could simply accept the worst, in the
silence. Or one could hope for the best, but resist responsibility.
And in between . . ." Now he shrugs as he looks at me. "There, I
think, is the hardest choice, perhaps."

I am glad for the clattering in the kitchen, I am glad for the voices all around us and the sounds from the street. I look down at the lines in my hands, the white mountains my knuckles make through thin skin.

In October, there was the letter from the embassy in Paris:

Dear Mr. Tobak:

Given the number of inquiries received in recent months, we are unable to devote a great deal of time to individual cases. I regret to inform you that we cannot at this time provide any information on the persons named in your letter.

Sincerely, etc.

I tell Schwartz, "I don't know that it's anything more or less than a compulsion."

And he sighs and waves his hands and says, "Ah, well . . ."

I don't mean to sound hopeless.

Friedrich wrote it in his letter, early in the autumn. He also wrote:

I don't write what I write out of despair or to cast my own morbid shadow across the world. I only mean to tell you the truth, Josef. I hate that I must insist on this. Your hope is like a knife in me. Understand, please: they tried so hard to take everyone. They tore houses apart. It was systematic.

I wrote back:

> *But remember, you were*
> *able to save someone.*

He said:

But see how much freedom I had, and
how little even I did.

> *Is it about what you did?*
> *I didn't do enough, either,*
> *while I was there. If we'd all*
> *done enough, perhaps this*
> *would never have happened.*
> *For your sake, for everyone's*
> *sake: be a better man now,*
> *but don't despise yourself.*

And his next letter, dropping this line of conversation (or perhaps, in his way, hammering a full stop on the end of it), said only,

> *I spoke to a man who said he knew Anna's family. He believes*
> *her mother, her aunt and Jakob were deported several years ago,*
> *most likely to Mauthausen. It seems most probable that Chaim*
> *died in police custody.*
> *I send my most heartfelt condolences to your family, and to*
> *Anna especially. There is no kind way of delivering this news,*
> *but I felt obliged to tell you. If I hear anything more, I will let*
> *you know right away.*

And then, how to pass this on to Anna—how to write it?

My darling,

Friedrich has written with some terrible news.

Anna,

I need to tell you at the start that this letter bears bad news.

Anna, my love,

This letter, I am so sorry to say, will contain very sad news.

I had to keep throwing out the letters I began to write; in the end, I tossed my pen in the bin. My mind unable to fix on its task: reaching east to argue with Friedrich. Who was this person who claimed to know them? How could he have known? How did he remember? Perhaps, I wanted to cry, they lived, they're recovering, they're making do in refugee camps and awaiting the day they'll be able to find us, or that we'll find them.

I wrote it again and again: *Anna, I'm so sorry, but I must tell you—*

But now that's passed; now it is December, and I am with Schwartz in the delicatessen in the city, and he is telling me that he understands why I have to go back to Vienna.

"Everything I hear tells me there's barely any hope," I tell him. "When I think of what we know, I could run away from everyone, everything."

Schwartz peers at me through squinted eyes. "Still, there's some chance, isn't there?"

My hands rise and fall again into my lap. "I have to act as if there is."

A month earlier Friedrich wrote, in a scrawl that seemed to speak of grief or drink:

Josef, I have held back writing this. I have no right to say it. But I wish so desperately that you were here! You can't imagine this terrible, soft hell: everyone is excused, but no one is forgiven. I need you to look at me, Josef, and see me, and understand the person I am and decide whether you can forgive me or not. I don't know who is left to do this besides you.

Do you know that no one goes to your graveyards anymore? I think of you every time I walk by the walls in the park. I haven't told you: those walls were partially damaged, but not destroyed, and though I think more of the trees and branches have fallen, I don't think anyone went to dig up the graves, thank God. And I don't think I would really notice or care about this—that's the kind of person I am, you see—unless it all made me think of you.

Josef, I wish you were here! I will go to my villa if they let me, I can't stand the city any longer. Please write to me. Let me know when you might be able to come back to Austria. I am sure I could help somehow with the paperwork. I could expedite things.

Tell me soon what you want. There is nothing to do here but wait.

I wrote to Anna: I can look for our families in Austria, and Friedrich can help me. It was as true as anything I'd ever put into words. But there was behind all this, also, that tug from across the water, almost enough to drive me mad in my helplessness— the tug that hardened into pain when I read "no one goes to your graveyards anymore." Faces filling from ghostly almost into flesh. Already Edith has caught me twice in the hallway with my hand clenched against my chest, my body bent partway to the floor, and asked me if she should call a doctor. No, no, I told her, no, I'm all right, it's just faintness, it's nothing. (A barbed hook through my heart, but it's true, it's nothing.)

Dear Josef,

Lena does not want to be in touch with you right now. That's all I could gather. She wrote back to me, "No, thank you—not yet."
   I know this must be hard for you, but it's what she thinks she needs. I know you'll honour that. I made sure she knew she could ask for help here if ever she needed it. Perhaps someday she'll be ready to talk to you, but not now.

I recall her mother's message to me from a decade ago, which said, No, thank you; which seemed to say, You failed me, all of you. I tell myself: That's not what Lena said. It's not that. But the ache still comes. I carry it along with everything else.

Anna has said, in her letters: I had thought we might meet you in America. And I wrote to her: Of course you will, certainly. But first, does it not make sense . . . And then a foolish rush of words, whatever I thought of saying: repeated rumours of refugees reunited in Red Cross camps, or the things Friedrich's said to me, or what I imagine, or things only half-true, or things truer than what I ought to know. I crossed out half of it before I sent it to her; I wrote "I'm sorry" in the margins.

But she wrote back: Perhaps you understand it better than I do. And later she wrote again: Perhaps you are right.

I have sent her a photo of myself and the Schwartzes. Herschel's and Edith's faces in it are kind and broad, if shy. My own face always looks odd to me: pale, pointed, somehow embarrassed, and with eyes that might be either childish or suspicious—through glasses, in black and white, it's hard to tell which. But when our friend took the photo, I tried to imagine it was Anna and Tobias behind the camera, and I looked into the lens as I wished I could look at them. Could they understand that?

Then, in Friedrich's last letter to me:

I want you to know that this isn't a beautiful place right now, nor am I beautiful, nor lovable, nor half-respectable. I have heard someone say that this is when people need love the most, and I would agree with him—only I hate myself for being this way, and I can hardly hope that you might feel differently.

Josef, I want you to come. I will be terrible company when you arrive, but I will be better for you being here, and after a while I'll be well again, you'll see.

Now Schwartz says to me, "You wouldn't think of doing it if it weren't for the good."

The sadness in his eyes—I want to meet him in it, take his hands and say, Herschel Schwartz, I know it too! I know it too! But instead I say, "It's still very surreal. And anyway, the whole continent's in crisis right now. They can barely feed themselves. I imagine I won't stay for long." (Do I imagine that? Do I believe it?)

Schwartz sighs; he leans forward onto his elbows. The human rumble all around us is American and English and beautiful as things in a film are beautiful, and also foreign. "Well, a man will fight for his family," he says. "And his home, if he can find one."

10

S O MUCH CAN BE CONDENSED INTO SO LITTLE, AS I
recall it. It must have been a long trip back to Vienna. I
remember it as dark sea, cramped passenger cars, terrible
food and not much of it. Anxiety that swelled inside me as my train
wormed deeper into Europe; a thought that someone would grab
me by the arm and arrest me for nothing. An instinct that I should
not tell anyone my name.

A real passport with my real name tucked into my coat: that I
do remember—the trouble getting it, the fear of showing it. But
see, little Tobak: it's all right, they don't care much anyway. They
stamp it with very few questions. They let you through.

In the train station, in my city, there's dirt and rubble, true, but
at this threshold I encounter also the shock of recognition. The
arches in the high walls (three above each lower set of two), the
shallow angle of iron beams in the roof—all the same. These places
kept existing; the city went on all these years. It strikes me at first
as a cruel joke.

Friedrich Zimmel, when he meets me, is not the same. When
I step off the train, he's twenty feet from me, and I see him at
once. We stare at each other a long time without moving. He's so

much heavier-set than I remember. His hair is thinning. There's a ruddy puffiness about his cheeks and eyes. I feel, all of a sudden, so very tired.

"My God," Friedrich says then, "you're exactly the same."

Later, when I go with him to see about ration cards, a man in line with us misunderstands and takes me for an American. He tells me, "It's a shame you've come to the city now. We've had a terrible time since the invasion."

"Since thirty-eight, in fact," Friedrich corrects him.

"Yes, that's what I meant," the man says, and peers at me a moment with narrowed eyes.

I remember the weather in those months as variations on grey. What we get as rations leaves me feeling always empty.

IN THE FIRST while, and then over time, certain things become clear.

I learn that Friedrich's source on Anna's family is a man who lived on their street, a Gentile who was the only man in his building for all of 1943. Anna's mother and Jakob were taken to Mauthausen, where Ella died and Jakob, having survived the first two years there, was taken on a train to the death camps in the east. Chaim was arrested earlier on. Executed, perhaps by hanging, perhaps at gunpoint. My Babka also has vanished, with no record to be found. And I pray, and cling to some small hope, that she died peacefully in her apartment with her cats. Is it fair to believe this?

In Paris, it seems Zilla and my mother and father were arrested by the French gendarmes in 1941 and sent to the Drancy internment camp and then to the eastern reaches of the Reich by train. Certainly there is no record I can find of them alive after this year.

Of Giorgio Repaci, we can find nothing—whether because he too is dead or simply vanished to another corner of the world, there's no hint.

Sarah Kostner and her mother were taken on the transports to the east. From Lena Kostner, the girl who survived, I hear nothing. She's emigrated, Friedrich says. I try to make peace with this. It's good that she's free—free to separate herself from all of this, if she chooses. Believe that, Josef Tobak. Put away that old shame.

I have folded in a book a list of family and friends who are gone, and I go through it sometimes, or add to it, or make notes as things become more clear, but I hate this list. I walk in the old cemetery on Seegasse, where the earth lies naked, and the bones that remain, unmarked. During the occupation, the community buried the stones to stop them being destroyed, so now, in this courtyard, or perhaps in a secret place in the Zentralfriedhof, Simeon's stone fish lurks in darkness. And I find I prefer the memory of these stones (stones that are real; could be unearthed in a moment, like a magic trick, ball beneath a silk handkerchief) to my list in black ink that seems to murder each name as I write it. There is another kind of information I would rather receive about each person, the types of things we rarely spoke about, but individual and beautiful, blessed.

In the Seegasse cemetery, and in the Zentralfriedhof, the headstones await their resurrection. Under the earth, Simeon's fish still curls up at the clouds. But I am alone here, as I usually am. The squirrels make their nests in the trees up above, the grass is green, and the earth under everything is cold, and dark, and still.

11

Anna,

I write, in the autumn of 1946.

*Anna, my love, how do I say this to you? Here is the simple truth:
I believe that the easiest and fastest way for us to be together is
to be here, in this new Austria. Would you come back to Vienna?
My love, it's so strange here, but stranger by far without you. Yet
more and more I feel it to be still my home, though changed—
like anything is, after a long time away. I know you would feel
the same. And I can't help thinking that if (by some miracle)
some person we knew were living, he might seek us out here. It
may be that someone would come back.*

*Is that sensible? Oh, it's unlikely—my mind's all muddled,
Anna. But I feel rooted here, despite everything. I thought we'd
been uprooted, really and completely, and all the dirt shaken off;
but I see now that it wasn't so. I find myself fairly fluent in this
city, changed though it is. Would you come back here? Would
Tobias want to live here? There are children here, young children, despite everything.*

Josef, you crazy fellow—
Are you sick again? Are
you insisting, or are you
only pondering it?

I won't insist. If you hate the
thought, write to me and tell me,
and I'll kill this yearning with a
word. (Bad, silly heart.) But really,
it isn't so terrible, love. I know this
city. I know the roads and the lan-
guage. You understand the difference
it makes—not to be a foreigner in
a place.

I think you would really feel
at home.

(But there is always New York, or
perhaps Canada. There are ways of
getting us all there. It wouldn't kill
me. It could do me good, perhaps.)

(But please consider.)

I wish I understood.

I wish I could explain.

*We want to be with
you, Josef.
My Josef, I want to
be with you.*

*Come be with me. Here I am,
right here. It needn't be forever.
But for now.*

*For now.
All right, then, Josef.
For now.*

12

I N THAT TIME, I AM STAYING WITH FRIEDRICH ZIMMEL. His old house is changed: all the upstairs and most of the rooms he used for entertaining are closed off, and we eat together in his kitchen. It is because he can't afford to heat it all, he tells me, and also because the new occupiers took most of his furniture. In this new way of experiencing old things, so much is overturned—for now I've walked in on my friend brewing black market coffee, or heating canned beans on the stove. It hadn't occurred to me before that I'd never seen him, even in my mind's eye, cook anything.

My friend is a man like the bombed-out parts of our city. I don't know how else to see it. The hammocks of skin beneath his eyes, his trembling hands: this is his very self.

Since I arrived in Vienna, Friedrich has told me next to nothing of his experiences during the war, has in fact avoided me in his own house. I thought, from his letters, that he meant to unburden himself as soon as he could. That he'd sit with me long hours and tell me everything that made him doubt himself. (And: "Friedrich," I'd tell him, "you were only a man. Only a man."—I'm sure I would.) But he doesn't say anything. Or—he cannot, I conjecture. The way he looks at me, that slow glance from odd angles: I sense it is a door in his loneliness nudged open, barely, but he does not press it further.

About my friend, how the war has changed him, there remains much to be said. And I will lay these things out; I will find a way and a place. But in that time, it was not my first concern; and now, in writing it, I find I have to gather myself to examine it. I will; indeed, I must. But a little while longer. For now: the business of his help, and my wife and child who must be brought from so far away.

Friedrich does not, in those days, have much money at his disposal. When, seated in his kitchen, I tell him I have persuaded Anna and Tobias to join me, but that I must now find a means to help them get here, he says, "Just think how simple that would have been a decade ago."

My heart falls a little at this. Without considering it seriously, I'd come to count on the promises in his early letters—that he could help us reunite. "You don't think it's possible?"

"That's not it. It's quite possible." He offers me a smile that seems to strain against heaviness. "But not by the same means. We'll have to speak with the authorities, that's all. I'm sure I can put it to them in a way that makes sense."

As I sit considering this, he says, "Here, Josef—don't worry. It's exactly the right thing. I promised I would help you come back. I don't say such things idly. I still have some leverage here."

He says it so simply—he doesn't doubt it. I don't see how this could be, and yet consider: despite everything, he is allowed to live in his old house, and host guests; and in the time since I joined him, I've seen him leave for meetings with French, American, British police officers and diplomats. No large proportion of these meetings interrogations, either, from what I can tell.

"Yes, don't worry." He reaches out to rap his knuckles on the table, and in his eyes some light of purpose such as I haven't seen in him since I arrived here. "We'll sort it out. They'll be here before you know it."

SNOW ON THE roads when we meet Friedrich's contacts in a café downtown. Despite the gasoline rationing, they have sent a car. I can't ride through this city with Friedrich, on a day late in the year, without reflecting on a previous time we made such a drive—when I was leaving Vienna, when I still had no sense of what would be lost or saved.

The snow is greying in the gutters. We pass checkpoints where the driver offers papers, speaks loudly in English or bad French. He's American, our driver. He's not from New York, I can tell, and yet to hear him speak makes me feel for a disorienting moment as though we're back on the other side of the Atlantic.

We are to meet with diplomatic authorities about Friedrich's role in the city's restoration. To my bewilderment, they are proposing that he take over a new Austrian manufacturing company. It is something I dare not protest to Friedrich's face. When he brings it up, he tells me freely: "Of course, there's the question of my reputation. It must be clear I'm not what I was." But what can one do, I wonder, to erase all that in the public eye? Can the world forgive and forget so quickly? Impossible, surely—but Friedrich has presented it as a route by which to ensure he can bring my family here. (To show he's no anti-Semite, it occurs to me—as if sponsoring one small family might prove this.) I don't argue.

At the café, I follow Friedrich to a table where two men sit waiting for us. Under dim lights we shake hands, say hello in German, though Mr. Henderson is American and Mr. Magnin French. I will not be called upon to speak much, Friedrich has told me. It's quickly clear he's right. These men are here to speak to Friedrich. The waiter brings us a litre of bad wine and then there is nothing for me to do for a while but drink it and listen.

Henderson is near fifty, trim and handsome, in a good suit. He speaks German poorly and switches often to French, sometimes to English. He is talking about Hungary and Czechoslovakia. Magnin, thinner and more soft-spoken, with slick black hair, interjects occasionally in clear French that I nonetheless strain to follow. Their talk is political, though framed in terms I can't fully grasp.

"I'm under a lot of pressure about this," Henderson says, after a while, in German. "Austria—you understand—our government sees it as a Western country. We like Mozart, you know? We understand you people. You understand democracy—yes, perhaps within limits." (Laughs once at this.) "We can work with Austria."

"I'm glad," Friedrich says. They have been talking for ten minutes and he has not mentioned my family yet. He barely looks at me.

"It won't be easy right away," Henderson says. "There's the matter of the German occupation, yes. But we understand how it was. For you, Mr. Zimmel, and for the country—none of it was freely chosen." He goes on in English: "Seen in the proper light, really, it's all very forgivable."

None of them seems shocked by this statement. How small I've become, all of a sudden.

"I appreciate your understanding," Friedrich says, still in German. "It has not been easy for us."

"Nor is it easy now," this man carries on. "There isn't much to live on in this country, is there, and that's putting it lightly."

"All over Europe, this is how it is," Magnin says, and shrugs.

"We're concerned," Henderson tells my friend. "The people are not easy. The workers especially. You understand what I mean."

Friedrich looks at the window a moment, and I follow his gaze, watch the shadow of an old woman pass by with shoulders hunched, face invisible.

"I understand," Friedrich says, quiet. "Ten years ago National Socialism looked like a solution, and now . . ."

He trails off, and Mr. Henderson says, in English: "The Soviet army liberated this city, I appreciate, and it's true that they're allies of ours—"

Friedrich speaks to him then in English for the first time: "The people here did not feel it so much as liberation, what they did."

A strange thing, to hear my friend speak English, when now it's a language I know well—for his accent is thickly Austrian, coloured with something British, and in that moment he sounds foreign, even to my ears. It strikes me that my English is better than his.

"You understand this. There is the risk," Henderson says quietly, now in German again, "that the workers will be . . . how do I say . . . vulnerable."

Friedrich nods. For a moment it seems as if the conversation has carried on among the three of them in silence, with a vague sense of understanding settling over the table, though I myself am excluded from it.

(There are things that, now, I think I understand a little: In these postwar years, any money that comes into Austria is aid money, and aid money comes in from East and West by different avenues. When there are food riots—and food riots there are, with the crops failing, and the people starved—we hear from

Western news sources that they were incited by Communists. Do I believe this? I don't know. I recall now a strike at a factory, not Friedrich's; in the newspapers there were photos of smashed windows. Some of those men, it was said, invoked the East. So it could be that these foreigners, Henderson and Magnin, were sent to recruit anti-Communist Austrians to keep our country from tilting towards the Kremlin. But could a man like Friedrich Zimmel ever quell a workers' movement?—he, who was so much a stranger to a hungry factory worker. Yet in all his endeavours, it's true, he knew how to make friends. There were perhaps a host of such men in our country. And after all, I admit it: the Soviets did eventually leave.)

"And yet it may be hard to justify to our chiefs," Magnin says, "this recommending a former Party member to oversee a major manufacturer."

"I appreciate the difficulty," Friedrich says. "I am ever humbled by the generosity I encounter."

Something about what he says, or the tone of it, sounds to me like a line in a play.

"But as I say," Henderson says, "we appreciate that you were not exactly free. And given your record of resistance, the ways you used your influence"—and here for the first time he nods at me—"there is a strong argument to be made. And the people respect you. You're—how do I say—a real Austrian."

"Mr. Zimmel understands what the people want," Magnin says. "And how they see themselves, yes?"

Friedrich shrugs. I feel he is about to say something of significance, but instead: "I expect I do," is all.

Henderson regards him for a while, and then looks at me. "So you were in America, I take it," he says to me in English.

"That's right." I am glad, absurdly, that I can answer him so readily in his own language, as if it is proof of something. "It is a wonderful country. I was treated very well."

"And yet you come running back here," he says, one eyebrow raised—and for a moment it occurs to me that I have insulted him, except that I recognize, thank the Lord, the accent of dry humour in his tone.

"You understand," I say, and open my palms to them, "my family, my sister, my parents, my in-laws—they had to stay here. From across the ocean, it was impossible to know anything. I had to find out if they were waiting."

"But your friend tells us you want to settle here again," Henderson says. "Bring your family back and everything. You're the first Jew I've heard of who wanted back in after all this. Smells funny to me."

And indeed, as he says, to me too it has the scent of madness. But the earth revolves around this place for me. It has reeled me back in. I cannot explain this, neither in English nor in German.

I say instead, "I was a guest in America, but I am a citizen here."

The American likes this, I can tell. He nods to himself, smiles a little. "Your friend here, too, he's a citizen," he says after a while. "And he was a Nazi. That doesn't bother you?"

But I sense this isn't about me. From Friedrich's posture, the way he sits so still, and with no attempt to enter the exchange, it's clear his own future is what we're discussing. And yet it's clear to me too that before this meeting Friedrich had already discussed with this man the matter of my family's migration to Vienna. So I am not as conflicted as I might have expected. It is easy to reply.

"Certainly it bothers me," I tell this American. "But there are other things to consider. I have always trusted Friedrich Zimmel, and he has always proven himself trustworthy. As you put it, he used his influence for the good, and in the midst of a situation where good was all but dead. This is what I care to remember."

"He helped you escape," Mr. Henderson offers. "You and your family."

"Yes, indeed. And others, I understand. And there is the matter of the girl he protected." I feel suddenly as if everything has led to this moment: not just this conversation, but the entirety of my friendship with Friedrich Zimmel. "She was my cousin. Before I escaped, I told that girl's mother that he was a man she could trust. I meant it then. I would repeat it now with a clear conscience. He is a righteous man. He is an honourable man. I am grateful to him."

Despite all this greyness, a feeling almost of elation at saying these words; as if with them I've come to testify against despair. I can feel my cheeks flush. I don't smile at Mr. Henderson, but he can feel, I am certain, the heat in me. And he nods. "That's very good. Very good," he says.

I turn to peer at Friedrich. I'm not certain what I expect. And perhaps I'm not certain even what it is I see; for who could say how this man now experiences gratitude, or humility, or relief. His face, though, is very white. His eyes are wide, but he is looking at nothing. He is hunched in on himself. He does not seem capable of speech.

Henderson says to Magnin, "I understand your people could help arrange for passage from Shanghai."

"It is likely. The settlement, well . . ." Magnin shrugs. "The East is another world now. Many people are leaving. Migration, a berth on a vessel for the passage—these things can be managed."

"But my family isn't French."

"Ah." Magnin smiles at Henderson. "Monsieur Henderson, he

has let me know that there will be funds available. To be covered by Monsieur Zimmel in good time, of course—for Monsieur Zimmel, he will soon be back at work, and better able to help you with such matters. So. It all looks very well, doesn't it?"

"Well, now. I'd call that a productive meeting," Mr. Henderson says in English. And then, in German: "Here, Mr. Zimmel, are you feeling well?"

Friedrich looks up at him. "Quite well, thank you," he says in English. He reaches for his wineglass. Sips from it with a hand that barely trembles.

OUR DRIVER STEERS us back through streets a little darker than before, snow still falling on roads and windshields. I am watching out the window; I have my Anna and Tobias in mind; I am conjuring them to me, telling them, One last long trip and we'll be together—only please do reach me.

From beside me, Friedrich says, "You were too generous back there."

He's spoken it into silence; we haven't said anything these last five minutes. I tell him, "About you, you mean?" He is looking at his knees. He nods, and I say, "Not at all. I meant every word."

"You don't know how it was," he says.

He has barely spoken about the war since I arrived—always statements made in the vaguest terms: it was awful, but we know this. He has told me none of the things I expected he might, and in this moment it strikes me that I might at last be able to offer him a listening ear.

"You might try to explain it," I tell him. "I would do my best to understand."

He does not reply right away. He looks out the window on his side of the car, and after a moment I look out mine. We are climbing the hill to his house, other people's windows through snow beginning to glow like candles, when he says at last:

"You told Lena Kostner's mother she ought to trust me."

Perhaps it is a taste of something lingering; perhaps I am ill. There is the feeling of bile rising. But I say, "Of course I did. She needed some convincing."

"I am glad she trusted me." He sits there awhile, lips parted, before he adds, "Only I wish you understood that it was not all so . . . simple."

"What do you mean?"

The car is stopping, the driver pulling over to the curb. He peers at us in the rear-view mirror, and Friedrich nods at him, says, in English, "A moment, please."

He leans in closer to me. "I just wish I had done better for her daughter," he tells me, quiet.

"That's all?" At this I might smile. "Think of what awaited her without you. What expectations do you imagine she had?" And, because he is still hovering there, in a lower voice I ask: "What is it you're so troubled by, then?"

He leans in closer. This whole time he has not really looked at me. But now he stares into my eyes, his own quite blue, wide, beseeching. He puts a hand on my shoulder, and after a moment in which it seems his breath is blocked, he whispers, "Josef—consider me. What you know of me."

All this while (weeks, years; since the *Anschluss*, perhaps), so much of everything terrible I've kept just barely at bay: I have striven to manage it. And now, when my friend says this to me, I don't know why—there breaks through some still-unarticulated horror, shadow without shape. I don't know what he means, but there is in my unknowing the form of things I haven't let myself think.

I am not proud of it. I do not set this down with pleasure. But in the moment my friend asks me to consider him as he is, an attack of nerves comes on me so desperately that I turn from him, fumble for the door handle and all but throw myself out into the evening air.

Here winter trees hang black; here is the cold with its tender sting. For a minute I stand gulping breaths beside the car, face turned up to receive the snow. Relief from nausea followed so quickly by shame.

And after a minute or two his door opens, and he gets out.

"Please, excuse me," is all I can say.

But his face is very quiet, almost blank. He says, "Never mind." He waves at the driver. I step onto the curb and the car pulls away.

"Honestly, Friedrich, if you want to tell me—"

"It's quite all right," he interrupts. "It was nothing." And he smiles at me. I would like to trust that smile.

I follow him to his house with a weight of something in me, and—yes—a little of a half-ashamed relief.

"I was quite pleased with that meeting," he says, unlocking his front door with a key from his pocket. "You'll see Anna and Tobias in the spring, I don't doubt."

And this is enough to put all other thoughts out of my head, and enough to make me put my hand on my friend's back as he opens his door, and mean it as nothing but thanks.

13

I N THOSE DAYS, IN THE WÄHRING CEMETERY—A LITTLE more smashed than before, but saved, perhaps, by its own obscurity—there is work enough to keep me busy. Here is a forgotten corner where the gravestones lie in heaps like the unburied dead. Alone but for the foxes, the rabbits and the birds.

My fox doesn't imagine the last fear of the voles he eats, and in this respect he is innocent. In the shrubs pawing earth, dripping rain, brush-tail chewed through with wet and a rodent body still warm in his teeth, he is good. As he should be. And he doesn't imagine beyond his own last fear, beyond the hound or the fisher chasing him down; he doesn't know yet that his legs will go stiffer, that he won't be so nimble always. He does his shopping and he puts it in his larder, to keep. He imagines it's my larder, filled with my dinner, that I've buried here—because why else guard it, why chase down thieves?

Under the trees in the cemetery, the fox will live forever, in his mind.

FORGIVE ME FOR lapsing again into abstraction, but I find I must set this down. More and more it seems to me that a world to come, unless it is more than a story told to children, unless it is somehow a good big enough to make up for the evil we do in this life, is only an insult to our suffering here and now. There are answers I want, but I can ask and ask forever and the questions just dig deeper into an earth that has no bedrock.

If I can put in a request for perfect justice, if you'll listen to me, if it counts for anything, this is what my heart demands: When we die, that we would know each other human person perfectly, in every detail, every fear, every minute victory of courage and every act regretted. That we would see each other's lives, and know one another's minds, better than we could ever know our own in this life. And if our afterlife could consist of nothing beyond this perfect and infinite intimacy, then I know what it would be: for every moment we had loved another person in life, it would be ecstasy, unburdening and communion; and for every moment we'd failed to love them, the keenest possible torment and the most just condemnation.

14

CONSIDER THE HAUPTBAHNHOF IN SALZBURG, EARLY spring of 1947, and the man approaching in a train from the east. He sits with his suitcase on his lap, a seat removed from the window in a crowded compartment. A sickly-looking fellow; since 1938 he has never been really well. The landscape beyond the glass, since he left the city, has blurred by in green-brown and grey: the fields are bare of crops, the trees still stand naked in winter blacks, and the pines in the higher places are blackish, cold in their prickly coats. In every town or city they pass there is the shock of mangled buildings, holes in storefronts made all the more ghoulish by the way they appear suddenly between untouched neighbours. The train rattles by these scenes without pause.

Already the train is grinding down into its platform at the Hauptbahnhof. Josef Tobak takes his suitcase by the handle; he stands when the passenger across from him stands.

He is meant to meet his wife and child in the station. They are going to stay with Friedrich in his father's villa for a little while. (When Friedrich requested to leave the city for the winter, no one, not even his friend Josef, protested too much.) In the country-side it's (one could argue) a little less devastated—though, really, they're meeting here because Friedrich has invited the family with such transparent yearning, and Josef feels he can deny Friedrich nothing.

He follows the other passengers down the aisle towards the door and tries to feel hope—but it is as if in his heart a wall has been built between the realms of reasonable and unreasonable hope. Reasonable: to get here, to Austria, safely; to make inquiries; and now to make one's way unmolested to a country villa. Reasonable: to make plans to find an apartment in some strange Viennese neighbourhood, safe enough, surrounded by unknown but benign faces. Unreasonable: to see the people one loved before, alive. To see a wife and child, in the flesh, nearly a decade older than they were when last one saw them.

He would like his hopes to press past this wall, but it's high and wide and it doesn't give. He shuffles past train compartments with cramping legs and a heart that bruises itself against a wall of no.

The air on the platform is cold and sharp. Coal smoke bitter in the air; stone walls blackened. His fingers around the suitcase handle are numb. When he enters the station lobby, his glasses fog up. He stands aside by the wall and takes them off, and he cleans them without looking around him.

Somewhere beneath this dark vault of space, he knows, if the world could conspire to let such a thing be, Anna and Tobias may already be waiting. Their train was meant to arrive half a day before his. True, he hasn't heard from them since they left Shanghai; true, their journey would have been even longer and more harrowing than his when he came from America. Anything and everything, ordinary or unprecedented, might have happened to prevent or delay their arrival. And yet, Josef Tobak thinks, one must dare to act as if they'll be here.

He carries his bag through the mass of people. This mass of people! Gazes slide off one another instead of locking. Here is an old man's face turned topographical with weariness, and this woman with a look that says nothing, nothing; she is arm in arm with one who must be her sister, who stares at the floor, who does not look up as she walks. That boy leaning by the wall—the darting alertness to his eyes that makes Josef Tobak think, There are likely pickpockets here. He does not have much money, this man Tobak, but this makes him all the more anxious not to lose it: he has it tucked in his breast pocket. He has considered stitching this pocket shut. But sometimes (and now) another part of him reaches out to say, But you escaped!—and at this he wants to hand his money out to these people until it's gone, every coin.

He crosses the lobby again; he scans these strange faces. That little family, with a small girl in a yellow sweater. Another family: a teenaged girl with her two brothers' hands in hers (the parents are speaking quickly to one another, brandishing passports between them). And there, a man with his wife leaning on his shoulder, and there, a woman checking the station clock while her son reads a book, and there, eight red-haired children tugging at the coat of an old man (their grandfather?), and there, a group of children who don't look related, huddled round a grey parrot in a birdcage—they call, "Good day! Good day!" at it over and over, and after a minute the bird squawks, "Day!" and they all fall silent.

A man there missing a leg; a youth there with his eye bandaged; a man there whose mouth hangs open at an angle (his hand held up against it); and a girl, and a girl, and a man and a woman and a man—face after face after face.

"Josef!"

His first thought, when he hears this, is: there are many men named Josef.

"Josef Tobak!"

It's a woman's voice, behind him. *Turn,* says his heart, *turn!* He must. He does. He turns.

There: the woman who was checking the station clock. Her face under the brim of a hat, her mouth ovaled in a half cry, her eyes wide and round and filled with garnet light—there.

"Anna!"

He has her arms. He has his arms, and around her, and her, here, her lips: his lips on hers, her love. Her taste. Her breath. And here. Tears on someone's cheek, and everything, and the world, and her, and here—he says, "Anna!" and kisses her again. She laughs and cries at once; her husband is laughing and crying as well.

He pulls back, and he looks at her (at her!), and he turns because the boy is there beside her. Back a few paces, with a book held against his chest. His eyes so bright and full beneath his very black hair.

Anna says, "Tobias recognized you first. From the photo you sent."

Josef bends his knee. (If the boy could know his father's shyness! The whole abyss of potential failure that opens up beneath the heights of love.) The boy is tall for his age, but Josef goes down to him. He holds out his hand. Tobias steps forward and places his right hand in his father's.

"I am very happy to meet you, Vater," the boy says. Voice like trembling glass.

Josef begins to say, "Tobias—" but his tongue fails him. He lifts a hand to this boy's cheek, to his soft, browned skin—this face he knows he knew once and (his mind says, Yes!) will know now, again.

He had leaned forward to kiss his son's cheeks. But now this boy's arms are around his neck. He holds him. He says, "Tobias!" and the boy says, "I saw you!" And he's laughing.

And now he can stand again and wind his arm around his wife, around Anna (she a pillar of light in the bend of his arm!), and this boy there so close and not yet embarrassed by their love. A man is peering at them, and a woman—he realizes there must be many people looking at them. But he will not yet look up, except inwardly. Inwardly he seems to see it: a fox, red flame, that alights at the top of a high wall, and the fox dances among the wires and glass, and he is not hurt, and he is not afraid.

PART III

1

TWO WEEKS AT FRIEDRICH'S VILLA IN THE COUNTRY-side, strange land. He says to us: "Please use everything as if it's yours," and then he disappears into a den whose walls once were dense with hunting trophies; he emerges at mealtimes smelling of tobacco and drink.

This place is new to us: an eighteenth-century estate in the green-brown hills east of the mountains. There is a farmer couple who occupy the opposite wing, who took up residence there after the war, and whom Friedrich has not evicted; they glare and pace and mutter in rural dialect as if we were foreign invaders. There are the three coveted chickens who are not allowed to wander, who are kept in the vestibule of the house in a pen made from bits of an old tin roof. There is Andreas, the groundskeeper, who sleeps in a hut with a loaded rifle in his cot. There are we three, and there is Friedrich.

In this new place, my friend tells Anna and Tobias that for a while the locals would raid these houses, armed with guns or scythes. Starved, he said. Or freezing. This was mostly before he arrived. The place now is stripped and bare. In the countryside one must walk a long way to find a tree, so many have been pulled down for firewood.

There is not much food, but there is enough. The nights are cold, but not unbearable.

In the daytime, Tobias runs everywhere. He comes back with things he should not have been able to find. (Old bottles of wine, knives and buckles in the fields and apples, somehow.) Once, Friedrich mentions that there might be unexploded shells in the ground, and Anna takes Tobias aside to warn him of this, and then for days Tobias seems determined to find one. ("I won't touch it, I promise.") I walk the grounds myself to try to find any first and forbid him from going near—as if I might be better at this than he is—but we're fortunate, and there are none to be found.

Tobias I love almost too much. I think he senses this. He acts a bit like a cat towards me, the first while. He glances at me sidelong and walks at angles around me, not without kindness, but as if my love were a field around me that his body glances off. I have to be still and not look at him, pretend I'm doing something else (writing a letter, or poking at the garden, or mending a sock), and then sometimes he will come and stand by my shoulder and speak very naturally, very freely, about a thing he's seen or a thing he wonders about. And then I must try not to look up, try not to attack him with my gaze, which betrays me always: "I love you!" it screams. "I don't know you at all, but I love you." No: look down at my work, and listen to him talk about a litter of kittens, or the axle of a rusted car, or the way rain comes over the hills. And say only, "Yes, I see. That's marvellous."

THIS TIME WITH Anna is another thing entirely. The first time we are alone, the first evening in our bedroom, she seems to turn her body away from mine and I have to go to her, stroke her through her dress with the backs of my fingers. And I want to touch her as I did when we were first married, but I am not certain she is the same as she was then, or that our love is the same.

In the dark, she says, "I can't help feeling I should be in mourning." And I rest my mouth against the angle of her neck because I have felt that too—and yet, and yet. The smell of her, her soap like a spice and then a richness that speaks of earth and musk. I know she can feel me pressed against her through our clothes, but I say, "We can wait as long as you need to," and try to mean it.

But here is the way her muscles slide beneath her skin, the softness and the give and then the gathering. She turns to me. Here is the whole world in the whites of her eyes, only a moment from mine.

She says, "Please, now." There is a creak to her voice like ice on a rooftop, melting.

Everything of us that was once familiar, now suddenly remembered, or changed. These clothes that slide away from us like old skins. Her chest thinner, her breasts lower and less full (but then also the same—the way to caress her into tenderness, and her scent). The hollow beneath her ribs, deeper than before, and the darkness filling more of the space between our bones (but no, but see, there need not now be space between us). And I am a stranger to myself, my blood is a stranger to me, the way it rushes to my skin and leaves me light-headed. And she is here, and she is she, and everything of her is warmth and tenderness and fullness, a jug of hot wine poured through me in the night.

When I'm spent, she's still clinging to me, her breath hot on my ear, and so I caress her and murmur and move in her until she shudders beneath me like a little boat come to ground on a pebble strand. And this small cry that she seems to make in spite of herself—oh, everything of you, my Anna, I would bottle up, I'd keep forever.

I am half-asleep, curled into her in the dark, when she whispers, "Shall we have another baby, Josef?" And though my tongue feels too thick to speak with and I'm sinking into a sleep too sweet for words, I say to her, "Hmm," and nuzzle her hair. And I feel as I drift off that she must understand everything I could mean by that sound, all of it, the world of us two made suddenly simple in the fullness of everything yes.

2

I N A VILLA IN THE AUSTRIAN COUNTRYSIDE, A MAN ASKS his wife where in Vienna she would most like to live. She answers, "I don't think I ever really thought of anyplace besides the Leopoldstadt."

Friedrich has confirmed Josef's suspicion that the second district, now in the Soviet-occupied quarter of the city, is not the right place. Find a place in the third district, Friedrich says, or the ninth. Josef wonders, though, whether his friend has things wrong, as regards the Soviet occupiers: Josef and Anna were never the enemy, after all.

Still, the other neighbourhoods are ones he's walked through, and they do seem safe; and so Josef writes a letter to a contact of Friedrich's in Vienna.

It has occurred to Josef many times—and he wonders at it—that Friedrich kept a lot of friends after the war. These can't, Josef thinks, be every one of them the type of man who wears his Party arm band now in secret against his skin. And if his friends are men and women who were not disappointed to greet the early end of the Thousand-Year Reich, then it must be that they knew Friedrich was not, at heart, what he seemed to be in public. But if this is true, then the question of what it is that makes him condemn himself surfaces implicitly in every encounter—for he does condemn himself. Josef sees this; Anna softens to their friend in response to it; even Tobias, who trusts this man more than Josef dared hope, leaves him little gifts that seem to suggest concern (a bright-backed beetle, the rusted rim of a helmet from the Great War, a snake's skin three feet long). But this, to his discredit, is not a question Josef Tobak is eager to dwell upon.

A little more than a week, and then a letter comes back: there is a suitable flat for rent in the ninth district, the top floor of a little row house, owned by a middle-aged widow who lives by herself on the main floor. Josef asks Anna, what about schools for Tobias? But she answers, "He's bright enough, and very adaptable. There are schools everywhere. Don't worry about it." And Tobias echoes her. He adds only, "Mutti said I could have a dog when we got a house."

"Ah." His mother glances at Josef.

Josef shrugs. "I'll ask if that's all right."

He decides that if the widow doesn't want dogs in her house, they won't take the flat—simple. This is something he can tell Anna. He can tell her too about his worries regarding work. Friedrich has said that he will hire Josef, but it isn't clear to them exactly what this means.

But there are also things he can't tell her. This knowledge that his city will makes its silent demands on his heart—the Seegasse and Währing cemeteries, and all the dead who seem to wait in thundering muteness. How it tears him one way and then the other, across water, over walls—and in the ninth district, if they are to live there, will he bear up under it? These strange new points on his mind's compass. He does not know, he can't ask.

═

THE WIDOW IN Vienna writes back before the week is up: she welcomes a family with a dog! Her late husband loved animals, she tells them, and there are several parks near the house where people walk their pets. She admits that she prefers male dogs to female, but says she will not make a point of this.

ANNA HAS TOBIAS read books in German, tries to have him sit and study and be ready for school again, but Tobias cannot stay still here. He appears and disappears, comes home muddy or scraped, and seems not to notice the difference. Once, he finds an old nest of squirrel kittens, dead and mummified, in a hole in one of the upstairs walls of the villa. Anna makes sympathetic noises when he shows her, even as she shoos him outside with it. But Friedrich, when he sees it, slips into paleness like a sudden disease and says, "Really, I ought to burn this place to the ground." He retreats to his den and does not come out for lunch or supper. When Anna goes to him in the evening she finds him asleep on the carpet, and can only cover him with a blanket, and stoke the failing fire in the hearth.

NOT LONG AFTER this, Tobias comes home with his dog. In his arms it's curled small as a melon: a brown, skinny mutt with a mangled ear. Three other dogs were chasing it, he says. He scared them off, throwing rocks. Pulled this pup out of the ditch where it lay shaking, wrapped it in his coat and carried it home. He'll feed it, he says, and wash its ear.

"But I don't have any camomile," Anna says—automatically, and then she touches her mouth and laughs; for it's a thought that trips them backwards through the years to a time when it was easy to think of themselves as Austrian. Tobias gives her a puzzled look.

He names the puppy Peng. When Tobias speaks to his dog, he speaks in Shanghainese.

ON AN AFTERNOON with Josef in his sitting room, Friedrich produces an envelope and says, "Go to this address at nine o'clock on your first day. Give them the letter. It shouldn't be a problem."

Josef, after a pause, says: "Why don't you come back to the city with us?"

But Friedrich coughs, and looks away, and raises his newspaper between his face and Josef's. It's a French paper, printed a week ago. And all Josef can see now are his friend's discoloured hands, fingers gripping this yellow paper, and the space between them stretched and crowded by columns of text. (He thinks suddenly— he can't say exactly why—of a shadow box full of tiny insects, perhaps ants, arranged in rows and on pins fine as hair.) He leaves Friedrich alone.

ON THE MORNING they are to leave, the whole world is erased to white: snow, fine as dust, almost an inch thick. Tobias steps out into it as if trying not to wake it. Turns to watch his footprints blacken and melt into the mud. The puppy winds in loops around him and licks up mouthfuls of snow, tail flapping, and Josef and Anna watch them from the doorway.

Anna says, "He's never touched snow before."

And Josef almost says, before catching himself: But he was born in winter.

The sun is already up, already wetting with melt this perfect coat of white. Tobias picks up handfuls of it, touches his tongue to it.

Josef scoops up his own ball of snow and packs it between his hands. This cold, this good sting—something from his boyhood. He suddenly sees a possibility: that he might shout Tobias's name, and see the boy turn, even as Josef hurled the snowball at him, catching him in the chest. That look of surprise, and sudden delight—and the boy would throw one back, and another. And they'd play together. It would be freedom between them, the years of exile erased and undone, the way this snow undoes the details in the world.

But he feels a welling of shyness. He cannot believe that the father in this fantasy could ever be him. He pats the snowball in his hands once more before he drops it, and Tobias wanders out across the field with the puppy frisking at his heels.

"So beautiful," Anna says, to Josef and out at the white hills. "It helps me remember that I loved this country."

Josef draws her close against him in the doorway. He says, "Will he like Vienna?"

"Ah." Anna pauses. (Her cheek against his shoulder, scent of her hair in the cold air.) "He will after a while. He's very willing to be happy." And then glances at Josef, seeming with her eyes to apologize—but no, my Anna; Josef says it with a kiss to her forehead: I too can be happy, dear love.

Friedrich will not be awake for a few hours yet. Meanwhile there is such a small amount of packing to be done that everything gets checked over three times. Andreas checks in the house now and then, grunts at them when he sees them with suitcases still not gathered.

The car is pulled up near the house; the chickens in their tin pen by the doorway skitter and squawk. The farmer woman who lives in the wing opposite them steps outside with her broom, muttering a little, and sweeps the snow from her steps and then from her garden.

At last Friedrich comes down, blinking and red-eyed, and says, "You're ready to go, then."

"There was snow this morning," Tobias tells him. They look out the window: only wet now.

Anna turns back to say, "Yes, we're all packed." She rubs Friedrich's arm. "You've been so good to us. It's hard to go."

"Well." Friedrich shrugs. "You should have a proper home. And a proper life." But there is something in his face: that tautness, like a readiness to scream. Josef would like to say to him: "I know you've been miserable, and I was a fool before, but if you need me to listen, I will listen"—but how does one say these things? Not in these moments, with Andreas tramping around outside the door and the suitcases already waiting to be hefted into the car. He decides he will write to Friedrich after they get to town.

By ten o'clock they are all in the car, and Friedrich has been kissed goodbye and stands leaning in the doorway. The puppy sits in the back seat of the car with Tobias and Anna, panting out at the cold, wet hills. Josef calls to Friedrich, "See you soon," and Friedrich smiles a little, and waves, and then the car twists rumbling away from the villa and out towards the road.

This first home falls away behind them. The station is an hour away, and then there is the ride to Vienna, and then the drive to their new home, little apartment with yellow walls that (Tobias will remark) smell a bit like fried meat. In a new house, secure with the people he belongs to, a man can set aside hard questions and imagine them buried. His nights he can spend twined with a woman he loves, and his mornings on walks with his boy and a little dog, who find flowers growing on so many of these streets, and their city at war with no one.

3

H ERE, TOBAK—DON'T REST YET. I'VE CYCLED ALMOST back, at last, to that night I first remembered, but I find my hand hesitates. Why should it be so? I haven't come all this way to tread in circles. There's an interval, certainly; but let me set it down lightly.

The time between our return to Austria and the night Friedrich calls me is made up of years, understand. It's made of Anna dancing with me in our kitchen in a green dress, Anna holding my hand on a street corner while a violinist plays Schubert, Anna burning a chicken and then conjuring a foreign recipe for stir-fried vegetables. And my son with us: Tobias with grass-stained knees, with eyes strained from studying—always with his dog Peng panting up at him, adoring.

It is, in the dark, my wife and her tenderness. She wakes some mornings to me examining her hands on our sheets, and she laughs at me. (I discover, every day, what a woman is like.)

These years are marked also, yes, with inexpressible grief, and by traumas that hobble each of us in unexpected moments. By betrayal and cynicism on top of that, when we see Nazi collaborators named to government posts. A long, cold public standoff between former allies while our country remains occupied; a private acceptance, as New Year's Eves cycle past, that there will be no brother or sister for Tobias, no matter how great our love.

Meanwhile, we make our shy observance of faith among strangers. We have a synagogue again, with a Hungarian rabbi who speaks almost no German, and a congregation that is half Russian, and not one face I knew before the war.

Through all this, we grow older; and there is the hidden Seegasse cemetery, in its nakedness, and the forgotten Währing cemetery, hooded in green. Back among these places, I could be sixteen again, or twenty, or a young father. The weeds and the vines grow, spring after spring. The fish cries out from the dark of the earth. The fox darts along the top of the wall.

The faces that wait don't forget me, though the world forgets them. Who will carry us, they seem to ask, even as I am asking that same question of God, and receiving all the weight of silence, as if perhaps it is not the right question, only I don't know the right question.

Always, in the back of the mind: this haunted nearness. One doesn't dare turn around, unless it's to confront it all plainly: What? I might ask. What, after all this? Here I am. Tell me, what?

4

O N THE NIGHT WHEN FRIEDRICH CALLS ME, I'M SIT-
ting in the kitchen with the newspaper while Anna
finishes the washing-up. It's dark, past eight o'clock. I
am starting to read her something from an article when Tobias
appears in the kitchen doorway. How quickly time has passed, see:
my son is taller than me, in his teens; his body hangs loose-jointed
and easy, but his forehead seems stitched tight.

"Vater, Theresa says it's Friedrich on the phone for you."

Anna is wearing a yellow dress that night. In her hand there's
a blue dish covered in soap, white puffs like clouds on a clear sky.

"You ought to hurry down," she says, and I say, "Of course."

I fold the newspaper in quarters and leave it on the corner of
the table. I hear Tobias behind me, as I head out, saying to Anna,
"If he needs my room, I'd be happy to stay on the couch."

Theresa, our landlady, waits at the base of the staircase with
the telephone receiver in one hand. She hands me the phone and
mouths the word, "Drunk."

"Friedrich," I say into the phone.

"Josef, thank God."

He is slurring his words, but it's more than that—he's holding
back tears, I realize.

"Are you busy?"

"No, not particularly. We just finished supper," I tell him.

He sputters something into the phone. I turn closer towards the wall.

"What is it, Friedrich?"

"I need to speak with you. I need to speak with someone and I mustn't . . . I mustn't put it off any longer. Please."

"Over the phone?" I peer at the clock on the wall.

"No. Please, if you can, I'd rather see you. I know it's a long way to come. I'll pay for your taxi if you need it."

It occurs to me I haven't heard him plead like this except in old letters. A flash of nausea, but: "I'll come. Just sit down and wait for me. I'll let Anna know."

"The door's unlocked. Let yourself in. There's no one here but me."

"I'll be about half an hour, I expect. But I'll do my best to hurry."

"Thank you, Josef. Thank you. I can't . . ."

But he breaks down again, and I stand there with the receiver in my hand for a moment before I say, "Just stay put, Friedrich. I'm on my way."

I hang up as Theresa comes out from her room.

"I can't stand drunks," she says. "I know Mr. Zimmel did some fine things during the war, but it's not manly, succumbing to one's emotions in that way. I'm almost ashamed of him."

I say to her, patting my pockets, "He's ill, I think."

"We all went through it, you know. He wasn't the only one."

And perhaps I should say more for my friend, but already she's turned back and gone into her room, closed the door behind her.

I tell Anna, and she says, "Stay over if you need to. I don't like the thought of you wandering the streets this time of night." She wraps my scarf around my neck for me.

Tobias has taken my place at the table. He looks up at me from under a wisp of hair that's fallen across his eyes. "I was telling Mutti that if he needs to stay here—"

"Oh, yes, Tobias. I heard. That's good of you. I'll let him know."

"Here's an extra twenty schillings," Anna says. "Just in case."

I bend over and kiss her lips, and as I do I inhale her smell, her breath. For a moment I wish I could tell them Friedrich didn't really need me, that I could stay home, read with my arm around my wife and call Peng in to sit with us; but instead I sigh and say, "I'll try not to be too long."

I TAKE THE tram to the base of Friedrich's street and walk up the hill to his house. The gate is open, and upstairs there's a single window lit from inside. At the door, I knock and let myself in.

"Up here." Friedrich's voice, carrying down the stairs. He sounds almost calm.

Upstairs, in the kitchen, a ceiling lamp casts a wedge of light into the hallway. Friedrich sits near his stove with a glass in one hand.

He rubs his eyes as I greet him. "I haven't been well," he says.

I pull a chair up to his kitchen table. "You haven't seemed well. Have you seen a doctor?"

"God knows I don't need one. I know exactly what it is. It's very simple."

He isn't looking at me, and I can't tell whether he's talking nonsense or I'm forgetting something. "You wanted to talk to me," is all I can think to say.

"I did." He shifts his weight in the chair. "It's not that I haven't meant to before. But I keep hearing these stories on the news, about children and men and all these terrible—these awful . . . and men who hid . . . but it never ends. I don't know how to talk about it."

"You can tell me anything," I say to him, say it because it seems the right thing to say, but my heart is a hammer and I wonder if I shouldn't get up and find a doctor for him right away.

"It's all the things that happened while you were gone. During the war."

A rushing in and out of heat from my body. "Yes. You tried to tell me once, I think."

"Ah, but Lord, Josef, it's so hard. I've wanted to tell you, but it makes me ill."

"You should let someone help you." I'd like to reach out to him, touch his shoulder—but, Just wait, says my mind.

I say, "Maybe I should make some coffee."

He shakes his head and sips from his glass.

I tell him, "No good thing you did for me will ever be wiped out."

And he says, "I will understand if you change your mind about that."

In Friedrich's face: a deeper species of darkness, somewhere and something I cannot reach from safety. So we sit staring at each other under the wax-yellow electric light.

"You're truly going to hate me," Friedrich says.

"I won't," I tell him. "Please."

He has his hands wrapped round his little tumbler, and his hands are thick and red, and the drink in his tumbler is the same dark as the waxy shadows in the corners.

"You know about my Lena," he says into his hands.

She flashes through my mind, a girl's face painted over Sarah Kostner's face: sharp cheekbones, bright, dark eyes. A catch in my heart. The one who lived.

"Yes, of course."

"You know, perhaps, that she was fourteen when her mother brought her to me."

Some unknown muscle in my belly goes tight as he says it. A part of my mind floating above this room and beyond this moment begins to pray without my prompting it.

And one must try to lay such a history down with delicacy—moreover, with justice, but compassion also. Here is the man who saved us, and here also are the things he did. And one must set them down and stare into them until the heart can accept them as truth, and ask all its questions, and see the souls behind them no less human than they were before—if it's possible, if we can be such creatures in this life.

5

CONSIDER, FIRST, THAT FRIEDRICH WAS NOT ALWAYS AS he is now, and consider that this bulk and breadth and weight of him was once a young man. Consider him this way: tall—taller than me, an inch or two over six feet, at least—and with his hair thick, black, slicked smooth above his forehead. His eyes clear blue, nearly grey; his jaw strong and set. His nose in profile might have been dashed off along a straightedge. His shoulders fill out a dinner jacket, and his back is straight. Of all this picture I think there may only be his oddly soft and full lips to throw off the perfect model of Austrian manhood (though some, I suppose, might wish him fairer).

Consider that this younger man can dance. Consider that he can speak well when he's not cowed by that mix of envy and admiration that seem to visit him when faced with someone better educated, or more self-consciously intellectual, or more confident. Consider that he's very wealthy, that he's always been very wealthy, has been raised by a mother and father who were always wealthy and who have, it must be remembered, worked for their money. Consider that his clothes are expensive and simple and his voice is low, and that his friends run the gamut from artist to banker to prince. Consider his three-storey mansion in the suburbs, his flat downtown, his villa in the countryside.

And consider, I suppose, that he's never married. That he has a new woman every second week. But recall also the two or three months out of the year when he renounces his habits, swears off girlfriends and lovers, lives a life almost monkish, celibate (though still in his mansion, still with wine on the table)—that he swims awhile in guilt, which turns after a time into fresh energy and resolution, until after a few weeks a nice girl at a party demands his attention and then the resolution slips down towards good intentions and then into nothing at all, until the next year when he remembers again. He feels a little guilt when he slides back, I think. He spends a few weeks away from friends. But then everything is as it was before.

But now consider the year 1939. Some force has thrown a switch on his life, sent him onto a sidetrack. His closest friends are gone, or changed; he doesn't know them, these changed ones. Whether because they are glad at heart to see Austria annexed and the Nuremberg racial laws enacted, or whether they read in his Party arm band a heart-deep complicity and mistrust him because of it, walls have gone up around him. One does not speak plainly.

He cannot leave Vienna, though he would like to go to Paris, see Zilla, even be French awhile. He has a duty to his factory and to the nation. He attends the proper parties, shakes the right hands and learns to salute. He drinks more than he used to. If he goes home alone, upon arriving he draws the curtains in his sitting rooms. He half-reads his books. He keeps one eye on the hearth. He falls asleep in his seat most nights.

So then, during days between fall and winter, cold and wet,

Sarah Kostner and her daughter appear at the small door by the laneway. The mother has been here before, has stood before this very door and met with her sick fugitive cousin. She comes this time at night, when there is no one else at home; Friedrich's family's servants no longer live with them. So they are alone. It's raining.

The mother is thin, hands on her daughter's shoulders in the old servants' entryway out of the cold, and though she holds her voice steady she is pleading with him. She's grateful, she says, for the help he's given her—the work, that rare security in these strange times. Only soon, she believes, it won't be enough.

She won't leave Vienna, she says. Her mother is ill and can't be moved. She doesn't trust the *Kindertransport* with her daughter—nor anyone, it seems, outside the city. "England," she says, "is much too far away, too foreign. She won't get on. She did awfully in English lessons." Does he glance at the daughter then? Is she blushing? And her mother adds, "Nowhere in Europe is safe for people like us. It's no good."

We can imagine him there with the two of them—tall man, a couple of drinks in him already; it's on his breath. Is he wearing his Party arm band? Is that part of the picture? We can wonder. And this mother, slight but hard-faced—she won't cry now. She won't allow the idea of crying. And the daughter.

Her name is Lena. She's fourteen. And she looks at him. The things he sees looking into her eyes, how he describes her to me later ("I had so much time to think up poetry for her, you see"): a slant of light through water; secret angle of gold in the dark. Something to the tilt of her eyes—something that reminds him of another woman, a relation of hers. She doesn't smile.

And he says yes to them. He says, "Very well." Friedrich Zimmel says yes to this, and let the record show it. You can number the men and women who gave such yeses in Vienna; you wouldn't need half a sheet of paper for the names.

He tells the mother he can take the girl. There's space for her in the attic. He wouldn't arouse suspicion asking the cook to prepare a few bites' extra food every day. He cannot take the whole family, of course. And in a little while it may be impossible to keep her in this country—though of course one hopes it will not come to that, he adds.

The mother understands. She thanks him. She breaks a little at his yes—doesn't cry, but bends, takes his hand and kisses it. This with her daughter watching. (And what does Lena think of it? How does she see this man then?)

He tells the mother to wait an hour before leaving, as it might be that anyone who saw them come will have stopped watching by then. But he knows it's a worthless precaution. If they do go unnoticed it's thanks to luck or providence.

In the meantime he shows them both the little windowless attic room where Lena can hide. It's a hot space, tiny and cramped, and it smells of mice and mothballs. But with the trunks piled up just so in the adjoining crawl space, it's almost impossible to tell there's a room there at all.

Lena says goodbye to her mother. He gives them some privacy, waits in the next room over. He tries not to listen, and it isn't hard—they're quiet together. He doesn't hear weeping.

The mother, when she appears, has the same straight face as before. She nods.

"That's settled," she says.

He asks her if she would like to leave any contact information for him. She tells him, "Lena knows," and shrugs. There. That's all. He nods and escorts her down the stairs, to the old servants' entrance, to the rain. She straightens her coat and her hat before she steps outside, and Friedrich feels suddenly as if it's he who is stepping outside, as if the cold is about to swallow him, and the cold goes on forever and makes you into nothing and no one. But the woman just turns to him, offers him her hand, and he shakes it.

She says, "Thank you, Mr. Zimmel." And with her back held straight, she walks away into the night.

So Lena is fourteen when her mother leaves her with him. And Friedrich is thirty-eight. He carries her little bag into the attic for her, and he spreads a mattress on the floor for her—sheets and blankets and a pillow that smells a little of mothballs (but perhaps there will be moths, after all, he thinks). She doesn't say anything to him that night. He doesn't say much to her.

In the beginning he finds himself trying to pretend she isn't there. Sometimes he goes a day without bringing her food, and then he tells her when he does go up that it was impossible, that there wasn't enough food, or that there were guests downstairs. And she trusts him. He sees that she trusts him. She doesn't complain. Sometimes she asks to go downstairs or to step onto the balcony at night, but, "No," Friedrich says, "no, it's impossible." Suicidal, he tells her. She doesn't argue.

A very, very few times, though, in those early days, he lets her come down. And he walks with her, hand low on her back as he escorts her through unlit rooms and up to half-opened windows where the air comes in fresh and cool, and she breathes it as if swallowing cold water after a desert passage. He finds himself surprised always by the materiality of her: her thin fingers on the windowsill, the chewed stubs of her fingernails, and the smell of her unwashed hair in the apricot breeze.

But up in the attic she doesn't exist. There's the whole top floor between her and the rooms where he entertains, and no sound reaches through either way. So he doesn't stop entertaining; he keeps everything the way it always has been: he hosts friends from the old days, Rudolph Steyer and Franz Blinne, and with them a new type of person—Neubacher's wife, and Bürckel, and some of the other occupiers. They've grown friendly with him. The Gauleiter comes once or twice too, when he visits Vienna, and he sits on Friedrich's sofa and drinks wine Hans Zimmel laid down when Germany was still a democracy. He talks openly about the plans for transports to Poland, and Friedrich's head nods up and down on instinct, his whole will pitted against this latent hysteria, terror that wells up from his bowels.

The Gauleiter's jackets are tailored tight across his belly, and the whole front of his body seems to jerk up and down when he says, "You see how much trouble it is, smoking the rats out of Germany." And they nod or stretch or stare at walls, his guests, and drink their wine. A tug, now, at Friedrich's nerves, a tug upwards through ceilings and rugs and rafters and to the place where the Jewish girl is hiding, above all of them, through all of this. He takes a long drink.

These days of hiding are, he knows, dull for Lena, perhaps sickeningly so. For Friedrich, at first, they are only terrifying. This fear clings to him, slips into him and seems to grey his skin. He is afraid she will do something to draw attention to herself. That someone will go upstairs and hear her moving about. That his cook will begin to wonder, or that there will be something that makes her flee the attic. This last fear hooks him, snares his mind and makes him stare sometimes at the divide between the main attic room and the crawl space where she hides—is there a way to block it? A way to keep her locked in?

A poison drip in his mind—the idea of stacking bricks, sealing the space permanently, forgetting about all of it forever. And if the house should burn down, or if a bomb should fall on it . . .

But when he snaps to, he splashes cold water over his face. Later he tells Lena that if there's ever a fire, she must use the old servants' stairway to escape, and never run into the street.

Once, when he comes to her, he finds her drawing on the wall with a pencil: ladies in party dresses, gentlemen in tailcoats, the swirl of the dance, everyone slender and dark-haired. She's shy of her drawings and starts to smudge them with the heel of her palm when he peers at them.

She says, "I'm sorry. I shouldn't have, not on the walls."

He sets down her supper and he says, "I'll bring you more paper." He heads downstairs with her swimming in his mind and he sits without reading, a long while, by the fire.

He starts to lend her his books. Some of them she can't possibly understand—those written in Russian, or in English, or those propounding philosophies so abstruse that there aren't likely a half-dozen minds in the world that could make something of them. But she thanks him, she thanks him over and over, and she reads them almost as quickly as he can pick them out for her. Philosophy, history, science—"It ought to be novels, for someone your age," he says once to her, but, "No, no," she says, "this is what I want." Nose-deep in a volume on Heidegger, and her knees folded together under her skirt; her hair up in braids, these days.

He has, as well, a collection of monographs and works by friends in his psychoanalyst circles: ancients in translation, contemporary theses, texts that capture a moment in an ongoing debate among the city's leading psychologists. He's reluctant, at first, to lend her these texts. Some of these are books that make even him—him, with his instruction, his experience—mistrust his body or his mind or that of his fellow man. He senses, holding a stack of them and peering down at long titles written in German and French, that they require context and explanation, and that the loan of these texts would demand an investment of time on his part.

A few evenings like this; a few evenings with her wet eyes staring out of the dark of his mind, the charcoal ladies that dance by candlelight.

He says to her at last, "What if I were to help you with these ones?" as he hands them to her.

She doesn't look at the monographs; she looks at him. "But you don't have time."

He shrugs. "I might have time."

Now in the evenings she sits with him in the music room overlooking the garden, with the curtains pulled shut, and just one light between them. She reads and she asks him questions: questions she's spent days asking herself, turning them over and over and feeling them out with her mind—nothing shallow or obvious. He thinks: What if I had had a daughter? Would she be like this? The glow of amber warmth in him, like candlelight.

She prefers Adler to Freud, but he and she agree that neither doctor captured the full complexity of the human individual. Their agreement is like strong spirits racing to his brain, and he sees by her eyes, he hears in her voice, that for her it's the same. He thinks: I am a capitalist and a capitalist's son and it was not for me to be counted among geniuses—but see here: alone with a fugitive child, I am at last becoming a man of original insight. When he looks at the girl through this feeling she glows like rows of candles at the feet of a painted saint.

The other things he tries not to notice about her then: her

blouses growing tight across her chest. The way her fingers run over and over through her hair. The smell of his bathroom after he's let her bathe in it, the dark hairs on his towel. He leans towards his half-steamed mirror with the towel in his hands and tells his reflection: She's not one of your dancing girls.

He writes letters to Zilla in this period. He greets her as "Jacqueline" out of fear or fantasy, and says, "Don't write back, I'm in a silly state." Writes narratives of Mr. Zimmel and His Wife Who Isn't. The wife is a little woman full of spark, dark-haired and laughing. In his letters he's with His Wife Who Isn't in Egypt, in Tibet. They ride camels, they fall off camels and are rescued by Bedouin herdsmen; they climb mountains and kiss in strange temples. Zilla writes back only rarely, and then on unsigned postcards (a cartoon of a cancan girl, or a monkey with an accordion); says, "I wish there were such a wife for you and I wish I could meet her. Giorgio sends his love along with mine." He keeps these postcards in a drawer by his bed, but he seldom reads them.

One night, after they have read together and Lena is padding away towards the stairs, he sees that she's left a folded piece of paper on the table. (The outside of it covered in sketches, a lady bent down her middle, her left leg amputated by the crease.) He almost calls the girl back—"You forgot something," he nearly says. But she is walking quickly. She's already gone. He picks up the paper and unfolds it. He reads the words on the reverse. Words meant, he sees, for him.

He thinks right away, reading it: I must have done something to invite this. She is so shy of me, she wouldn't dare, otherwise. He folds it back, touches his face. Watches the fire flickering and thinks of tossing the note into the flames: it would be gone. It would be nothing, it never happened. ("The maid must have swept it up," he could say, if she were to ask if he saw her note—and then of course he would have to be very stern.) He could do this, but instead he folds the paper over and over until it's smaller than the palm of his hand, and then he tucks it into his pocket and goes to pour himself a drink.

In his bed that night he opens it again. He reads and rereads it. Before he sleeps, he knows each sentence by heart.

In the morning he brings her breakfast but does not say a word to her. In her face then (though he glances at her sidelong, though he hardly lets himself see it): that terrible flush of mortification. It twists in him like nausea. He runs from her, almost, back down to his quiet rooms with their tall windows.

All day it follows him, to work, with friends, over his meals. I have wounded her, he thinks. I could have behaved like an adult. I am the adult in this situation. Why not be gentle? Why not acknowledge that, of course, she has nothing else to do with her affections?

After work, in the evening, he laughs at his friends' jokes over beers and he leans back in his chair like a man surveying a thriving empire and he shrugs at disasters. And feels through all of it the worm that gnaws his belly. When he comes home he climbs the steps to his front door as if through thick mud.

Later, when he has almost reached the narrow stepladder he will use to access the attic, he hears a sound like swallows in the eaves. It's her crying, he realizes. And the first thing that seizes him is a yellow rage: he grips the thin railings and is ready to tear her cubby apart, throw her out on the street—"It could have been someone else coming up! And if they'd heard you . . . !" But his grip on the railings trembles, and he finds his breath slowing; he hasn't lifted a foot to climb in over a minute. He rubs his forehead. He goes to her without anger.

She is lying on the floor when he finds her. She hasn't touched her breakfast: toast curls at the corners, and the jam sizzles with flies. She turns her face away from him. Shakes as if she expects him to be violent.

He sits against the wall—these beams now decorated, every square inch, in charcoal or pencil drawings that will (he is certain, but doesn't especially mind) rub off on his jacket. He gazes at his hands awhile, and then he tells her, as gently as he can, "I'm so sorry, Lena."

Her trembling is quieter, but still she's crying. He wonders if it's all about him; perhaps she's thinking of her mother, it occurs to him. And this makes his heart twist with a deeper grief.

He tells her it doesn't matter what they feel for each other: she's a young girl, and he is old enough to be her father. Besides, he says, he's responsible for her. It wouldn't be right.

It's only as he hears himself say it that he admits it to his own mind: she was not alone in wanting this. But he has never dared speak of it, or even hope for it consciously. And now she is rolling over, meeting his eyes, peering at him out from the shadows (soft little creature, like a fawn curled among fallen leaves—something found by accident that would leave one feeling blessed). He can't find a way not to look at her. And she reaches out and touches his knee with her fingers.

"But you shouldn't feel guilty," she says. "You wouldn't be taking advantage. I asked you."

She tells him that she thought about it for a very long time before writing the note. Friedrich feels his tongue thick in his mouth. He can't speak. He is suspended in warm water. It's a minute before he finds he can lift his hand and brush her fingers from his leg. He says, "Still, you're much too young."

She swallows and then she says, "It's true I've never been with a man. But I'm not a little girl. And you've loaned me so many books, I think I must know more about these things than many women twice my age."

His head swimming at this: Did I mean for this to come about, all along? Impossible not to wonder now. He stands slowly and says, "It can't happen, Lena." And he adds, as he picks up her breakfast dishes, "Come down and have something to eat."

He makes her camomile tea and an egg on toast. Sits with his drink, across from her, and neither of them says anything. He cleans up after her. Doesn't say good night as she goes.

He still brings her books, and he still lets her come downstairs now and again to read with him—hopes, perhaps, that by reverting to the way things were she'll forget her infatuation. But she sits nearer to him now than she used to, and gazes at him while he speaks to her, even if he points to lines in a book, even if he hasn't looked at her in half an hour—and at the end of the evening she says always, in her voice like cool water over stones: "I love you, Friedrich."

He nods and swallows. Says good night and stands. And she goes.

But he knows, when he finds himself, at work, lost in dreaming about the soft tendrils that curl up against the back of her neck, with her hair up in braids—and the dimple under her lips, above her chin—that he's lost. And he floats through it, like secret joy, like agony: I am in love, he thinks. At last, when it's most impossible, and most foolish—in love. The sound of her voice in everything, and the silhouette of her little body: perfect. When he sits beside these big blond Viennese women at dinners, he smiles at them and sees their delight, but he thinks inwardly, and with sparks of exultation: They're nothing, compared to her.

Still, it is a few weeks before he lets it become anything. A while before, at her "I love you" (grown a little sadder with every day he resists it), he turns to her and cups his hand against her cheek, presses his mouth so hard against hers he knows (through the heat and the rush) that it must hurt her neck to bear back against him. He lays her on the couch and kisses her chest through the thin cotton of her blouse, and then (her voice, as she clutches at his hair and his shoulders, crying, "Friedrich, oh, I love you") through her brassiere, and then nothing. But he stops then, pulls back, gasping, and says, "Lena, it's too much."

She reaches towards him, but he stands—he says, "Please, I can't." Everything in him shaking. She goes. He sinks back into the couch, and then later into bed, caught up in swells of fantasy in the dark.

He buys her roses before he makes love to her. He thinks, If this were under more ordinary circumstances, I would be buying her a house. No—asking her to live with me. Forever, he thinks. This is that kind of love. Her cubby is so small it smells like a garden of roses, with the little vase standing in it. He sees the way her eyes invite him, even then: here, on her little mattress, she would like to be his. But now he finds himself disgusted by the cramped little space, the smell of sweat under the rose perfume, and the heat. He takes her to his bedroom and pours a little wine for both of them. Tells her it's very important that they always take precautions. But now already (as if no minutes have passed in between, as if time is moving in fits and starts) here she is beneath him, and he is afraid at watching his own hunger, how it finds or makes a way to move in her through everything tensed and tight and she so small in his arms.

He kisses her afterwards, all up and down her belly, saying, "Oh, love, I wasn't gentle," but she only strokes his hair and says, "I don't mind. I don't mind." He lets her spend the night there, finds her curled into him in the morning, awake but absolutely still. And embarrassed, after, by how she's bled on his sheets, but he tells her, with a tenderness he's never known until he finds himself now putting it to use, that it's normal, and it won't always happen. He kisses her before he sends her upstairs. Thinks then of the shame of it, that she can't walk hand in hand with him in the park—but who knows, perhaps someday, he thinks. When all of this is over.

Now work is like sleep, and he feels every part of himself tugged back towards home, and upstairs, to this girl (this woman) who is so suddenly everything. She is eager, always, to see him, and so tender with him, and so free. He buys her little things, little treats and jewels, reads her love poetry. (He writes his own, too, in moments of insanity, and she doesn't laugh at it.) She wants him to show her everything he likes to do with a woman. She looks up at him with angled amber eyes and some part of him finds itself consoled. Her every gesture pierces him with its solemnity. He believes that, for her, he could be a better kind of man.

But still sometimes he must host Party members or colleagues or friends, and he must have parties, and in all this Lena must not exist. He dances with tall women who wear diamonds, who have husbands, and who have affairs, and who smile at him in a way his body makes him understand. One night after all of this, when the guests have gone home and he goes to Lena (a little drunk on champagne, and happy), she seems quiet. She does not turn towards him when he kisses her.

When he asks her what's wrong, she says, "You never think of inviting me to your parties." And he laughs without thinking. She starts as if stung, and her eyes grow wetter.

He puts his arms around her and kisses her cheeks and says, "Love, you know it's not possible. It's not that I don't want you there, but it's impossible! You must understand that."

"You could disguise me," she says, and wipes her eyes on the back of her hand. "No one would know I live with you. I could be anyone."

"Oh, darling, you know I can't. They know everyone in town." He strokes her tangled black hair with the back of his fingers. "I have to keep up appearances, you know. To keep us both safe."

"For how long?" She peers at him.

He opens his mouth, but then closes it again. Says, after a moment, "I don't know."

She seems to curl tighter into herself. "I see."

"Come down to my room for a while," he says to her. "There's plenty left over from the party. See if I don't make it up to you."

Without making eye contact, she says, "No, thank you," softly. And it takes him a while to grasp this; she's never said no before.

But he pulls away, and shrugs, and says, simply, "All right." And he stands to go.

Before he goes he hears her behind him, with a kind of solemn dignity, say (to him or to the night, he doesn't know): "Today I am sixteen."

His first—his physical—reaction to this is a kind of revulsion. He would like to rinse his mouth out; he would like to take a long and scalding shower. But then this feeling softens to guilt, and he turns back and kisses her. "Happy birthday, my love," he says. But still she doesn't turn to him. So he says good night to her, and she says good night to him, and he finds himself, as he traipses back towards his bed, wishing he hadn't let go of Eva von Rathsburg's hand when she tried to lead him out towards the darker corners of his garden.

BUT IN THE morning, when he's sober, and his head is clear and aching, he thinks of her loneliness and is ashamed. He considers buying her a dress, but can't think of a good-enough excuse for anyone who might ask what he wanted it for. He takes one of his mother's rings—these ones she left at the mansion, ones she doesn't wear now on account of her arthritis—and sets it aside. Buys pastries in the afternoon, makes a little tray of cakes and opens a bottle of champagne, and when he takes her to him, he plucks her up in his arms and carries her into his bedroom—and she laughs—and he sets her down against the bed, in the midst of the picnic he's set on the floor.

He kisses and caresses her while they lie there together, and then he takes his mother's ring out of his pocket and slips it onto her right ring finger. She stares at it awhile, and he says, "I am going to marry you, Lena, as soon as I can."

She looks up at him now, eyes like jewels—says, "I hoped you would, Friedrich. I hoped so much that you would." And takes his face in her soft, thin hands. And kisses him. And is so tender with him in bed, so tender he is drunk on love, and declares to himself in the throes of his bliss: I will defy them all, I'll marry her now; we'll run away and to hell with them if they catch us, I am not afraid to die.

So for a while again between them it is this happiness. He rocks her in his arms, and he listens to her tell their fantasies to the night every evening in his bedroom—the future they'll have together, their house in a country far away, their friends and their children. He has not found a way to marry her yet, it's true; but he feels it's good to be prudent, and every night with her he feels new courage. And after some time has passed, he thinks, After all, they're already married, as one might say, in the eyes of God— isn't it so?

THERE IS A night when he hosts another party. His guests spill out from the conservatory into the garden, the summer air is hot but lifting with the evening, and a lithe if intense little Bavarian woman, Clara, is dancing up against him, making him laugh with her boldness, making him reel—and the whole world is laughing, he could believe. The whole world powerful and young and beautiful. His eyes rise up on his giddiness, up through the apricot branches, along the back wall of his house, the tall windows dark, reflecting dusk and starlight. But there: in his bedroom window, you can see it, if only just—against the inner dark, another darkness, the shape of a woman's head and shoulders at the window, looking out.

"Excuse me," he says to Clara, who sighs as he squeezes her hand and says to him, "Don't take up with anyone else. I'm paying attention."

He pushes past friends without faces, he bumps through them all with a pulse pounding in his ears, louder and louder, a throb that out-thunders the whole world and the taste of fear so bitter in his throat that when he bursts into his room, and finds Lena crouched there in the dark, he cannot rightly hear the words he says, and he cannot discern the taste of them on his tongue, and through the dark can barely see the face of the girl who cowers and cowers and cries. He has her arm gripped tight in his hand all the way down the hallway and up the little stepladder; he flings her back into her cubby, spit flying now between them as he curses her. When he comes out, when he's coming down the stairs, he finds his legs shaking so badly he can't walk, and folds down onto the step behind him, his face in his hands. It's five minutes before he can stand and go back to his guests.

His blood still hot in him when Clara brings him a fresh drink, and whispers, almost into his mouth, "I want to show you my husband's new car."

Down the street, in the dark, he is rough and fierce with this woman in the back seat of her husband's Mercedes. She grips him and moans with him and, when he's finished, takes his lower lip between her teeth, and later says, "When can I see you again, Mr. Zimmel?"

In the days after this he brings Lena food, but he does not speak to her. And she is so wounded by this, so frightened—he finds in his anger that her attempts to coax him back to her nauseate him. Her tears and the way she offers herself to him: A child with no self-respect, he thinks. I was mad to begin this. He meets Clara in a hotel near his work, where his anger becomes a roughness she seems to translate as passion: she talks about going into the country with him, spending a week together, just the two of them.

And in this time, too, he begins to see the world as a beast hungry for his life—sees it in every resistance member accused and condemned, every old man beaten to death and every family shipped off on trains that seem to steam straight out of the land of the living. Hangings and shootings. Executions by the dozen. The very munitions his factory manufactures: churning up the earth, shredding bone and flesh and the mess of it roiling its way towards him like the crest of a flood. He feels strapped to the ground; he wakes gasping from nightmares in which a creature comes to devour him and he cannot move to escape it.

Then, late in the summer of 1941, this news comes: in occupied Paris any Jew who registers with a foreign passport will be detained and interned. When Friedrich hears this, it's already too late to warn anyone. He wonders, for a little while, if perhaps Zilla has escaped already—but she seemed so confident, he remembers, that her connection to Giorgio would protect her. Or could he make a special petition, he wonders, to have her freed?—but he knows what this would look like, and knows too that his influence only extends as far as the Party authorities like it to. And he knows better than most (and, standing on a street corner near his office, is suddenly paralyzed by) what the intention is for any person interned.

At home he lies on his couch, his face in the cushions. He does not weep; he finds he can't. He feels hollowed out and filled again with yellow-grey fog. When he brings Lena her supper he doesn't think about her one way or the other, and she sees this change in him: she goes to him, touches his cheek with her hand. He stands a moment under this touch, and then he melts into her. He cries out into her shoulder; he screams muffled and wordless into her flesh, and all the while this girl holds him, and rocks him, and lowers him onto the musty sheets of her little bed. Kisses him until he softens and relaxes into her arms. She whispers as she strokes him, loosens his shirt and trousers (he won't resist it now; he forgets being mad at this girl, forgets almost who she is). There is her touch and her kiss and the smell of this room, which is mothballs and sweat and old flowers. He lies in her bed with his eyes shut, these unwashed sheets rough against his skin but her lovely mouth so tender and warm and wet. Lets her comfort him any way she likes. Rolls in towards her when at last she puts her arms around him and tucks her blanket around them both. Falls asleep against her breast with Lena humming softly to him in the dark, some strange, wild song.

A NIGHT IN December when she asks him if he could find a prayer book for her: "My mother always said the prayers on Fridays," she tells him, and, "When did you become so Jewish?" he asks her.

She only shrugs and says, "I miss it."

Of course, there are no prayer books to be had; he tells her this. "Why don't you just make it up? Some people just talk to God," he says, "like He might understand what you're saying."

She looks at him awhile, and then she says, "You've got a strange kind of faith, Friedrich."

He laughs. They're in his bedroom, and the clock reaching towards one o'clock in the morning. "I don't have one, you mean," he says.

She shrugs, and nestles into her pillow. "If you say so."

He tells her he could probably find her a Christian bible with the Old Testament written in Hebrew.

"It's not like it would make much difference anyway." She sighs. "I don't read Hebrew very well."

"Well, tell me if you've got something better to do than practise," he says, and she laughs a little, and he wonders, as he sinks into sleep beside her, whether this is what marriage would be like: a softening of passion, perhaps, but a laughter that might flow in to take its place.

She is a bit sick the next day, though—and then strange with him. And stranger still the day after, and seems for the entirety of the following week to be distracted and withdrawn from him. He asks her for the first little while if there's anything the matter, and then, when she doesn't explain, decides to leave her alone until she comes around: he brings her food and lets her use his bathroom to wash up, but they hardly speak and he doesn't kiss her.

Then, after almost two weeks, he finds her sitting waiting up for him in the evening, her face streaked with the tracks of tears, and she tells him, in a thick, strange voice, "I'm worried I might be pregnant."

The first thing he feels is a fizzle of fear: a kind of bubbling up his back and into his brain that almost makes him giggle. And his first advice to her: "Perhaps not, though. Let's wait and see." He goes back downstairs. He finds his hands are shaking when he holds his book. He tries to think back about whether there was any time they didn't take proper precautions or if these might have failed, but this thinking makes him feel faint. He mixes two very strong drinks and lets these dull him out of his wondering and to sleep.

But he finds, soon, that her "I'm worried" meant something closer to "I'm nearly certain." She's almost a month late on her cycle, she tells him. She's been sick into her chamber pot most mornings. And each time she mentions something she apologizes so profusely, often with tears, that he has no trouble thinking this is her fault, that this is something she's done to him.

And still for the first few months his strategy remains: do nothing. Willed ignorance, he realizes, is like a well-worn suit for him at this point. The shaking in his hands he attributes to political stress, or his drinking too much these days. He lives his life as usual, he goes to Lena in the evenings and brings her supper and, as often as not, takes her to bed. He says to her look of concern, "Never mind, my dear, it's nothing." And sometimes laughs to himself when he says this—a feeling like drunkenness, or dreaming.

When she becomes visibly swollen, and pretending becomes harder for him, he begins to take her to bed less often. He calls on Clara and meets her many evenings after work. He begins to join in her talk about a holiday in the countryside ("If it weren't for this damned war," she says).

He tells himself he'll get a doctor to come deal with Lena—any day now, he thinks. But knows, behind that thought, that it's impossible. There is no one he can trust. So he tells Lena to drink herbal teas he brings her, and to exercise in ways that seem unfriendly to pregnancy, and all the while feels as if he's watching a crazed, detached version of himself instruct the girl in this way. She tries to obey him for a little while, until one evening she bursts into tears and says, "I'm sorry, Friedrich, I can't. Please don't make me."

Without really being aware of it, he brings her less and less to eat.

At the same time circumstances in the city are becoming harder: the war intensifying, all resources directed towards the two fronts, where the Reich seems only to expand and expand. Friedrich is terrified and amazed by it; he sits with his colleagues and watches the newsreels, the spread of the empire like water spilled across a floor. Dizzying, he thinks. And in the midst of this there is the sense that the new declaration of war with the Americans is only exciting, and inevitable, and that—perhaps—the patriotic mania that gripped the first, sincerest Party members was not only reasonable, but prophetic.

Friedrich thinks about these things to make himself stop thinking of the girl. In a corner of his heart that he hardly dares examine, he hopes that she might, somehow, simply disappear. He knows that if he were to climb up to her attic one day and find her gone, with no explanation, he would dance. He would laugh like a madman. He would thank God, whose existence he'd confess, willingly, in his delirium. But he cannot bring himself to tell her this is what he wants. He senses that she would leave, if she believed he really wanted it. But then, he knows, it would be his fault: it would be he who killed her.

Almost without thinking, and without letting his mind fix fully on the things he fears, he finds that he's defending himself against practical dangers. The sight of the girl growing bigger and less comfortable triggers it. He is afraid that she will go into labour suddenly, and make a lot of noise, and that someone on the street, or someone who happens to be visiting, might hear it. He starts to gauge how soundproof her little room is. He stacks newspapers all around her walls (paper that, he knows, he ought to keep for kindling). He wonders if he could make her bite onto a stick to keep from screaming. More than once, in the worst, the darkest moments—ones that come upon him unannounced, when he's opening a window or reading a book—he fantasizes about killing her. When these moments pass he fantasizes still more vividly about killing himself.

Now, walking down the sidewalk towards his office, or sitting in his living room, or at dinner with friends, he finds he exists in such a perfect state of terror it's like a novel kind of calm. This detachment, he senses (but cannot make himself address), might be a species of insanity. He has never imagined what might become of Lena, or her baby, but he sees constantly before his eyes his own show trial, his prison cell, the hangman's noose framing a teardrop of pale morning sky.

Without mentioning it to Lena beforehand, in the first week of June he locks up the house, and he goes with Clara to her cottage outside the city. He drinks with her until the days blur and he forgets how long they've been there. Here he finds in Clara the same kind of detached terror that cripples him. Their affair does nothing to bring them back into a state of calm; he realizes one night that he knows nothing about her beyond her wealth and her name and certain ways to please her in bed. Still he tries to fling himself into this passion, in a faith that it can sometimes be a stirring in the present that lets one forget the future.

He returns home in tatters after five days away. If he had hoped to find Lena gone, he is disappointed: she's there, in hysterics, weeping that she thought he'd left her, or died suddenly. She's trembling from weakness; she's hardly eaten all week. (He left the kitchen almost empty, he realizes.) She nearly faints as she's crying to him and though he himself can barely walk, he drags his feet beside her to get her back into bed.

"There isn't any food," he tells her the next morning. "I'll bring some to you as soon as there is any. Don't come downstairs again."

He will wonder, later, if it might have made a difference if he'd still pretended to love her. Here in front of him she dissolves into a state almost animal, starved and frightened. Her belly strikes him as grotesque beneath her bony face with its wide, hungered eyes.

There is then the night she sneaks downstairs to find food, but he hears her (her steps on the staircase, the banister that squeaks when she grips it), and he follows her and catches her in his kitchen. She's seen already that his pantries are not empty, as he's told her. Now he grabs her wrist. He raises his fist as if to strike her, and she looks up at him. Then she collapses—without a cry, without protest. He has to carry her, half-conscious, back up to the attic.

He has no idea until he comes to find her the following evening that she's gone into labour, and by this time it's already over. In the sitting room, on the main floor, he didn't hear a sound.

There is a mess, and the smell of blood and filth. She will not move. She won't look at him, or at anything, and she doesn't speak. He takes her sheets and uses them to sop up the mess on the floor, concerned at first that something might seep through the ceiling of the floor below. He cannot now make himself look at the curled, stillborn body beside her.

She doesn't look at him through all of this. It is not, this erasure, a thing simply done. He has to leave and go back down for more sheets; he comes back up looking for a stain on the ceiling. At last he gathers everything up in his arms and brings it all downstairs.

The sheets he burns on a hot fire in his hearth. He sees it will take more wood, and he doesn't have much. Still by his feet there's the little body wrapped in sheets soaked through with blood, cut from the afterbirth with kitchen shears. He decides to carry it into the backyard. He takes a baking tin from the kitchen, which the cook will miss, but it doesn't matter. He goes to the very back corner of the garden, into the dark under the apricot trees near the high fence, and he digs a hole as deep as he can manage in the hours before the world awakes. He lays the bundle in it with the baking tin on top (to keep the foxes from digging it up, he thinks) and he covers it over with soil, and pats it down, and sets atop a stone or two, and see, it's done.

IN THE YEARS before the war ends, there is less and less to live on. The winters are colder, and Friedrich's colleagues less and less confident. Before the end of 1944, one knows. Some men have talked of leaving the country. Friedrich has withdrawn from most of them. Still he smiles sometimes, but less and less often is invited to visit friends (and it's all right, the world seems to say, because this isn't the proper time for parties).

He has decided that the girl in his attic must survive this war, and that she must go free. And this is all there is for him.

There are nights when the bombs fall on Vienna, he says to me, when you can hear the crack of them and, far away, the buildings centuries old disintegrating into rubble, vomited across streets; nights when he sees again in his mind the flood of churned earth rushing towards him. Only now it doesn't scare him. Only now he sometimes wishes, tucked into his great, dark, lonely house, that such a flood could sweep up everything, and wipe away the stars from above his home and every other light from his eyes, and in the dark make the world over, everything once again new.

6

WHILE FRIEDRICH SPEAKS I FEEL THE SWEAT ON ME, cold, a trickle down my back and sides that seems to leach balance. He cannot tell this thing straight, nor all at once, but opens sometimes into details that seem trivial (the smell of flowers, or what the weather was like on a particular evening). He loses track of what he means and falls silent, staring into the space between us with his lip dangling, looking like a very old man. And I have to call him back, to find a context: "What happened when you told her that?" or, "Did this part happen before or after you knew?"—though I don't want to talk, though the words in my mouth feel false.

He sniffles. "I never told anyone. She never told anyone, as far as I know."

My collar is damp, and I feel feverish and strange, pasted into my own clothes. I am afraid it is the flash of heat before extreme nausea.

"You helped her emigrate."

"Yes. She lived, and she left. It doesn't count for much, but I wonder, sometimes, if she's happy." He wipes his nose on the back of his hand. "No matter. She'd never want to hear from me. She knows what I am."

"And she didn't want to talk to me—"

"I may—Josef." His eyes wide, his lips hanging loose. "I was . . . I was afraid. I was afraid of you speaking to her. I didn't want you to."

I press my hands over my nose and mouth and close my eyes, and I breathe slowly, in and out. My palms smell like Anna's soap.

"Please don't leave me."

He says it so quiet, with a boy's voice, full of fear.

I stare at him across the table. Purple tear-stained liquor-ravaged pig face and dark shining eyes and monstrous, says a part of me. What a beast this man has become. But he blinks and a tear rolls down his cheek, and a dog barks outside, and I put that part of me aside.

I say to him, "Friedrich—" But the words to comfort him lodge in my throat. A long hot wound runs down my heart. I can say: "But she had no other family, Friedrich."

"I know. I know! But she went away in safety. I can promise you that. I will be sorry forever. Josef, I'll be sorry forever, believe it."

What does that matter? The word *sorry* drops through my mind like a shadow and impacts nothing. "And what do you want from me?"

He sucks in a breath. "I have to put myself in your hands. I don't know if I ought to confess publicly. I think . . . I think I shouldn't."

I don't know the answer to this. I can't imagine what it was like to be this girl, whom I know only from Friedrich's understanding of her (and that limited, I think, despite everything). Would she want this brought into the light? "I don't know," I tell him. "Perhaps it ought to be up to her."

"I don't know what she wants. I don't dare contact her. I don't dare presume. If she accuses me, I won't deny it. But if she has decided to forget . . . I think I'm the last person in the world with a right to remind her. This was my sin." He swallows. "No part of it was hers."

I hang my head. "What a nightmare."

"But I had wondered, lately—" A pause. I look up. "I had hoped very much that there might be something . . . a kind of gesture . . . that you could make." His hand extends across the table in front of me, trembling a little, as if reaching for something, but his eyes aren't on mine. "All this time I've known her child was back there. In the garden."

I peer at him. "Where you buried it."

"Yes, and . . . Well. It just makes it all the more barbaric. What I did to her—to both of them, I mean." His left hand finds his right and his fingers interlace, tremble less as they hold one another. "Like a murdered creature, hidden back there—but she's not, Josef! I am ashamed beyond words of myself, but I can't make myself be ashamed of her."

I'm not sure whether he's speaking of Lena or their child. "What is it you want me to do?" I ask him, for it seems so strange, and I can't imagine how I could change anything—and is it even true? A part of me now wonders. Has he made up this story to torture himself for some other real or imagined crime? If one could look beneath the earth, would anything be buried there?

"I want—" He seems to shiver in his seat. "You could—and oh, Josef, I don't know how I dare ask this of you—I don't deserve it— nothing makes it right—but you could perhaps . . ." (I want to take hold of him and say: Just tell me!) At last he says: "I was hoping you could bury her in the Währing cemetery." A silence. And then, "You know: properly."

My throat is dry. Strange thrill of sickness and cold. "You want me to dig up the child and . . . and rebury her?" I cough. "In the cemetery?"

"Yes, yes—I thought of it, you know, right from the beginning. But I didn't dare try to go there. I felt"—he coughs—"unworthy. Yes. And I didn't know how to do it, after all. But you, Josef—you know that place so well, and no one ever goes in there. You could bury her. You could give her a little marker and say the proper prayers. I am certain you could. And perhaps it would atone—I don't know." His shoulders collapse. He seems to shrink before me. "For something."

I swallow and hold my hands on my lap so he won't see them shaking. "I don't know if I'm prepared to say yes to that, Friedrich."

"Josef, I'm very sure you could do it!" Again his voice catches in his throat. "I know how you look after the dead. You go after the foxes when they steal the little bones. You make sure those people have their dignity when everyone else forgets them." Now my own eyes are wet, and this man's face blurring around the edges. "I've asked myself, doesn't she deserve that too? I'd never tell anyone you knew. You know I wouldn't. Even if Lena tells the world what I did, I won't tell them you were here. I'll tell them I took her there. But I can't do it. I don't know what to do. I'm scared, Josef!" And he folds his arms on the table and buries his face in them, shaking.

Under this light, watching him, I feel completely empty and clear inside, as if washed out after a rain. I don't even know if it would be a crime to do what he's asking me. But surely it would be, I think. But does that matter?

I wish I could ask Anna what to do. I wish I could ask her father.

I tell Friedrich, "I can't imagine doing anything like that. And in secret!"

"Oh, Josef, I won't ever make you lie for me."

"I certainly won't lie. But this seems like you want me to help you conceal it."

"No! Not to hide her. That's not what I meant. You can put a proper marker there. Write whatever you want. 'Stillborn daughter of Lena Kostner and Friedrich Zimmel: she lived and died because her father was a selfish man.' It happened in forty-two. You can write that. Anything. Or—don't even mention me. I don't deserve it. She would have been Lena's. I wouldn't have deserved to kiss her feet. You could write—"

"Friedrich, stop." I hold up a hand. My heart is a boot kicking my ribs. "This has to stop. I can't think straight. This is too much to take in. And you're not in your right mind." I look into his eyes as I say it, trying to hold on to the good in him, trying to sustain him. (I feel, watching him in this stained twilight, as if I am slipping down a steep hill into the mouth of something vile; but I swallow, and then: might this not also be the way up and out of darkness?) "I think you need something other than what you're asking for. It seems to me you need"—I am about to say *a holy man*, but instead—"a doctor."

He stares at me, and I know somehow I am watching a light in his eyes go dimmer, dimmer, deeper, gone. He hangs his head.

"I understand. I shouldn't have asked."

I hold out a hand to him across the table, but he either doesn't want it or doesn't see it.

"Listen, Friedrich. I need some time to receive all this," I tell him. "And please reflect that I'm still indebted to you for what you did for my family. This doesn't change that. Nothing can erase that."

His body so frail, so limp again; he isn't meeting my gaze. "Yes," he says, weak as a man twice his age.

"Perhaps you should stay at our house." I make myself say it because here he is like a hospital patient in need of fluids and rest. But there is this nausea in me that threatens to bubble over, and I wish, in a deep place, that he might say no, and leave me be, and let me go out alone with all my grief.

"No, I'll stay." He touches the table with his fingertips and peers into his glass.

"Or"—I make myself say it—"I could stay here." Though it makes me reel to imagine it.

But Friedrich shakes his head. "I think I would like to be alone for a while. To get some sleep."

We sit for a moment, saying nothing. He is hunched like a stone, and the shadows on his face are like bruises. I feel my head spinning a little, a tilt across my ears. It will be hard to stand, it will be hard to walk, but I don't want to stay here. I push myself up from my chair.

"Well, if you can manage, I'll see myself out."

Friedrich only nods, still not looking at me. It seems I should say something to console him, but my throat feels tight and the right words seem lost in the thin night air.

"Are you sure you'll be all right?" I ask, and again he nods, shrugs. I have one hand on the back of my chair, and from this position, standing, the room does not seem so huge, but dark and small and grubby. I tell the both of us, and I'm not sure where I find the words: "You're my dear friend, Friedrich."

He puts one hand to his face, and with the other he seems to wave me away. I stand there for a few seconds, but then I turn and walk out towards the stairs.

"Josef—"

He says it so quiet, I might almost have imagined it. But I stop and turn.

He is like a mound of earth under an old, dying sun, but in the same instant so small, so nothing. I have trouble finding his eyes. His cheeks are wet.

"It's only that I never had anyone, Josef. Not really."

We stare at each other for a long moment, seeing and not seeing. At last he lowers his head to the table and waves me off, one last sweep of his hand.

I raise my hand to him because—I don't know the because, but I do it, and I say (though my voice is cracking, useless), "I will pray for your peace." And I turn and walk down the stairs, to the door, and out into the dark.

As the night air hits me, all of this hits me anew or perhaps for the first time. I have to take hold of the gate to keep upright. Everything is tilting to the right, the vertical bars themselves tilting, turning to point downhill.

It's not just Lena, I know; it's not just Friedrich. With the wind sweeping past me down the road as if it could not be bothered with what happened here, with the clouds overhead grey and blind and the whole street blue and black and grey, I can feel the countless silent faces pressing in around me, inches from me, watching, waiting, but I have no answer for them, nothing. I can walk out of the yard, down the street, down the hill. Still the world seems sometimes to tilt sideways and I have to grab a fence or a tree until it all goes level again.

In my heart Zilla is beside me, Zilla at ten and fifteen and twenty, and Zilla the last time I saw her, blessed and in love, happy. (Zilla's script from her last letters—*Help her* and *Make her trust you*—as if burned into the back of my eyes.) Her own eyes are the same in every season, fire and light, but now they are asking me something, and I can't hear the question. She is holding a bundle to her chest and the blood seeps through it. And I can't speak to tell her why or who or how, or to say I'm sorry, I'm sorry.

But right now I'm walking towards the Währing cemetery, through the dark, with things alive and rustling in the trees, leaves shaking in the wind and the air cold. My footsteps aren't steady, but they are a solid kind of sound in a night that might otherwise feel unreal enough for me to fall straight through it.

Through the park and up to the brick wall, to the solidness of this place. I let my body fall against it. The wind shakes the trees so that they sigh a little above me: *Oh, well.* I can close my eyes and press my forehead into the stone until I feel the grit scratching the rims of my glasses, biting through my skin.

My Lord, I pray. *Aren't you done with us yet.*

A cat mewls, a block away, and then it hisses. A car backfires.

I can lean into this wall, and it can take all of my weight, all of my grief, everything, as if I didn't exist. Coolness and stone against me. I can beat against this stone, but some small voice is saying, deep into my heart, that the stone is the same stone whether or not I remember any of them.

My God, why don't you wash the earth clean. Why don't you start over completely anew.

The night sleeps around me. I lean there a long time.

At a certain point, I don't know when, a snuffling and rustling to my right makes me look up. Between the wall and a tree that hangs over it, two eyes are lights in the black and it takes me a moment to find the corners of a snout, to see the paws blacker than the wall or the earth and to see the little body hanging broken-backed from sharp teeth, somehow softer than any little body in life.

I stare at the fox, and he stares back. I feel I ought to shoo him off. Instead I put my hands on the wall and I push myself back. Still the fox doesn't move. I wipe my nose on my sleeve and back away.

When I'm perhaps thirty feet back, the fox drops his snout and trots forward. He seems to sniff the earth, and then he paws at it. It's hard to see him exactly in the dark. I didn't know that he kept a cache outside the wall, but perhaps that's my doing, after all. I've made it harder for him to depend on the cemetery.

He drops the little creature, vole or mole or rabbit kit, into the hole, rolls it over with a flick of his snout, and starts to bury it again. It doesn't take long, and I am amazed that he lets me watch him— though perhaps, I think, he knows he's shooed me off for now.

When he's done, he sniffs the earth, then turns and looks at me for a moment, and if I understand anything from that look it's only a sense of irritation or, perhaps, weariness. But as he trots away it's only my own weariness I'm left with. It's well past midnight and I have no strength left to stand watch here. I stuff my skinned hands into my pockets and I walk with my head down, slow, out of the park.

7

WHEN IN THE AFTERNOON OF THE FOLLOWING DAY I make myself knock at Friedrich's door with bandaged knuckles, he doesn't answer, and I try not to feel relief. I stand outside and look up at the windows, but I can't see anyone. There's nothing else to do. I go for a walk in the Türkenschanzpark. It's a fine day, cool but sunny. The white butterflies are visiting the flowers. I stop at the bakery on the way home and buy a bag of fresh rolls.

The next day, again, Friedrich is not there when I visit, and when I get home I make a phone call to his house, but there is no answer. I haven't told Anna what he told me—dare not tell her, I find. The feeling is still too big to process. It would split me in two, I feel.

The fine weather continues, and I worry about him, yes; but there is work for me to do and it's not unlikely he's left town without telling us, or has been visiting a friend or staying out late at a club of his. Certainly there are thoughts I almost have, and things I almost revisit, but I keep busy and breathe the good air and close certain gates in my mind. It isn't happiness, and—though it shames me to say it, knowing what I do now—perhaps that's what makes me so selfishly sad in some moments: that these are free, blue-skied days I have with my family and, smile as I might, I cannot be happy in them.

But five days after I saw Friedrich for the last time, I come home and find Anna and Tobias sitting together at the kitchen table, and the moment they look up at me with that sadness and yet also with that shieldedness that would try to spare me some measure of hurt, I do not sit down with them, but go straight back out into the street without saying a word. For an hour I walk with my hands in my pockets, thinking of nothing, feeling nothing, until the sky starts to go dark. When I get home again, Anna has made coffee and Tobias takes my coat from me. We sit together in the kitchen under a light from above the stove.

FRIEDRICH'S FAMILY HAD servants when I was a boy, but in these days he has only the woman who comes in on Thursdays to clean house. He leaves a key for her in the mailbox on Thursday mornings. When she came this week, the key wasn't there. This had happened before, however, and, as the neighbours in the next house knew her as Friedrich's long-time help, they loaned her their key to his house. It seemed he'd given it to them after a girlfriend of his had left her dog locked in the house while he was out of town, and the animal had torn up his furniture while the neighbours heard it howling through the second-storey window.

The woman let herself into his house and cleaned the two main floors without noticing anything amiss, other than that Friedrich had left some dishes unwashed for several days (but these she could dismiss as a bachelor's simple vice). When she went upstairs, however, there was in some rooms a terrible smell, but she could not find out where it was coming from. It was strongest in the hallway, but there was nothing she could see that might be giving off such a stench. It took her several minutes to notice the ceiling hatch leading into the attic.

She went to find a neighbour before going up into the attic, and for that I am grateful, for her sake. Even when they'd made it up there, however, it was a few minutes before they discovered the little crawl space leading into the hidden back room, a room half-filled with decades-old newspapers. It was in that little room that Friedrich Zimmel had, some days before, looped a winch chain over an exposed rafter and hanged himself.

8

THERE WAS A DAY WHEN I WAS TWELVE, PLAYING FOOT-
ball in the street with the children in the old neighbourhood, when Zilla came home with her hat pulled down over
one eye. I left the game and walked with her up the stairs, though
she told me to go away. One of the boys said something rude and
I swore at him.

I could see the swelling on her cheekbone, from up close, going
purple already. It was a fellow from the university who did it; not a
boyfriend, she said—he'd got the wrong idea. I told her I'd beat him
up, and I meant it, though I was small for twelve and the last time I'd
fought a boy in my class he'd pressed my nose into the sidewalk and
kicked me so that I couldn't sit properly for two weeks.

Zilla had a cut of beef out from the icebox by then (Mutti must
have been in the parlour, or out), and she was holding it on her eye,
and she sighed and told me not to bother: someone was likely calling a doctor for the bastard already, she said. Friedrich had broken
his nose and probably a few of his ribs and told him he'd murder
him if he ever laid eyes on him again.

And I don't know—perhaps my pride hurt a little, for my sister's sake as much as for mine; but through and within whatever I

was feeling right then, I loved Friedrich Zimmel to tears and I told Zilla she should marry him.

My sister laughed a little, and looked at her feet. Then she looked up at me with her one good eye and she told me she could never marry Friedrich. He was her brother, she said.

"He's who you would be for me, if you could," she said to me, and even peering out from under a red flank steak she was hazel and gold, shining. "You'd be just the same for me, if you were older. I know you would."

I went red, and I kissed her on the cheek. I suppose it was the kindest thing she'd ever said to me.

9

$\equiv$

I N THE BRIEF TIME BEFORE FRIEDRICH'S FUNERAL, I SPEND
a lot of time walking Tobias's dog in the park. (I take my mind
for a walk, and Peng pulls me.) On my own too, I walk once
towards the Seegasse cemetery, meaning to visit; but instead I walk
past the old doors without turning my head, and around the block
and then off on another errand, and home. The Währing cemetery
I do not venture near.

Still. I can walk and retrace the city's streets, repeat and reorder
the route so often it seems unfamiliar, like a word worn out to the
point of meaninglessness, but I cannot shake the hook in me. It
tugs and teases.

Under the sun of an afternoon, on a bridge over the canal,
listening to the clap of my own feet as I walk, it occurs to me: I am
the only one now who knows what he wanted.

The canal under the bridge is deep green, like bottle glass, and
my shadow an emptiness in its middle. Sunlight spearing colour,
scaffolding of gold in the green.

$\equiv$

ANNA COMES WITH me on one of these walks. She holds my arm. She has been so quiet since she and Tobias told me my friend was dead. I have felt it as kindness. And now I walk with her on a street near our home. It's mid-afternoon, warm. The sidewalks under our feet are uneven, and we have to part arms now and then to negotiate a hole in the pavement. (But most of these have been repaired, it occurs to me; not nearly so bad as it once was.)

Anna says to me, after some minutes, "I've been thinking."

This could be anything, I think. So: "Yes?" I say. "Go on."

"It's about the Währing cemetery," she says.

(How to describe this feeling? Something cool that starts beneath the collar and trickles down the back; it makes me want to twitch away from my own clothing.)

"Almost no one goes there," she says. "And barely anyone seems to care what goes on there. It's terrible, I know—and I do feel terrible about it. But also—and Josef, just listen to me for a moment, that's all I'm asking—doesn't it mean that one could, if one wanted, set up a small memorial there? Without having to ask, I mean."

I stop and stare at her. Has a curtain been pulled back, does my wife hear everything that happens in my brain?

"What are you talking about?" I ask her.

She sighs and gazes off down the road, then at her hands clasped in front of her. "For our families, I meant, Josef. Or—if you didn't think it felt quite right—for my family, then."

This is a cut to my heart, and it lets the heat pour out. I take Anna's hands (although another part of me still is watching this situation, saying, How very strange. And so . . . ?).

"You've been thinking about this a long time," I say.

"Of course. And yet—" Fixing her eyes on mine. Her hat shades the knot in her brow, but I can read it. "Now I've been thinking about Friedrich being buried. Don't misunderstand—I begrudge him nothing. But his friends will always have a place to go. And even when they're gone, strangers will walk by it and see, and they'll know about him. But my mother doesn't have that. My brothers don't have that. Your family. Every—"

She stares off down the street again. She will not cry, this wife of mine. But my chest aches. My eyes prickle.

"I have been thinking about it," she says at last.

I take her arm. We walk again. Walking is like a mother stroking one's back, like rocking a child. I have been walking so much these days.

"One could do it," I say. My throat is tight, but it comes out soft. "No one would be particularly bothered by it, I imagine."

She is quiet. Listening, I know. She doesn't look at me.

"Although," I say, "almost no one will see it. Not a marvellous memorial, Anna. A secret one. I don't know. Is it what's needed, I wonder."

Anna sighs. She squeezes my arm, makes me stop and look at her. "Listen, Josef— It is— Listen. Tobias was speaking to me once." I can barely tell now whether it's her eyes brimming with wet or mine. "He said, 'Mama, we don't know. It could be that someone was kind to them at the end. Or that someone tried to remember them. We don't know.'" She is almost smiling when she says it—but oh, it's a smile like a wound, and I wish I could heal it. "Such a good boy, my Tobias. And he's right, it's true, we'll never know. But Josef—*I know*. And these people"—nodding at the windows that look onto the street—"they know. We're all too old now to tell each other fairy tales. So you're right, yes, it isn't what we need. But understand that I am surviving on every small, poor scrap of justice or truth that's afforded to me. So I am asking—"

She touches my cheek—which, yes, is wet; but so, I think, is hers. "Just for now. A little place. Some stones. A word. It's not enough, you're right; but still—it's good."

NEITHER ANNA NOR I sleep regularly through the night, and this is not so strange—but on the evening before we bury Friedrich I am awake at all hours, bartering with the dark. There is something I do not want to offer. But it will not stop tugging, I know, no matter whether I dismiss it or try to forget it or watch it tear me apart. This is not fully sane, says a sober part of me, from some high and solid place, but in the silent dark I can barely hear. It occurs to me at length that I am free to end this. I am free to offer anything.

I can roll towards my dear wife in the dark; I can speak into the curve of her neck, a little rough with sunburn, and say, "You see everything so clearly, dear love." So that teeth and tongue brush this spot of skin—so that I have touched this piece of her with affirmation. And she will not wake; but I will stroke her arm and call her wise, wise. So: her family, and mine, and that of a woman who once trusted me—it is not so very many to have to care for. Consider the shadows, consider the numberless dead—see how few my special charges, and how light they are to carry.

For my Anna has made me face this fact: that my friend buried his crime under an apricot tree in the dark, and it's there, I know, that this hook is tugging me, regardless of whether I consent to look where I am going.

10

THERE'S A BRIGHT SUN AND A COOL BREEZE ON THE DAY Friedrich's body is buried. His mother, Katrin, is very elderly and worn through by life, and she stands, tiny creature of bark and air, by her son's grave without a word. That he was refused a Catholic funeral seems to have shaken her more than anything, though the fact that her priest has come with her today and is standing beside her now, and that he promises to offer a Mass for Friedrich on Friday morning, seems to help her stay rooted in the moment. She doesn't sob, but from the first moment I see her, tears run in a steady stream from her eyes to her chin and she doesn't try to wipe them.

Tobias and Anna are with me, of course, at the burial, as are so many strangers. They are silent when the coffin is being lowered, but in the other moments they talk in earnest whispers to one another, tutting and conferring and consoling.

One woman with a feather in her grey hat wrings my hand and tells me what a terrible misunderstanding it's been, the fact that some people would have his death taken for a suicide when he was such a pillar of the community, so noble and so good. I pat her hand and say, "He was very good to his friends," and she says with eyes full of heartbreak, "Yes, yes; and you know, he did even more for the Jews than they deserved."

And another man tells me that he'd known for years that Mr. Zimmel's resolve was failing, but that Friedrich would never take his advice and see his psychologist, who would have cured him within a month.

"The point is to get to the root of things. You have to remember the things you've repressed, the root traumas." He leans in closer to me and my eyes catch on his one silver tooth. "It's because of things his father did to him before he was at school, I'd bet my life on it. It always is." And he shakes his head at the grave. "Shame."

And another man, an old fellow two heads shorter than me, just barely grunts out as I walk by, "And finally we know what sort of man he was all along." For a moment my mouth goes dry, but the man's wife says to him, "He had a hard time of it, dear," and he replies, "The war ended years ago, but everyone's still talking about it. I've managed not to kill myself. He was a coward."

Anna, when I come back to her, is pressing the hand of Katrin Zimmel, who is talking in low tones and cannot seem to meet my wife's gaze. Tobias is standing a stride off from her, arms crossed across his chest, staring down at the freshly turned earth. He is red around the eyes, and it surprises me: it's not that I doubt his affection for Friedrich, but that he seems always so capable of hiding his heart. I did not think he would cry.

When I come up beside him I lay my hand on my son's shoulder, almost at the level of my cheek. He looks at me out of the corner of his eye, and he nods. The air smells like summer.

Anna turns from Katrin to me at last, takes my hand, and says, "Mrs. Zimmel has just told me the most incredible thing."

I have never been able to predict the changes coming; I have never once been prepared. I am like a blind man before stepping into traffic, saying simply to my wife, "What is it?"

Anna points across the turned earth, points to a woman I'd barely noted—brown-haired, perhaps as many years older than Tobias as she is younger than me. Something familiar to her face, though I can't place it. This woman is looking at the new grave. She does not turn to greet anyone. Her expression is strained, almost anxious.

"That woman," Anna says, "is the young woman Friedrich protected all those years. Your little cousin—what's her name—Lena something."

I can set this down sincerely: not since years and years earlier, not since I was a creature forced to eat grass on the grounds of the Prater, have I felt the feeling drain so suddenly from me. It must show on my face, it must, and yet my wife carries on:

"Mrs. Zimmel says she's married to a London banker. She moved to England a few years ago. Her husband has been in touch with Mrs. Zimmel a time or two. It seems Lena's health has been poor—or something like that, I didn't quite follow." Anna is patting my hand, not looking at me, and so she does not remark on what I look like as the feeling goes out of my feet; as I become a man whose spirit is fighting to escape his own body. "So Mrs. Zimmel sent them notice of Friedrich's death, and here, you see—she took the train all the way to Vienna, all by herself. She arrived just this morning. We must say hello to her."

"Vater," says a voice, "are you all right?"

Tobias puts a hand on his father's shoulder and almost makes the man collapse. He can't know the nightmare that fills Josef's whole world: the possibility that this woman will turn, will see him—see on him the mark of decades of failed responsibility—and it is a blow to the gut; it is blindness come like murky water from alien thunderclouds. There was a sparrow perched on the gravestone only a moment ago, he thinks, but it is the last thing he sees clearly before he all but faints against Tobias.

"Vater, you're not well—"

"Oh, Josef, I'm sorry—I didn't think—"

Thank the Lord his son is taller than him now, can bear up against him, help him back towards the street. They had meant to take the tram home. Tobias says he will find them a cab.

Anna sits with her husband on a bench, his body slumped into her like one pulled out of charred rubble on a bombed street.

"Dear Josef," she says, stroking his hair. "I didn't think how it might shock you. I didn't guess. I'm sorry."

He would like to say, "I am sorry," but there isn't any connection now between desire and doing, and so he sits there dumb and blind.

THEY TAKE HIM home, sad man, and put him to bed in the dark.

Understand that he'd meant to go that very night to Friedrich Zimmel's house to reinter the buried child. Before the funeral, early in the morning, he'd gone to see the place: saw the front door open, men beyond the door shouting, sounds of moving furniture. Josef Tobak, untried grave robber, had gone to get a sense of the risk, but had found himself wondering instead whether a new resident could stand to know what had happened in that attic (or even a small part of that story, true). If someone died in a house, Josef thought, he might be there forever: huge and formless, filling the emptiness under the eaves.

But now all the ghosts are here, in his bedroom, crowding in on him and clouding his vision. So Lena is here. Real. With that look on her face—like her mother in a doorway out of the cold, and Josef Tobak responsible for everything that happens next.

Anna lies beside him for a while on the bed. She says, "Mrs. Zimmel said Lena was planning to be in town a few days, if it would help you to speak to her." And at his silence: "But if it would make things worse, love, never mind, never mind."

That evening, when Josef's vision is a little clearer, when the world seems quiet around him, he breathes deep, and he imagines what petition he would like to make to God. He is sure he has an argument. He is not sure what its object is. To be freed, he supposes. To be no longer responsible. Responsible, guilty—he realizes the concepts have twined together in him like old roots. Take an axe to them, then, he prays.

He can shuffle down the stairs in front of their house, and he can look up at blurred clouds, and he can say this in prayer—but the world will still shadow over, come night, and there will be no word sent back, and his own dry mouth filling with silence.

11

You are listening to me, Tobias?

The light's so dim.

I think you're listening. Stay there
a moment. I was telling you:

This man Simeon, he goes out to
the river before sunrise, remember—almost no one is awake. His
fishing rod is over his shoulder,
and he praises the Lord for the
coming morning—

Mama said you ought to
get some rest, Vater.

I have to go wash up.

You can stay with me a minute.

I was saying—and you know, this
is a real story, Tobias. If you go to
the Seegasse cemetery, right there,
you could find the fish's grave.

I know, Vater. You've
shown me the place.

But let me tell this right—I don't
think I've told it right yet.

Vater, I have to—

It was the early morning—the sun
just starting to come up, and he
goes to the river, a special place he
knows, just outside the city: bend
in the water, there, and the shore
sloping down as sand. And he casts
his line—*whish*, like that—far out
into the water, just as it starts to
glint in the morning—

Vater. For goodness'
sake, you weren't there.

305

Shh, Tobias. Where was I—

Oh, yes. So the line flicks out into
the water, and the whole world is
beautiful in the new light, and he
prays to the Lord: "I shall praise
your power and kindness at dawn,
for you have been a place of refuge
to me."

                                        A very pious fisherman.

What do you want? He was a good
Jew; it was the Middle Ages; the
Lord was very near to earth then.

                                        I've heard it another way,
                                        to be honest.

You don't know so much, my boy.

Anyway, he's praying. And then all
of a sudden, *poof*—a great strong
pull on the line, like a man in the
water has grabbed hold of the hook,
is pulling with great strong arms.

So he pulls and he pulls, this
Simeon—he reels and he reels,
fighting this strong man in the

306

water. He teases the line back and
forth, he lets it go, he pulls it in,
battle and battle, will against will,
and then, at last, in the beautiful
morning light—

Watch your arm, Vater.
You'll knock over the
lamp.

It's all right.

As I said—this fish: he flops out
of the water, he's huge. Made
absolutely of silver, scales like
armour—shining—beautiful. He's
big as the man's arm. His muscles
—he's thrashing, he isn't dead,
only panting, like the fisherman.

But Simeon, here, he's won the
battle—and so he heaves this fish
into his net, thinking, I hope it
holds—and it does, thank the
Lord. He carries the great big fish
in his net all the way back to the
city, smiles at the other folk who
are awake now, all pleased with
himself, with his good catch that
morning. How good a fisherman

he is, how good the Lord has
been to him.

And which is it—that
he's a good fisherman, or
that God is good?

Tobias, you don't really ask that.

You know these things. Be sincere.

So he's got this fish.

He has the big fish, yes, and he
carries it in his net back to his
house, and there his children are
waiting, all awake now. They
gather around him there to watch
him kill it.

So he takes the fish, and he takes
his great big knife, you know—

Like a cleaving knife.

Yes, precisely. He raises his big
knife over the fish, and he swings
it down hard to cut off the fish's
head—but just before the blade

makes contact, in the moment
before it dies, the fish screams out,
in a voice like a man: *Shema Ysrael!*

Oof.

Yes, "oof." So Simeon, now, he's
terrified, and his children are
terrified, and the fish is dead, and
no one understands why a fish
should scream so, like a man, in
the moment before it dies. So he
runs up to his wife, who is nursing
the baby—

So many kids.

Well, what do you want.
They're blessed.

Are you still blessed if
you have only one child?

Ah, go on. If he is good, he's
worth ten.

"If he's good," he says.

You are good, Tobias.

309

Well. Finish quick,
Vater—I said I'd help
Mutti.

So the mama, Simeon's wife, she
tells him, You take this fish to the
rabbi, and he'll tell you what to
do. And so he goes.

Good man.

And you know, Tobias, he's carrying this fish through the streets,
through the busy morning crowds,
all wrapped in a sheet, and he
feels, now, so ashamed. To be
carrying this thing, or to have
killed it—whatever it is, that he
has done his part so wrongly.

He is so ashamed.

Why?

Well, because—it's so natural, you
see. Because he is so ignorant and
small, and he doesn't know how to
proceed. And he has done something, maybe, very wrong, because
he didn't know. Like you might
feel, as a child, when you've broken

something by accident, and you
have to go tell your papa, and you
think, Oh, he'll see how bad I am.

Or you tell your mother.

Or—yes.

Anyway, he goes to this rabbi's
house. And they look at the fish,
and they discuss and discuss . . .
and then at last this rabbi tells
Simeon, It was a dybbuk, you have
to bury it.

So they bury it.

That's the story.

All right, Vater, I'm
going to go wash up.

Tobias, just wait a moment—
I want to say something, but I
don't know what.

Well, tell me later.

No, just this—I didn't get along
so well with my father, and now
he's gone, and it's awful, Tobias.

Not to have had that. I want you
to have that.

Yes . . . well.

Who knows how long I'll be
around.

I wish you wouldn't say
that.

Well, it's true.

Think of Mutti, Vater.
Think how you'd hurt
her, saying that.

I don't want to hurt her! I want to
not hurt her. But you go on now.
Go wash up. Only bring me my
slippers before you go. My feet are
frozen. Thank you, Tobias. You're
a good boy. Tobias—

(But the room, this man Josef Tobak will find, is empty, and his
son doesn't hear him. He sits alone in his soft chair. His boy's dog
sleeps at his feet. The walls creak, and the haunted world grows
strange and grey.)

12

JOSEF'S BOY, IN THE DAYLIGHT, IS A SHADOW IN THE canal. Here is a green-grey deepening into black, and the lampposts and bridges like figures in it. Elsewhere the father, bundled and blanketed at home, still stricken, cannot know his boy's thoughts, nor exactly what pull the lonely city has on his son. It may be (and wouldn't we like to imagine it) that the young Tobias can feel his father's childhood in footprints beneath his feet, somehow preserved in cobblestone and concrete. Mystery and hope that crept beside this water, just there, on the far side. That massive Ferris wheel leaning over everything, only a short walk from here.

Is he thinking of his father? Tobias is a lamp cupped in the palm of his family's sorrow. He can lean over the canal and dream of peace.

But it isn't only dreams that draw Josef's son this day. He has been holding a particular grief to his heart, through everything, despite and within his father's crumbling. He is peering into a persistent evil, Josef's son. He is making his feet lift as if heaving himself through a bog.

He has an idea in mind, as if it could fix something. (Scrape the mud off his feet and leave him light again.) He has felt his family's grief, felt it thickening around him and moulding him in its own image. Yet here, adamant, in his centre, is a part that says: We are survivors, aren't we? And he would like for that to mean more than shell-shocked hauntedness—he would like it to mean victory.

Because he is a young man with a future, this Tobias Tobak. And his family, he has decided, has a future as well.

IN THE EVENING, Tobias asks Josef to take a walk with him and Peng. It's such a rare offer that Josef, half-asleep on the sofa, stirs almost at once and asks for his jacket. Anna doesn't say anything, and though one might catch her glancing at Tobias for the shortest of instants, otherwise her gaze is steady on her book, open in front of her. Peng pants up at his master by the door as he dances in and out from between human legs.

Tobias takes his father's arm, and they walk in quiet for the first block. Josef keeps swallowing, blinking; Tobias stoops once or twice to pet his dog and Peng runs back and forth across the sidewalk in front of them, claws like tap shoes on the pavement. When a man in a cap pulled low over his forehead passes them going the other way, Tobias raises a hand to greet him, and the man startles as if he wonders if he is supposed to know these two.

As they pass under a street lamp, Tobias says, "I wanted to talk to you about Friedrich."

God, no, Josef pleads—but: "What is it, Tobias?" He tugs his jacket closer around his neck. It isn't at all cold, but he wants something wrapped round him.

Tobias sighs. "I just keep thinking there might have been some way we could have known."

And now a shiver down the back, a cold sickness. Josef says, "Known . . . you mean, that he meant to kill himself."

His son nods. "I wonder if a person would try to . . . try to warn someone, even against his intentions. You know. Subconsciously." He holds Josef's arm steady by his side. "Is it possible that Friedrich said something, or did something, I mean, and we missed it?"

Josef coughs. "Tobias—I wouldn't want you blaming yourself. Or anyone. When someone wants to . . . to do that, they'll do it, and you can't stop them unless they want to be stopped."

A moment of silence before Tobias says:

"But say he *did* want to be stopped."

"He didn't, Tobias. We can be sure of that," Josef tells him. But is this what he'd dare tell the ghosts that trail him? He doesn't know, but he finds himself insisting: "He went somewhere where he was sure no one would find him until it was too late. He didn't leave a note. He made very certain that no one would stop him."

Tobias stares down at the sidewalk, and his fist clenches and unclenches. His father can feel the muscles move in the young man's arm. Tobias's pace has quickened a little and Josef breathes a little heavier, keeping up with him.

"But he had so long," Tobias says. "You don't know what he was thinking, all that time."

(It is suddenly before this poor man's eyes—Friedrich falling through all those years, those nights alone, the darkness and the poison of it—but Josef Tobak can't guess what his son is thinking, how much he knows.)

Tobias says, "I can't imagine how he must have suffered, all alone."

"You can't heal someone who won't let you see how he's wounded"—Josef's voice hoarse to his own ears, and strange.

Tobias glances at his father. "I meant in the attic, Vati."

At this, Josef says nothing.

"Mrs. Zimmel's priest," Tobias says, "at the burial, he was trying to tell her that Friedrich might have decided he wanted to live, after he did it. I didn't realize his hands weren't bound, but of course they weren't. They couldn't be. And of course he couldn't have broken his neck—such a short drop. The ceiling was about seven feet at the peak. His toes must have almost brushed the floor." The words are falling out of his mouth and Josef wants to stop him, wants to reach up and clap a hand over Tobias's mouth, but he can't. Josef rubs his throat, swallows hard. So it's this grief that cracks Tobias open like an egg; but all the father can feel now is sickness, not a bit of what's precious in this moment.

Tobias is still telling Josef, as if he can't not say it: "I think you must have your instincts at that moment. You must try to live. You must. He would have tried to pull himself up on the chain, or on the wall, to stop it, but he couldn't. He would have tried to call for someone, but . . . he couldn't. God. I wish . . . Vater." Josef squints up at Tobias and sees the young man's face like a monument, a stone soldier's face, his sister, Zilla, resurrected as a young man. But there is water in his son's eyes. "I wish someone could have helped him."

And how much more beautiful a story, in Josef's mind, is the one where someone bursts into that room and cuts Friedrich Zimmel down, rushes him to a hospital; the story where Josef sees his friend again, weeping and humbled, broken-throated but alive.

"I just wonder if that part of him—that part that wanted to live—might have made him say something, or do something, when you were with him." His voice trembles, and he turns his face from

Josef as if glancing up at the houses. "Maybe when he called you, that night."

Shut up, you damned boy, shut up, shut *up*, say the gut and the throat, but Josef's lips say, "I don't think he said anything about meaning to kill himself, if that's what you mean. I wouldn't have left him there if he had."

"I know you couldn't have done anything, Vater, but I wish . . . God. I wish he'd asked for help."

Josef lays a hand on his boy's arm, though it is as much to hold himself steady as to comfort.

"Of course you do, Tobias. We all do."

"I think I want to do something for people like him," Tobias says now, "to help them. Perhaps I would like to be that kind of doctor."

"Oh," says his father. New information. "A psychiatrist, you mean."

"Whatever it is," Tobias says. "There must be something. If there is that reflex to survive at the last moment, perhaps it's there earlier on. Perhaps you can detect it. Maybe no one's tried."

Josef wants to think of Tobias in a white coat, he wants to let his chest swell for this son who means to be a doctor, but the street lights are yellow haze above them and here is Friedrich's face before him, a mass of puckered, ruined flesh, and he says *Do this for me* as Josef turns away from him.

"I wouldn't want you to think you could really stop someone who was determined," Josef says. "I wouldn't want you to take that burden on yourself. It's too much. It would crush you."

Tobias swallows. "But you have to fight, Vater."

Peng has stopped to sniff a tree and they wait, not speaking, not looking at each other. The faces of the buildings don't see them; these windows are blind. It is occurring to Josef that perhaps—just perhaps—there is something more to this conversation than he'd realized.

"There was a man in Shanghai, I remember, who killed himself," Tobias says as they start walking again. "I've been thinking about him, on and off, the last few years. I don't know if Mutti told you about him."

Josef shakes his head. She never did.

"He was a tailor. He lived in the building next to ours. I don't know what I thought of it when I was five," Tobias said, "but lately I keep thinking of him. How he fought so hard to survive—he ran away from people who wanted to kill him. He made it to China." (While Josef's son talks, Peng *ruffs* and trots against a fence with his ears pricked. Perhaps there's a rat.) "He beat them. He'd survived. But then he gave it all up. He handed them just what they wanted. And why? Why let them win in the end?" Josef is listening for the judgment in Tobias's tone, but it's only the question he hears, the pain of it. "I just can't imagine why. Can you?"

In the soup of Josef's thoughts he isn't sure who it is he's speaking with, the little boy who is somehow sure his father will have the right answers, or the man who wants to pick over an idea with an equal intellect. Or even, perhaps, a healer trying to probe a wound—could it be?

But Josef says only, "Perhaps he wanted death on his own terms, then."

"I've wondered that," Tobias says. "It's an idea. But he didn't seem strong in it. He seemed defeated, like he had no other way out. Not that I remember him very well. But I thought the same thing with Friedrich. That he wasn't himself, in the end. Do you think it feels like being driven over a cliff?"

318

Such a strange thing to say, but Tobias is peering at his father and Josef observes with a gaze that so often fails that his son has Anna's deep eyes. And Josef's mind is asking, Do you think that is how he felt, Josef?

Josef says, "I don't know," because it's all his throat can manage, but he wants to say no, no; like you're drowning and you would grab on to anything that might pull you out of it.

"It's horrible." Sharp now; Tobias sounds almost angry (and Josef's own blood too is going hot, as if he is fighting some jeering someone). "That a person could fight so hard against something so evil and see it driven out, and then run back into it willingly. It's like they keep getting what they wanted. Friedrich survived; we survived. So why now, after all these years—why do what they would have done to us?"

And before Josef can think: "But he was one of them, Tobias. Friedrich was a Nazi."

And immediately he takes it back, in his mind, but it's too late. Tobias is silent. Peng is panting and bouncing along in the dark, and Josef's stomach is a lead weight.

"He never was," Tobias says, even-voiced. "He wasn't really."

Josef coughs. "Well. You're right—not really."

Tobias says, "You can't think . . . You don't think he deserved it." He swallows. "I know you don't think that."

Josef barely knows what he thinks. But a moment ago he was wishing Friedrich were still alive, and so he says, quiet, "No. Of course I don't think that."

"And if there had been anything you could have done, you would have done it," Tobias tells his father.

"Yes." Josef Tobak takes these words into himself, places them at the centre, tries to make a lamp of them. "If there had been anything I could have done in good conscience, I would have done it."

They walk the rest of the way side by side, silent.

IN HIS BED, in the dark, Josef Tobak feels his boy's words stir inside him. All these others, these faces that have haunted him since his childhood, have gathered around him, but he will not meet their eyes. He is looking for the face of an angel who can carry a message to God, but whatever angels there are must hang back in darkness.

But he has read before that should one run to the ends of the earth, or crawl to the depths of hell, yet would the Lord be there. And so he knows he can speak now, in his heart of hearts, and be heard: I am so tired, says this man's old heart. I have so little left of good to offer. I can do, perhaps, one further thing, he tells the night, but that is all, and I am not strong, so help me—and in the silence trusts that the message has echoed upwards, outwards, into the knowledge of one who hears.

I DON'T KNOW how disease affects the mind, or why the body, so fragile, reacts the way it does. But I can tell you this about the man I was: when he awakes the next morning, there is a clarity to the air like purified water. He holds his hands before his face, lying in bed, and prays, *Very well, Lord. I will use this.*

13

THE FOLLOWING NIGHT IS AS DARK AS CITY NIGHTS EVER are. I am certain when I tell Anna ("I need to visit the Währing cemetery." She says: "So late?") that she knows I have something unusual in mind, but she lets me go. I have a prayer book, a small torch and an old key tucked in my coat pocket; I have a wide, fringed shawl the weather doesn't demand draped round my neck, hidden under my coat. By our landlady Theresa's front door I pick up a garden trowel I left in her umbrella stand. I don't know what Anna guesses. I hardly know what to think myself.

My eyes are clear, and my stomach is all but settled. The streets are quiet. I take the bus from our home and climb the hill towards Friedrich's old house. Trees a deeper black against an overcast sky—street lamps every few houses. Myself perhaps suspicious-looking, I think: thin fellow in a long coat, hunched, striding quickly. But there is no one to see or guess.

All the windows of Friedrich's house are dark. His gate is locked. The fence is iron and spiked, but I have already decided I might climb over it. Halfway over I realize this was foolish: my arms might be strong enough to pull me over, but then the stretch and the tension of getting both legs over the top—and I am not as young as I need to be. I gouge my ankle half-tumbling down the far side of the fence, pull a muscle in my groin, hunch in the shadow at the base of the fence in determination not to moan or curse. A sad sight, I'm sure. I can see this man, his face hidden in dark, small in his muffled pain and his heart a kick drum pounding—how ridiculous he is. And whether this makes his foolishness more or less maddening, I can't rightly judge.

The pain feels somehow correct, though, like a form of reverence. I ought never to have proceeded without it, some part of me decides.

Limp into the backyard. The air here is rich with summer—greenery and black soil, and last lingering perfume of flowers asleep for the night.

The apricot trees are in the back corner of the yard. Their fruit is young and green. Here I will test, for the first time, my dead friend's faith in me: for there is no way I will know where to look unless he thought to show me somehow.

It isn't hard to admit that I half-hope to be foiled at this point. If I have come here in good faith, and if it proves impossible to proceed, then, I'm sure, I can take my freedom and leave in peace. The torch beam finds roots in the hard soil, the creased and cracked bark like old skin. Two tired men, I think: myself and this tree, facing each other in the dark.

But now, see, in the beam of light—something I would prefer not to have seen. A stone pressed into the soil. Crouching to touch it, I already understand: for here is another little stone resting on it, almost—but not quite—as if by accident. There are no other such stones in this place.

Oh, Friedrich! I want to say. Perhaps you were lying to yourself. Perhaps, my friend, you created this story as a penance, and paid it tribute with your life.

The feeling of dirt under my fingernails is one I've known almost nowhere besides cemeteries: we never had a garden, and I've lived always in cities. In digging, I am a child, and a youth, and a young man and a middle-aged man all in a moment, in the midst of a silence deep as a well. An awareness of faces peering over my shoulder—just here, so near they might lean in and touch me. We all stare together into the dark earth.

How much is enough? I am bartering—even as I begin to sweat, as the little mounds grow beside me, as my hands turn black. I'll try only a little farther! And then, when the silence deepens: Fine, a little farther still.

When my trowel strikes metal I stop a long while and lean my head against the tree. I would like to cry. The tears seem to be drawn from a very long way away, and are long in coming.

It is a baking tin or a square roasting pan, rusted and caked with earth. It is long as my forearm, elbow to fingertip.

Bundle of cloth beneath it. Nothing gruesome, nothing accusing, nothing awful: this scrap of dirty linen like old laundry under the earth. Something that might once have been white.

Here is what I do: take off my coat. Awkward, a moment, as I remove things from the pockets, try to fit all of it into my trouser pockets. Shivering through a thin shirt, despite the summer. I lay the jacket out flat on the grass, like a scarecrow belly-up to the sky. Loosen all the edges of the buried cloth in the earth with the trowel—this is not difficult; everything is light and easy. When I gather the cloth in my arms at last, I'm terrified of what I might feel, but there is nothing—it weighs nothing. Only ancient, and smelling of earth. I lay the bundle in the open jacket, fold the jacket around the dirty cloth.

The tin and the turned-up earth I pat back down in the hole. Flattened over, the earth still looks disturbed, but why, I ask myself, would anyone suspect anything?

The bundle held against my chest is light. I hold it so that it can rest against me.

From the inside of the yard, with a little effort, the front gate can be opened without a key—and it swings open without much noise, nothing that would disturb anyone.

I have made this walk so many times; I've seen this path through joy and despair; I could trace every tree and break in the sidewalk from memory, but tonight I wander along it as if through a foreign land. Maybe it is the feeling that I'm young again, a young father, and my city not yet touched by war. Maybe it is the train of followers I cannot turn to acknowledge—everything is strained with the weight of their patience. Or perhaps the world is different because my role in it is different.

At the gate of the Währing cemetery, I fumble through various pockets for the key and find it finally inside my bundled jacket. This gate is a struggle to open, but it seems wrong to lay down the little weight in my arms to wrestle with the lock two-handed. It grates open at last. The black space beyond enfolds my burden and me, and with us the whole ghostly trailing multitude.

There is a space halfway to the far wall from the entrance of the cemetery, a place where the earth is thrown up in little hills to trip you up. It's shady here during the day, among tangled trees that dip their branches low, and the mat of vines hanging over them like sleep. Sometimes I surprise a partridge here, sometimes a squirrel. This is the place that beckons.

Lay the bundle (this—can a person think it?—this child!) on the earth. One can dig with hands shaking, with head almost empty, almost faint. The earth opens up. There is room here. One can pray without words. One can watch himself praying and think, That man is praying—and not know what he is praying, and consider it right.

I take the bundle out of the jacket to bury it. Wishing now, for a moment, that I'd brought a fresh shroud—but it's all right, I feel. Just tuck the cloth as carefully as one can. Pat it gently (afraid to feel the press of bone, afraid to feel anything inside it), let it rest there while one finds the old prayer book and prays an older, far older prayer, standing under the branches in the quiet; how one's voice sounds strange, wavering, as if here is a man who has not spoken in years. A fringed shawl lifting and falling in a little breeze.

I don't know her name, Lena's child—or even if I understood Friedrich correctly in thinking it was a girl. I'm alone a moment, sober and clear—peering straight up through the branches at the black sky, then down at the black earth where the bundled cloth lies. How strange this is, but also how simple.

As I bury the child, I am turning myself into a memory. Here now is my sister, taking my mittened hand in hers; here a young Jakob Dükmann pats me on the back; here my mother touches my hair as she pads past me, her eyes on a letter. A thickness in my throat; something of longing unstoppered, but I mustn't yet allow it to flow freely. The earth can be flattened over the body I'm burying. A big stone can be placed there at the head, and a smaller stone laid atop it, to prevent any of it looking accidental. I wish I'd thought to bring something better, but it's all very poor, very small. Still: this is an earth rich with sleeping bones—nothing ignoble, nothing lonely, about resting here. A family waiting to receive its newest child, it occurs to me.

I sit on the earth here awhile. My heart beats heavy but slow. And now it seems that everything that just happened has been done by a different man, a long time ago.

What does he imagine, this man? That he will be allowed, now, to walk away from everything entrusted to him? Perhaps a part of him believes it. But another, deeper part must understand.

For he is ready to leave this place and put the whole thing behind him. And in the moment this fact spells itself clearly in his mind, he hears words spoken in his wife's voice: *We don't know.* How none of them know what became of their dead, and how this unwritten page becomes a wound—so here now are eyes that stare out at him from another time, asking, *Can I trust?* Lena, he realizes, does not know what became of her own dead, her child.

So, so—he feels it welling in him as his vision swims (stumbling a little on his way towards the cemetery gate). One must allow one's self to be seen. In his mind's eye, a man picks a fish's head off a table, peers through its mouth and out the open portal of its throat into the light of a clear morning. It doesn't matter, it doesn't matter, he thinks—to be seen, then, if only to be emptied out at last, nothing but air and light.

14

THERE IS SUCH QUIET THE NEXT MORNING, AND WHITE light on the apartment walls through parted drapes. Tobias has received two cups of coffee from his mother, who said, "Your father came in so late last night," and he is carrying one of them to this old fellow who lies in bed. From his mother's face he's guessed already that his father is not well.

"Vater, a drink for you." He pushes the bedroom door open.

"Tobias! Come here." From the bed, Josef motions him close. The young man must dance a little to keep a hot mug safe from this grasping hand, to press the cup at last into his father's fingers without burning him. "Sit, sit," says Josef Tobak to his son.

"What is it?"

"Tobias, I need to write a letter." Josef's voice low, as if it is a secret between them. "But this morning I find—you know—my eyes—" He waves his hands before his face, and his vision seems not to focus. Tobias, kind young man, will not sigh at his father today.

"You want me to help you?"

"That would be perfect, Tobias. Yes—because who knows, who knows how long she'll—which is to say, if it isn't already . . . Tobias," Josef says. He takes a deep breath, and then: "I need to write a letter to Lena. The one Friedrich Zimmel looked after. You know."

Tobias does know. He says, "Of course, Vater. Of course. I think Mutti knows where she's staying, so I can just—"

"Please, no need to tell your mother just yet. Not yet." The man's hands tremble as he raises his coffee to his mouth, so much so that his son reaches out to help steady them. He swallows and he says, "You won't be upset, I hope, if what I have to say is a bit . . . strange?"

"It's fine, Vater."

"You're very good, Tobias. Thank you. Only please bring some paper. I have it all in mind. All here." (Tapping his head.) "I find looking at the paper makes me a little dizzy this morning, but if you help me . . ."

"I'll help you," Tobias says. And he goes.

Tobias, as I'll learn, had never imagined Lena in great detail as a person, before the funeral; he'd been limited to the fact of her—how she was an emblem of his father's friend's decency. He had hoped, perhaps, that seeing her might be a gift to his father—something they might all point to, to say, See, there is still so much of good in this world. What disappointment, then, at the fact Josef could not even meet this woman without fainting. But now it may be, it may be (one can imagine Tobias thinking it as he retrieves a pad of paper from the desk in his bedroom) that the man will consider another survivor and find strength.

"I don't know her married name," Josef says as his son sits down beside him on the bed.

"It's Lindner. Mutti told me after the funeral."

"Mrs. Lindner. Very well. You are ready? 'Dear Mrs. Lindner . . .'"

He says it, and he pauses. Tobias has written the words and sits with his pen poised above the page, waiting. Josef Tobak's lips are parted, his eyes scrolling back and forth as if reading an invisible ledger. He swallows.

"It's hard to know where to begin."

His son says, "Take your time, Vater."

"If I am a little unclear," Josef says, "I hope you'll forgive me."

In the almost half an hour they sit together, Anna comes in once to retrieve cups (says nothing but "Good morning," wise woman), and Tobias writes on and off as his father reaches for the words that might say just enough, just exactly enough to satisfy his secretary without scandalizing him.

Dear Mrs. Lindner,

I must ask you to forgive my reluctance to approach you at Friedrich Zimmel's funeral, but I hope very much that I might be allowed to meet you or correspond with you. My name is Josef Tobak. Your great-grandmother and my grandmother were sisters, I believe. Mr. Zimmel was a long-time friend of mine. He helped our family very much before the war. I also knew your mother, Sarah Kostner, but only a little; my sister knew her better. I wonder if already you know who I am? Perhaps one of them mentioned me.

You must allow me to apologize for never being in touch with you before. My understanding—what I was told—was that you didn't want to hear from us. Perhaps that was true, after all. It hurt me to believe it, but I believed it too easily. I wish we had been able to offer you help or friendship.

You are on my mind very much because shortly before Mr. Zimmel died, he let me know that there was a great deal that still distressed him about his choices during the war. He told me there was much that he wished he could undo from that time. Some of the things he told me it seemed he had never before revealed to anyone, and I wondered perhaps for a little while even if they were true. I don't wonder this anymore; I have seen enough for myself.

But there is much of what he said—and of what I now understand—that I would like to share with you. It is not an easy matter, I appreciate. Understand that I don't write this expecting gratitude or even acknowledgement; I don't expect you to forgive him (or me, come to think of it). If you choose not to reply to this letter, very well. I may still feel compelled to write once more to you—forgive me if this causes you pain. But if you were willing to meet, or if you would receive mail, it would be a great relief to me.

Mrs. Lindner, I leave this choice to you. You have my utmost respect. I wish you all happiness and blessing in your life.

With sincere admiration,
Josef Tobak

He has Tobias repeat it to him twice; he says, "It doesn't sound sinister, does it?" And, "No, I'd hardly say it does, Vater," his son replies.

Josef blinks, rubs his eyes. "I suppose you'll have to ask your mother about the address." And at Tobias's affirmative, Josef shrugs and says, "Well, what good does it do us to have secrets from each other, after all." Which leaves his son with a new and unfamiliar warmth, something that nestles into his ribs, and which will stay with him for several hours yet.

══

LISTEN: SUCH THINGS do happen. A boy who is almost a man can carry a letter across town to a woman half-ready to leave Vienna. She can receive it; she can reply. We can wonder what need or curiosity abides behind the words she offers: "Yes, I will meet him." How everything tilts towards this. This last piece that remains to be set down—open your hand, Tobak; let it fall.

15

I N A HIGH-CEILINGED COFFEE HOUSE NEAR THE CENTRE OF the city, the little family are huddled at a small round table. They are not so noticeable, these three: it's early afternoon, the sky outside is overcast, and all around them are other little groups ringed round small tables. Another generation's music plays above them. Many of these other patrons who surround them are tourists. (So there are tourists again, Josef reflects. So this city is a place worth visiting.) And there is the odour of coffee and baking, apples and marzipan beyond, and everywhere chatter and shifting, sounds shrunken by this wide, tall space.

"We are a little early," Anna says.

In the time since Tobias spoke to Lena, there has been a strangeness among them. Anna is half-shy at it, as if this news is of royalty she needs to entertain. Tobias is quiet at her quietness, and the father—well, the father! He has said, "I'll meet with her," and now he feels he has handed over his whole life to be weighed. There is no need to say anything more.

Anna and Tobias are looking about them. All these strangers, this noise. It occurs to Josef, in his silence, that it is possible she will not come. And here again is a shadow that reaches into him. For couldn't she, as her mother once did, decide she doesn't want to see him? And what then? He squeezes his wife's hand, once, very tight.

"Tsk, Josef. She'll be here soon." Anna's other hand comes to pat his arm.

It's impossible, of course, for him to look for her. Better to look down at the table, at his hands, anywhere. So it is Tobias who says, "There she is," and then, standing, calls, "Mrs. Lindner."

Anna also stands to greet her. (Josef finds he cannot.) This other woman's voice, in clear German but with a hint of a foreign accent, is saying, "Thank you, yes, such a pleasure to meet you."

Someone apologizes for Josef on his behalf, and this woman bends and kisses his two cheeks. A certain hesitancy to the gesture, despite its gentleness. (What are her eyes like? Josef finds he could not say.) Her perfume has a hint of lavender. It makes his throat go tight.

Tobias is catching the waiter's eye; Lena is settling herself across from Anna and Josef. "What an unlikely meeting this is," Anna exclaims, and it becomes, for a spell, a quietness draped over them.

Then, "It is really our pleasure to meet you," Anna continues. "I've thought about you so often."

"Oh!" Lena says. "That shames me. How lovely that you thought of me. I don't suppose I deserve it."

"It's not a question of deserving," says Anna (all of her gentleness)—she has reached out to touch this new friend. "To me it was always that you were a blessing to us. It's helped me keep a little of my faith."

This silences all of them. Something twists in Josef's middle, and Lena makes a small noise, not quite a laugh.

"It's strange, isn't it," Lena says at last, "how we all end up tangled in one another."

"It's so. Indeed. I'm very glad you've come—and do you like living in England?" Anna asks it suddenly, perhaps out of her sense of how grave they've all become.

"I do." (Her tone lighter.) "It's a good home for me. I met a very good man when I was in America—he was a displaced person too, as they say, but of course he's made a very good life for himself in England. We have three children. The eldest is seven years old." A slight creak to her voice when she says it.

"How wonderful," Anna says. "And you don't ever miss Vienna, then."

"Miss this city?" A short silence before she says, "You understand, Mrs. Tobak—there was so little left to miss."

She says it, and they all think: Very well; but see, after their friend died, how she's come to them.

"Josef and Friedrich Zimmel were good friends since they were young," Anna offers. "We tried to be family for him, but it's not quite the same."

"No, I suppose not." Lena's voice quiet. "That's very good of you, though. Very kind."

"We tried." Josef says it. They have not yet heard him speak; they listen to him, but he can only add, "It's so hard to know anything."

The waiter arrives, and for a minute after she orders, Lena turns to complimenting Anna on her beautiful son. ("He means to apply to medical school, I think," Anna tells Lena, and Tobias says, "Perhaps, yes." Both women make noises of approval at this. "You seem so steady, after all," Lena says to him.) Josef sits through this and waits. She has not begun by accusing him, he notes. Perhaps it is that she's waiting for him to speak. But how can he begin?

"It's been good to see Vienna again, after all," Lena says at last. "My memory of it is so strange—mainly from before the war, and all that when I was a girl. I left so soon afterwards."

"Oh, I've so wanted to ask. I hope you don't mind," Anna says. "What was it like for you, staying in that house all those years?"

Lena shifts in her seat. "Probably as you would expect. I feel I ought not to speak a word in complaint. I was one of the lucky ones, in the end."

Josef finds himself searching for her face. It is so hard to make his eyes settle on her. There are spaces between the words, and a silence she isn't speaking into. He is certain of this. He feels it.

"I think about my mother, what she wanted for me, and it seems like—perhaps—that is exactly how things worked out," Lena says. "Every so often I pause, with my babies, or when we're eating dinner, or even on some silly errand—the experience of life is so immense, despite everything—and I think, Mama, here I am. You gave me this. You chose well."

"In trusting him, you mean," Tobias says—and the words are a knife in his father that he doesn't see.

"In giving me up, in choosing him. Everything. I don't think I could have done the same for my own children. I can barely stand to be apart from them, even like this."

Anna says, "I don't imagine I could have done it either. Thank God I never had to find out."

But the next thing Lena says makes Josef want to clutch his chest:

"So Friedrich never had his own family, then. No children."

"Well, not that he knew of," Anna cracks, and now Josef feels his stomach like a marble, but though he sees it as if through shadow, Lena only smiles down at her hands.

"Oh, dear," Anna says. "I shouldn't have said that. Shame on me."

"Well—isn't it so?" Lena says to them. "He didn't consider it properly, I suppose, but I think he did want that. A family, I mean. I believe he did. Or perhaps I imagine it."

"I think he did," Anna says.

"I remember that—the loneliness," Lena says. "My own, yes, but also his. There was such loneliness in that house. I wonder if—and this isn't fair at all, I know—I'm sorry to bring it up to you—but I wonder if, maybe, he died of that loneliness."

"That loneliness," Josef says. And here, just beyond the dimness in him, is his friend who says to him, *It's only that I never had anyone, Josef. Not really.*

"My husband," Lena says, "would not have me think about Mr. Zimmel too much. He believes Friedrich was too lucky in the treatment he received. He's right, I know. And I have enough love to spend on memories of my mother and my grandmother—everyone. But my daughter asks me about the occupation, and what can I do? I think about it always. He's there, you see, just like a ghost. In my own house, despite everything."

It makes Josef raise a hand to his throat, this word *ghost*. The word seems to stir the air around him.

"I have trouble speaking about these things with my husband," Lena tells them. She rubs her stomach with her hand. Glances around at the strangers with their coffees and cakes.

And in her silence, when Anna says, "It's very hard," the words are like pebbles dropped into a still pond.

"Mr. Tobak," Lena says at last, turning to Josef, "I wonder if you would take a walk with me. Outside. I would be able to speak better, I think."

BENEATH UNLIT STREET lamps, in the shadow of these old imperial streets, Josef walks arm in arm with this woman. Her softness, just here, and the smell of lavender on her. His wife and his son walk behind them, far enough not to hear.

"I was so grateful for your letter," Lena says to him, "but I can see that discussing these things is painful to you. I suspect I'm asking you to remember things you don't want to remember."

"No," he says. He means this. "Please. It's better to say it."

She goes silent, and the world flows around them. She guides him gently by the arm. The light off the windows makes him feel as if he might see everything, see clearly at last, but for now the swirl and haziness will not cease.

"It still makes me sick, being indoors," Lena says. "After all this time. You'd think it would pass. I have a doctor, and he's very helpful. But there are things they can't do, after all." She pauses. "Your son will be a doctor, then."

"He says so," Josef says. And then: "We are very lucky."

"I miss my children," Lena tells him. They step down off the curb, cross cobbles, step up again. "My husband gets frustrated with me. I have such a hard time when they're born. Darkness, you understand? Like I am not a part of my own life. And I'm afraid to touch them." Another silence. "But after a few weeks it's better, and then I'm afraid instead to let them go."

And then she adds, as if responding to someone, "But it's true, I have a good life."

And in the silence that follows, they each of them reflect on the depth of things unsaid.

"It is difficult to leave your children, then," Josef says to her.

"Yes. Yes, it's hard." She holds his arm tighter; he is certain she doesn't notice that she does it. "But I had to. You understand. I had to. It was that or . . . or tear myself apart."

He feels it, the truth of her words, the very literal truth, and it chills him. "Because Friedrich died?"

"Yes." She squeezes him again. "And in that room. I thought so many times . . . I had envisioned myself . . ." She takes two deep breaths. A tension to her speaking that threatens to snap the air between them, and a rock set into Josef's middle, terrible weight.

And at last, in so small a whisper: "Did he tell you that there was a child?"

"Oh—he did," he says. "Yes."

In the air, the smell of water. This shadow that opens up in front of them, the canal stretching off in either direction. They arrive at a bench beside it. Josef knows Anna and Tobias will keep their distance, and is grateful for it. Both he and Lena sit beside the water.

"So he spoke of her," she says.

"Just once," Josef tells her. "At the end."

She shivers. "I named her after my mother—Sarah. I named her before she was born. That whole time, I dreamed—I was so lonely—to have her . . ." Her voice fades, and she says, "She was stillborn, though."

"Yes," Josef says.

"And my husband doesn't understand why I won't name a daughter of ours after my mother," she says. "I haven't told him. I've wanted to tell him. It's such . . . such a burden." Her voice small as she tells him this, and as she goes on it shrinks almost to nothing. "But in my heart it's as if I cast her aside. Same as he did."

He holds her arm tight. He has been braced, all this while, for interrogation, to beg forgiveness or to let her destroy him, but now he finds himself in quite another role.

"I suppose he burned the body," Lena says. "I never could ask him."

"He buried her." Josef finds himself lifted in saying it. "Under a tree behind the house. And then—" It may be his mind only, but it seems that one of the faces from his darkness has come to peer at him from Lena's eyes. "—and then later in the Währing cemetery."

She is watching him. "I don't understand. You're sure of this?"

He nods.

"He told you? He went into the cemetery with her body?"

Her hands on his arm, and he finds—this mercy—that he can say it.

"No—he asked me to do that. I did that. I buried her there."

Nearby is the water, which shimmers, green and gold, carrying shadows down through depths. All colours clear and bright. A simple beat to his heart, like a clock ticking in the next room. You could fall asleep to it.

At length, he feels her leaning into him.

"All this time," she says, in a voice he hasn't heard until now, "do you know—and it was a thorn in me—I've imagined her completely alone, and forgotten."

The voices behind them, the cars that grumble and spurt, colours flying by on both sides of the water, and a light held in the man's heart, a red glow.

When she sits straight at last, and she says to him, "What a strange chance it is to find you, Mr. Tobak," already he is holding between his ribs a heat he'd half-forgotten in the dark.

He is looking into her eyes, lights amber and bright. He says, "Well, sometimes—these things—" And whatever he meant to add (something that sounds, to his inward ear, almost rabbinical) is muted by the pain in his throat, and he only nods, lays a hand on her arm.

The canal is very green. There is light everywhere, late-afternoon light, and a richness as of gold. Windowpanes glinting like stars.

"I could not have guessed I would ever be allowed to know that," Lena tells him.

"Oh." Josef swallows. His whole self is saying, I am glad, and he hopes she can understand it.

But now place yourself in it, Tobak. Understand that this man is your very self. So: I sit beside her. And listen: she says, "If I could tell my husband, so many things might be better."

"Could you tell him?" I ask her.

She peers at the water. "I don't know. Perhaps I could," she says at last. And: "What a relief that might be."

And I think, holding her small weight against me—this so-innocent weight: Yes, indeed. Such a relief to set a burden down, if one is, at last, permitted.

Soon Tobias and my Anna will come to us. I am certain the new posture of my body invites them. But while there is time, I ask Lena if she would like to visit the Währing cemetery with me, to see the place where I buried the child. And while she sits beside the water, contemplating something beyond my understanding, it occurs to me that regardless of what she answers, her words become a blessing, and I am free to receive it.

16

ANOTHER DAY, SOME TIME AFTER THIS MEETING (Lena at home in London; Vienna mild in the months before the winter), I am with Tobias in the Seegasse cemetery. I know the timing is muddled in my mind. I must place myself in history—here, I suppose: about a decade and a half into peace, and five years since the new occupiers left us; four years since our Hungarian neighbours poured in, and three since a Soviet satellite first blinked by. A year, still, before an American president and a Soviet premier will arrive in our city to talk and talk and talk, and a year also before a wall in Germany cuts another city in two. And of all of this I'm only half-certain. You find yourself in it, you try to hold a place.

So begin with a sure fact: I am with my son Tobias in the Seegasse cemetery. We are poking about in the earth, since there are gravestones buried here, and we would like to know how deep. (All this while I have been piling other unhewn stones in the Währing cemetery for our families. I have been thinking of so many families. I have been looking for ways to hold it all.) I am surprised at how much the digging disturbs me. I dig with a little trowel and when, only a foot beneath the earth, I uncover carved stone, it is like bearing bones to the light. It is unearthing the dead, it seems to me, and I must resist the urge to ask forgiveness.

The air has a little of the spice of autumn in it, and digging makes me breathe heavier, so my throat has something of that good, raw hurt. It has become, since Lena came, easier to pray. I can recite psalms as I did as a young man. It isn't so much a feeling of being heard as a rootedness in prior knowing, and this like a stone foundation is, I think, a surer base than the transported feelings of my youth. In this confidence, and despite fear, I can come here with Tobias, scrape and dig a little.

I remark on my discomfort to Tobias, and he falls thoughtful. He says, after a pause, "It is strange, isn't it, since they're only markers. But perhaps they begin to stand in for what they mark. I can see that."

I scrape at soil, cool clay under my nails, and I hold these words of his. The distance between a marker and the thing it marks collapsing into nothing, and then separating again as I note the collapse. Collide and come apart: body and stone, spirit and bone. And it strikes me that I had better know which it is that I am caring for, and what I am carrying, or else it's all nonsense.

"It's terrible to think that people might forget these were here," I say to my boy, and I pat soil back down overtop this worn stone. Because of course no one sets markers up for buried gravestones. So how would you know?

"But someone would find them eventually," Tobias says, "even if by accident." He is not looking at me; he is prying at the soil. A squirrel bounds and springs against the brick beyond him. If the people behind the windows that look onto this courtyard are watching us, we cannot see them. "And whoever it was would know what it all meant."

"By the text, you mean?"

"They're gravestones, Vater—people understand." My son shrugs. Wipes his hands on his trousers. "It's all very clear. Right there on the stone." Back to digging, and he adds: "That's *why* people set it all down this way, isn't it?"

I dig awhile. Set it down, he says. Is it his German? (Still coloured by China, perhaps—I wonder about it.) I know what it is to want to set a thing down: some things so heavy, and yet one has to bear them. But to connect that longing to this memorial—I am looking for the link. I ask Tobias, "How do you mean, set down?"

"Recorded, I meant," he says. "It's all recorded. So even if I forget, or you forget, or everyone forgets, still it's written there."

He goes on digging. He's not watching me, and he does not see. But in this sharp air there is some invisible light that penetrates. That there is a fish buried here, and a stone that remembers him. That there are hundreds of years between us and these dead. So understand, Tobak: nothing you have carried of these souls have you ever carried on your own.

In the Seegasse cemetery, the stones lie sleeping, but they do not forget. Here is a prayer rising up from a man who forgot, for a while, what was asked of him. And the question he was afraid of is no longer a question: Come alongside, it says. You are not the only one who holds these things. Nothing need be carried alone.

17

Now I would like this to be finished, but I see it is not so simple. I am within it and apart from it, am watching a man who is and is not myself. Perhaps now that he is all laid out in front of me, I can pity him more gently. I suppose it might be so.

A thousand things I've neglected: about my mother, my father, my sister, the smell of winter, candlelight through frosted windows, foxes in the snow—all this begs pardon. There is time and space yet; I may still find the words to carry everything. If I reflect awhile longer, if I wonder deeper, will it all come at last? Everything accounted for—each piece with its marker. But it's never been so, of course. It slips away, and this (a part of me can grasp) is not always an evil.

So you would say to me, "Find the ending, Josef, the true ending"—but I don't know the ending; I am still waiting for it.

18

THERE ARE TIMES IN THE WÄHRING CEMETERY, WHEN the weather is fine and my knees are not stiff, when to chase the thieving fox away is no challenge. There may even be times when it seems I can be on him so fast as almost to brush his fur with my fingertips. How he drops his little bone then—quick as anything, preferring to save his life. (Though I wouldn't hurt him, I know; and wonder, sometimes, whether he knows.) And I can bury the bones he leaves behind, though between the tree roots and the animals, a man's bones might be spread over a half acre in this walled garden, if they haven't left the grounds completely.

But there are times, too, when the wind is high, and there is a bite of autumn to the air, or a scent of spring, and the fox's coat shimmers in the wind as he trots; and then it has been that as I hobble along behind him, he looks back at me, full in the eyes, and I am arrested.

So he holds that bone in his mouth; so he flicks his tail; so he peers at me awhile, to say: Will you chase me?

I suppose my eyes must give an answer. For then he is off again, little flicker of flame, under the wall with the pieces he carries.

I think, Fine, then. You have somewhere to take them. I will follow you there someday—someday, but not yet.

Acknowledgements

THANKS, FIRST OF ALL, TO RHEA TREGEBOV, WHO READ
sections of this book during its earliest stages of develop-
ment while I was studying at UBC, and without whose help
I doubt I would have had the confidence to undertake this project
or the insight to do it justice. Thanks also to Annabel Lyon and
Ruth Daniell, both of whom provided feedback on the manuscript
at key moments

Thanks to Rachel Letofsky and everyone at the Cooke Agency.
Thank you to Jane Warren for understanding this book before I
did, for believing in it and for steering it in the right direction.
Many thanks to Patrick Crean, who stepped in at a critical moment
and compelled me to make the book what it ought to be, despite
my protests. It really is a better book now.

Thanks to a series of patient roommates who shared my life in
Vancouver, Sudbury and Ottawa while this book was being written, and to all the friends who encouraged me in writing it.

My family, to whom this book is dedicated, have been a life-
long support in my writing life. Thanks to each one of you for
believing this book would be real someday. I hope you love it.

ACKNOWLEDGEMENTS

Special thanks to my grandmother Holly Martin, as enthusiastic and patient a supporter as I could ever hope to find. Biggest thanks to my biggest fans, Jane Morrill, Keith Morrill and André Morrill: for stories, for the graveyards of Vienna and for your love.